Heir
of
Roses

ISBN: 978-1-7365164-2-3 (Digital)

ISBN: 978-1-7365164-8-5 (Paperback)

Front cover image by Victoria McCombs

First printing edition 2022

This one is for you, J

Previously in Rowan's story:

Welcome back to the tale of the girl who ought to have been queen! I'm about to give a rundown of how the last book ended, so if you haven't read it, I recommend you stop reading now!

The Winter Charlatan brought a lot of growth to Rowan's character, and some hardships. Her goal was to break her curse so she could reclaim the throne, which otherwise would have gone to Cassian, the boy she ended up falling for. While she found a way to stop the curse by using a wish she'd acquired from a witch, the kingdom was in danger by an attack from ThornHigh that they could not survive. Rowan used her wish to save the people instead. With it, she sent everyone back to their homeland in the deep south and Rowan fell asleep for a hundred years—alone.

She woke to a stranger's kiss: Nicolas. He is the crown prince of Thames and is now bringing Rowan to his home as the ice palace of Elenvérs is falling. Anika and Christopher (characters from Woods of Silver and Light) were lured north by talk of magic and found them, and are now their traveling companions.

Key characters to remember: Cassian—the boy she had just fallen for, and Elis—her sister who betrayed Elenvérs by marrying Tarion (Prince of ThornHigh.)

You are caught up. Enjoy the end to Rowan's tale.

Chapter One

FALLING IN LOVE REQUIRED a certain art, I decided. And as much as I told my stubborn heart to do it, it refused to be coerced.

To love another with your entire soul needed more than an awakening kiss. It needed time. It needed passion. It needed connection. All things that couldn't be solved with a swing of a sword, unfortunately.

I shifted my aim of the arrow. I might not know how to force my heart to love, but hunting? This I could do.

Nicolas knelt at my side just as Elis had done so many times, though he peeked my way far more often than she ever did. I wasn't sure if he liked knowing I was there or if he feared me running off, but occasionally the corners of his lips tugged upward when he thought I couldn't see.

For now, we both kept our eyes ahead to scour through the forest. The thick stench of pine clouded my nose with a passing breeze, and I found myself leaning into the wind to find relief from the heavy heat. Sweat dripped from my skin and the wisps of hair on my arm were drenched from wiping my brow so often. I wasn't built for such relentless warmth, nor was I accustomed to the army of bugs keeping us company with loud chirps that made the quiet game of hunting more difficult.

There was plenty in this new terrain to get accustomed to.

I held the bow that Nicolas had whittled for me not long after we'd left the ruins of Elenvérs. He had carved my name into the side with a small heart next to it. I hadn't known what to say to that, so I'd said nothing.

"We might not find another deer in these parts," Nicolas whispered as he scanned the thickets.

"Something moved ahead, I'm certain of it," I said back. No sooner had I spoken than a small creature tumbled out of the nearby bushes with tall ears twisted in each direction. A tiny, pink nose sniffed a few times as it poked along the ground, and little paws turned over the soil. It hopped a few times before repeating the action.

Rabbit, I identified after a pause. Not something I came by often in the north, but it made a scrumptious stew if I recalled correctly. With how hungry I was right now, I'd eat it raw just as happily.

"At least we'll have something for dinner." I pulled the bowstring to the base of my jaw, letting the thin feathers brush my cheek. Normally I'd release right away, but this time extra care went into finding the heart, so I could impress Nicolas with my skill. If I couldn't rely on my charm to win his heart, perhaps my skill could cover some of the gap.

"Don't wait," Nicolas whispered. "He's likely to run off any moment."

Of course, as soon as he said that, the rabbit perked up, likely cautioned by the sound of his deep voice. Before my lungs drew another breath, the beast was halfway across the forest floor and out of sight.

My arrow stared at the empty space where he was. "Blast," I said, lowering my weapon. "I wouldn't have guessed such small legs could be so swift."

Nicolas grinned, the light in his eyes indicating that he held no bitterness over losing our best shot at a proper meal. He replaced his arrow into his quiver and stood. "Are rabbits slow in Elenvérs?"

I didn't put my weapon away, ambitiously hoping for another animal to come by so I could regain my pride. "Rabbits are dead before they come to Elenvérs. I've only eaten them a few times, and it didn't require putting an arrow through them first." The harsh cold of Elenvérs attracted few creatures, and none like the numerous ones found in the south which were all foreign to me. Nicolas claimed to be impressed with my hunting ability, but I'd done a poor job of proving myself since leaving my precious mountains.

Twigs snapped behind us. We turned our heads to the clearing where Christopher and Anika high stepped through tall grasses and overturned dirt with three plump squirrels in hand. Squirrels were nowhere near as fast as rabbits. "Look what we caught." Christopher proudly showed them off before nodding at Anika. "She hit two herself."

"Lucky shot," Anika admitted, while breaking through the thick overgrowth into the matted down soil of our little camp. My arrow tip scraped against my quiver as I put it away with a sigh to trudge after them empty-handed. My stomach grumbled to further shame for me losing the rabbit.

The hunger was only made worse by knowing that we could be dining in the presence of kings on our way to Nicolas's castle, but instead he'd suggested we trek home on horseback through back trails and fend for ourselves. He'd suggested it for me. This offered us the chance to familiarize ourselves with each other before he paraded me around the kingdoms as the girl he'd woken with true love's kiss. It was considerate, but it also felt like hiding. Hiding from our feelings that weren't growing and distracting ourselves with staying alive.

Most importantly, though neither of us would say it, this gave my heart time to fall in love.

Perhaps it was my mind that didn't want to love and be subject to a future that I didn't know. In truth, many things could be holding me back from feeling like my mother had so soon after she'd been awoken—in love from the moment she opened her eyes. Thoughts of my deceased mother brought a sharp pain to my chest, and I took a deep breath to expel it.

"Anyone would have missed that shot," Nicolas said.

He leaned so his shoulders grazed my braided hair. He did that often—got close but didn't touch. He kept near in case I needed him but always respected my space, finding the balance between persistent and gentle. The perfect gentleman.

I studied his nearness. Was I what he'd expected when he fought to wake me? Or was he disappointed with the girl from the ice palace?

We'd be at the gates of his kingdom, Thames, in a few weeks, and in the two months it took us to travel here, we'd yet to accomplish the bonding that I knew he'd hoped for.

"I usually hit my targets, I promise," I said, trying not to appear bothered by my lack of skills in this new environment.

"I believe you." Nicolas's smiles were freely given. He didn't sway toward me again, but kept his hands tucked into the pocket of his linen pants that were tied up with knitted horsehair. As we entered camp, Nicolas gathered a stack of wood and bent over the ashes of the fire while I stepped over the fraying bags of meager provisions to tuck the bows near our horses. By the time I'd faced Nicolas again, he'd already convinced the small embers back to life. Just like that, the fire obeyed him.

That was another thing I was dreadful at. Without the help of the cave mages' trinkets, I couldn't conjure flame from sticks.

Unbeckoned, thoughts of Tarion came to mind and of his amazement as I used the cave mages' gift to keep us warm against the ice. This time, I bit down hard to demand the feelings away. They were not welcome, especially the ones of him.

I drew near to Nicolas to divert my thoughts. Encouraged by my closeness, he grinned at me.

"Who taught you how to do all this?" I asked, gesturing to the fire as I folded my legs beneath me.

"My father did." Nicolas adjusted the last of the twigs then set up sticks to hold the squirrels over it. Recognizing something I could help with, I offered my hand for half, easing the sharp wood into the moist dirt. "We used to go on long hunting trips together when I was younger. He taught me everything I needed to know to survive, though I was quite unprepared for the harsh cold of Elenvérs."

It comforted me to know that just as I was struggling with the unfamiliarity of his country, he had struggled with mine. We shared the confusion. "Well," I said, brushing my hands on my knees and pulling back to my feet as the fire sparked, "thank you for rescuing me."

His unkept hair tumbled over his brow as he peeked up from the fire. "You're welcome. I'm glad I did."

I held his gaze, wondering how much he meant that. As much as I was placed into a future that was uncertain, he was too.

Nicolas was handsome, more so than I'd originally appreciated. A strong frame, thick lashes, freckles over the nose. The little hairs on the back of his head curled as the heat got to them, and he had a way of pulling his lip into his mouth and crinkling his forehead when he thought hard that I found attractive. His ears stuck out a little bit, and the wrinkles by his eyes pulled deep when he smiled in a way that showed he was really happy.

I hadn't brushed my hair in months, and the last bath I took involved less soap and more mud. I wore a pair of riding pants that I'd taken from Elenvérs, though now they were heavily stained with animal blood and soaked with sweat, and my tunic had a decent tear in the shoulder where branches had pulled at it. The revealed skin was becoming dangerously red from the sun, and the skin on my arms was peeling.

Not the beautiful princess he'd been promised.

"We're low on water," Anika called as she beat a stick against our canteens that hung from a low branch. They let out a hallow sound. "Christopher and I can fill these up, if you begin dinner." She strung the straps over her shoulder as Christopher tossed dead squirrels at our feet.

"It'll be the finest squirrel you've ever tasted," Nicolas promised.

"I don't know about that," Christopher said. He nudged Anika as she raked a hand over her wild hair. "Do you remember that dinner with Lord Ethner?"

"Yes, but we didn't catch those ourselves, and that's most of the fun," Anika said.

"I think eating is the fun."

"You would." She poked his belly. "I look forward to the best squirrel we've ever had when we return." She waved to us as she headed through the trees with her fiancée following as he rubbed where she'd poked him.

I caught Nicolas's expression as he glanced after them, one of slight envy. Their relationship came so naturally. And, I thought guiltily, I couldn't promise him that. The look passed as Nicolas pulled his knife from his side and laid one of the squirrels belly side up before handing me another.

I blinked at it in my hand, then back at him.

What in Elenvérs' name was I meant to do with this? Carving such a creature required a delicate touch. One harsh slice and I'd pass the meat and hit the bone. Give me a bear—that I could do.

A frightful thought came to mind. This would be my future, to be forever faced with tasks that I didn't know how to do. Love, creating fire, skinning a squirrel. I mimicked Nicolas's actions, unwilling to admit any further shortcomings.

"Christopher mentioned they are departing tomorrow," Nicolas said as he drew a line down the animal's abdomen. "Heading back to their own home. Their wedding is in a few months, and they need time to prepare it."

"It was nice of them to come with us so far." I observed his movements out of the corner of my eye as I worked. "I enjoy their company."

"Yes, but I enjoy yours more." He winked at me. He was so sure in his actions. No hesitation. If doubt lived in his mind, he guarded it carefully behind warm exchanges and fond comments, leaving me to constantly wonder about his true thoughts while I struggled to discern my own.

I grinned, so his wink wouldn't go unmet. "Same," I could honestly say.

Nicolas lowered his blade and fixed his eye on me. Without his guidance, I was unsure of the next cut to make, so I turned and allowed him to properly look. His gaze lingered as if intricate words were inscribed on my skin for only him to see. His eyes were the color of sap from the trees around us, while mine were like the ice I'd left behind.

"Do you?" His quiet voice drifted over me, bringing a hint of warm breath with them that rested on my cheek where his eyes had just been studying. "Do you care for my company?"

He shifted further. "I'm aware that our situation is...delicate. I woke you with true love's kiss, but that doesn't mean you owe me anything. If you aren't in love, or if you don't want a future with me, then you shouldn't feel obligated to remain here. We'll be upon Thames soon, and from there I can have my fastest horses carry you to Elenvérs."

The very name of my home kingdom caused something deep within me to arouse. But it wasn't home. It wasn't mine. It was the rebuilt land of my ancestors, the ones I'd sent there to save them from ThornHigh's army. There was nothing there for me.

"What do you want, Rowan?" He wasn't forceful with the question, but gentle as a first snow. And when I raised my head to see his, Nicolas's expression was soft, with lips slightly parted and eyes fixed on me as he patiently waited for my thoughts. He wouldn't pressure me into a life with him. He wouldn't ask something of me that I wasn't willing to give.

"I'm not in love with you," I confessed.

His lips closed and his brow drew up in a way that made him look like a sad animal, much like the squirrel in our hands. I had no doubt believing he felt as skinned as the creature, gutted by my indifference. I followed with my next words quickly. "But I think I could be. Forgive me, my heart moves slowly, and it's still broken over everything I just lost."

I couldn't say their names out loud. That pain was too deep. But I allowed thoughts of them to drift by.

My mother and father who I'd never gotten enough time with. Lord and Lady Trelluse who always cared for me like their own. Cassian, who I never got to explore things with. Elis, who broke my heart. It was a hundred years ago, but the pain was fresh for me, and it was hard to swallow.

I spoke slowly. "I need a few more months to decide if I want this, or if I will try to restart my life in Elenvérs."

His fingers brushed against my leg in a tender gesture. Despite the uncertainty of my answer, the relief on his face shown bright and he smiled. "That's enough for me. I think if you gave me the chance, I could make you happy. But I won't rush you. And if you decide to leave for Elenvérs, I will help you with anything you need."

Tears formed behind my lids and threatened to drown my cheeks in their sorrow, but I held them at bay. This moment felt perfect, so full of hope, that I didn't want to ruin it by making him think that the sadness was all that consumed me. Behind that rested a timid eagerness for the future that could be here.

The horses neighed, but it took a moment to realize they weren't ours. The sound came from the south. Nicolas's hands pulled from me as he flew to his feet, clutching his knife between white-knuckled fingers.

"It's likely a sentry," he said, but quick eyes still scouted the trees.

Any moment we might have just shared was ruined. I stood beside him.

A rider broke into view with a purple crest painted across his tight, gray tunic and a sword bouncing at his hip as the horse trotted near. The lion's crest of Thames marked his livery.

Behind him followed more riders, each bearing the same crest and weapons as they searched through the forest. At the sight of us, the one in the lead whistled loud enough to scatter birds from above as the sound was repeated several more times through the trees. Soldiers came from all sides in a loud thunder of horses.

Nicolas's grip on his blade had released, but the frown on his face deepened. "Mattias, what is this?" He spoke to the man in front, whose eyes glanced to him for no more than a moment before fixating themselves on me.

"So the girl was real," Mattias's voice boomed through the trees, and he laughed. "Must say I'm surprised. We thought you might have been mad."

Nicolas positioned himself in front of me. "She's real. What business do you come on?" By this point they'd surrounded us in a thick shield, and I turned my head to inspect them all as they stared down at us.

"I'm sorry, dear friend," Mattias spoke, pulling up on his reins. To his credit he did appear saddened by whatever news he brought. His wide lips curved downward. "I come at the bidding of the king. The queen has died, and unrest stirs within Thames. His Majesty says you've been gone long enough. You and your love are to return home with us."

Chapter Two

WE HARDLY HAD TIME to bid Christopher and Anika farewell before being whisked off on our horses and were surrounded by a company of thirty soldiers.

"Is this necessary?" Nicolas asked Mattias with a gesture over the number of men.

Mattias's dark eyes hardened. "It is. The towns are protesting, and we didn't deem it safe for you to travel back with anything less than this." To my right, a few guards exchanged glances over heavy-set frowns.

Nicolas's brows furrowed. "How did that happen? We were at peace when I left."

I stared at him. In one moment his entire demeanor had changed from the carefree man in the woods to a prince caring for his country. His back straightened, his shoulders drew back, and the little creases in the corner of his eye vanished as a blank expression swept over him.

Mattias's eyes wandered my way before back to Nicolas. "I'll explain more later," he said, leaving me with the impression that it was my presence that guarded his tongue. He nudged his horse forward to lead the group and left us behind. Nicolas's mouth set in a straight line, and his chest rose with a deep breath. When he caught me looking, he smiled.

"I'm sure it will be sorted quickly."

I knew nothing of his country, nor of the depth of the unrest that Mattias spoke of. There were no words of comfort I could offer him, so instead I returned the smile with a nod. "I'm sure it will."

Nicolas's claim to the throne wasn't the ordinary one. He was third in line as a lad, but then the prince fell down cliffs and perished. Later, the next in line died in a jousting accident, leaving Nicolas as the new crown prince of Thames. He moved into the castle with his uncle, King Silas, and his parents joined him.

He'd only been crown prince for two years, and much of that time had been focused on me.

Over the past month, Nicolas had unveiled an array of emotions, but the tight expression he wore now was unfamiliar, as was the blankness in his eye. I could only guess as to what the news of the queen's death and the unrest brought upon him. He hadn't spoken much of his parents—the sea merchants who left their seaside manor to join him at the castle. He spoke even less of the king and queen who took them in.

Though I wanted to ask him about it, the closeness of the men around us made further conversation difficult, so we rode in silence for a short while until the sun began to dip behind the tall trees.

At last the men halted.

"We'll make camp here," Mattias instructed.

Tents were raised and fires started. They'd brought meat with them, and they twisted it over flames while my mouth watered. Nicolas rolled the hems of his pants while kneeling to assist them as I brushed down the horses. It was the only task I could find that kept me at a distance from the men who glanced my way often enough that I was never not being watched.

Nicolas had done me a favor by keeping us in the countryside for the journey home. This was dreadful.

My horse whined. "Oh you think they are looking at you?" I joked. "That could be, you are very beautiful." I scratched under her chin. She was eyeing the other horses and shifting as if all she wanted was to run. I felt that.

Plumes of smoke brought the tender scent of venison drifting by, and my stomach growled in anticipation.

To my delight, the venison was soon served. I stayed by the horses to eat, my knees sinking into the damp ground as I feasted on the delicious meat. It made a much better dinner than the skinny squirrels would have, though it might have been my extreme hunger that exaggerated the savory flavor of the animal.

We never had meat this tender in Elenvérs. Everything there had been hearty and thick and dry.

"It looks delicious," Nicolas said as he settled next to me with his own meal. Either he was as famished as me or still lost in his thoughts, but we ate in silence. Before too long the golden light left the sky and we were directed to our own tents for the evening.

"We leave at first light," a guard said, half looking at us and half staring into the thick trees. I didn't miss his hand situated on his sword hilt as if prepared to be attacked at any moment. As the darkness settled in, the men turned their glanced from me and into the trees, and their nerves almost made me wish they were staring at me instead.

"Will we be safe?" I asked.

"You should be."

That was encouraging.

The guard tore his eyes from the darkness to acknowledge me. "We have guards stationed throughout the night to be sure of that."

Without getting another chance to speak, Nicolas said goodnight and ducked into his tent, the worry across his forehead manifesting into wrinkles so deep that he'd need his own hundred years of sleep to ease them out.

I watched until the folds of his tent had settled before retreating into my own.

Inside smelled of dirt and slight mildew, but the thick walls of fabric offered a night of freedom from hungry bugs, and my mat had been replaced by a thicker one that invited me into its softness. I shucked off my outer jacket and laid it next to my small bag before pulling my hand through the tangles in my hair.

Sleep beckoned me, but I didn't take it.

Instead, I busied myself with unknotting my hair and waiting several more minutes until the full darkness of night had set in before creeping out of my tent and into Nicolas's.

I whispered into the dark as I scoured the shadows to find his figure. He sat on his mat with his legs stretched out as he twiddled something between his fingers, until catching sight of me. He rose. "Rowan?"

"I wanted to see how you are doing," I said, bringing myself fully into the tent. "Care for a walk?"

In the dim light I made out a grin. "Thank you," he'd said like I just offered him his first taste of water in a week. I ducked back out and he followed me, his hand searching for mine in the moonlight. Ten tents sat around us as the remains of a fire crackled with its last bit of life while owls hooted from above. Rustles came from different directions, sometimes small as if from a creature and other times large enough to turn our heads.

One such time, Mattias stepped from around a tree and raised his brow.

"We'll only be a short while," Nicolas whispered to him, leading me by the hand further into the trees. The knowing smile on Mattias's face as we passed led me to believe he pictured this as more of a romantic getaway than it was, but I didn't care to make the correction. My focus was on Nicolas.

"Were you close with the queen?" I asked when the camp was behind us. The moon offered a silver hue to the forest around us, and we moved in and out of the speckled shadows of the branches. Even though our eyes had adjusted to our surroundings and we didn't move at a quick pace, Nicolas kept his hand locked in mine.

He thought before answering. "Not quite. She was a kind woman and I liked her, but we only knew each other for a short while. She fought in the war by my mother's side many years ago and the two of them were quite close. I imagine my mother is distraught right now."

I wondered if his mother being upset would make meeting her more tense but was glad to hear Nicolas wasn't thrown by the news. I wouldn't know how to comfort him if he was. I'd lost many people, but it wasn't the same.

"I'm more concerned about the unrest Mattias spoke of," Nicolas went on. "I knew there'd been squabbles as each of the heirs before me died, and rumors that their deaths were more than an accident, but it'd been nothing to worry the king."

We came upon a fallen tree where Nicolas rested himself against the wide trunk. The wrinkles in his forehead had eased, but only slightly.

"Do you suppose her death was murder?" I asked. As I did, another distressed look marred his face so painful that I almost took the idea back, but he nodded.

"It crossed my mind. I meant to ask Mattias more about it. I don't know the other lords enough to guess if they could plot something like this, but if the lords are revolting then the court is weak. My ascension to the throne could be in jeopardy." His free hand picked at the bark in the tree underneath him.

I draped my loose hair over one shoulder to see him better. "Is the king not a strong one?"

Once my question left my mouth, it sounded more blunt than I intended. Nicolas paused from picking at the bark. "He is, but the power is not solely in his hands."

I played with my lip between my teeth for a few moments as I tried to understand. "Who has control?"

He shifted, curling one leg up between us and resting his chin on his arm. A breeze ruffled his hair and brought the scent of pine with it. Nicolas's pupils were as dark as the night, and his blue tunic appeared black.

"I'll do my best to explain this," he said, stroking my fingers one by one. "Silas rules Thames, but the lords have a lot of the control. They have their own armies, their own small courts, and the lands pay taxes to them. In order to remain king, you must have the favor of the nobles, or else you could be easily overthrown. The queen was beloved, and her endorsement of me kept the lands together. But with both her and the rightful heir dead, I will need to fight for the approval of the nobles to keep my place secure."

The political system of Thames sounded far more complicated than Elenvérs, where the king ruled all. I couldn't fathom multiple courts in one kingdom, but then again, Elenvérs was small.

Thames would be a much larger beast to rule over.

Nicolas withdrew his hand from mine to drag his palms against his face and groan. "I'm sorry about all this. I meant us to have a few more calm weeks before reaching home."

I'd wanted that too. I felt wildly unprepared to begin socializing with other folk. But I shrugged. "It's fine; we can still steal moments like this."

"That might be the most romantic thing you've ever said."

"I've been practicing."

His expression relaxed, and he retook my hand with a chuckle. "I quite like stealing moments with you."

I wondered what it'd be like at the castle where he was crown prince. Would he have time to spend with me during the day or would our interactions be limited to minutes stolen in the night? It might be difficult to find privacy in the castle, and I loathed the idea of falling in love in front of the kingdom.

It was almost enough to make me flee.

The thought of all those eyes on us, scrutinizing our relationship while we still attempted to figure it out for ourselves, pressuring us from every side. I'd be on display, the princess awoken from a hundred-year sleep who now ought to be in love with their beloved prince. And I'd have to convince the nobles to support me.

My throat tightened while the air grew thinner, and my next breath didn't come as easily as the one before it.

I could imagine myself escaping in the night, taking my horse, and riding far away from pestering eyes. We'd travel like a wisp of wind, disappearing into the world until we'd found a quiet place to settle. I'd build a simple life for myself, perhaps on the edge of Elenvérs so I could see what had become of my beloved country.

The image in my head was a difficult one to banish, but I forced it out. *This is what you want. If you leave now, you lose Nicolas and your chance at love.*

My hand tightened in his, pressing the skin of his hand against mine as if I could soak him in and make him a part of myself. Force my heart to want him as much as it ought to. Compel myself to fall in love. As if that's all it would take to convince myself beyond any doubt that this future was the best one for me and to dismiss the fool-hearted daydreams of the life I could have, or of the life I ought to have had before the curse came.

Nicolas breathed calmly beside me, as if this were all he needed. A still night by my side. I envied the way he seemed so certain about what he wanted.

"Did you always want to be the crown prince?" I broke the silence to ask him, knowing the path to his position was far from usual.

To my surprise, he laughed. "Not at all. I was quite adamantly against it, in fact. I spent my childhood convincing the kingdom that I didn't want to be prince and was more surprised than anyone when it came upon me. Sometimes I still don't believe it."

I couldn't imagine. "I spent my childhood trying to reclaim the throne. I suppose things would have been far simpler if I hadn't wanted it. What was your plan, then? Take over your father's shipping company?"

He didn't take long to answer. "It's honest work, provides well, and I quite enjoy the sea. I could have done worse." A hint of remorse stirred in his voice for the path he might have been on, as if the future before him was one of his own doing instead of forces beyond his control.

For a moment, I wished that were what fate had brought to him, so we would be traveling to a seaside manor with salt in the air instead of a palace with relentless watching eyes. I'd never seen the sea before.

An idea came to mind. I gasped. "We are the same."

"What?" The moonlight fluttered off his lashes as he glanced to me.

I smiled. "We both had a different future planned. Both of us lost those futures, and both are on a path we didn't choose for ourselves." Though it wasn't a happy thought, it brought me unexplainable joy to know that he understood me in that way. I was not the only one who had lost the life I wanted for myself.

He matched my smile. "I suppose that's true. And we are both attempting to navigate this new future as well as can be. Thank goodness we get to navigate it together."

That was the feeling I'd been searching for, and it settled in my chest with a flicker of warmth trailing behind it, spreading until it tingled in my fingertips and touched my toes. For the first time since I'd woken, I didn't feel as alone.

I buried myself into his side and spread my arms around him, hoping he could feel how happy that made me. But just in case he couldn't, I whispered into the night, "Thank you. I'm glad to have you."

The deep sigh that followed told me he was happy, too.

A shuffling from the east turned my head, and Mattias came treading from the path. "I'm sorry sire. I must insist you return to your tents."

Nicolas's next sigh wasn't as happy. "As you wish." He straightened himself and held out his arm for me. "Thank you, Rowan, for the perfect night." He led me back to camp and kissed my hand before disappearing into his tent, and for the first time I missed him when he was gone.

Chapter Three

WE CAME UPON THAMES nine days later, and it left me breathless.

A castle as beautiful as this deserved an equally beautiful name, so it was no surprise to find it had two. First, it was called Green Pointe in tribute to the tall towers lining the east and west walls with lush, green ivy so dense I could hardly see the thick stone peering from beneath them, starting at the ground and clawing higher until they'd draped themselves around the turrets that kissed the clouds. Large pink flowers bloomed from these plants to add a flash of beauty to the impenetrable foliage.

"It's magnificent," I found myself whispering as we crossed the drawbridge over a slow-moving stream with iridescent pebbles along the banks that held pieces of the sun inside them.

The other name had nothing to do with the physical features of the structure, though there were plenty prime areas for inspiration. The scarves hanging from arched windows that greeted us upon arrival. The enormous courtyard with orange trees peeking over a wide golden gate to watch the horses as they approached with clicks over copper cobblestone. The turtles bathing on the bank of the moat.

Turtles. Little, cute turtles.

We weren't in Elenvérs anymore.

Despite all these ideas, the second name came from the glory of a king who ruled long ago. After further inquiry I discovered long ago meant about when I was born, which properly made me feel ancient. Quickly brushing by that fact, Nicolas explained that this such king was one who had been so loved that half the babies were named after him, and the castle renamed in his honor after he died. Heart of Bjorn. It wasn't a title used often, but when it was spoken it was said with pride for the king that had been theirs.

Nicolas confessed he hoped to be considered good enough to name something after once he was gone.

Guards dispersed as we entered the courtyard, each relinquishing their reins to dutiful squires in feathered hats before stretching their bones and bowing away. Mattias didn't leave us, but rather waited until we were alone and he had waved the squires away to step close to Nicolas and peek at me.

I pretended to be fascinated by an orange tree while I tuned my ears to hear his words.

"Be gentle with His Majesty. He is a broken man in the wake of losing his queen," he said. I peeked to see him rub his mustache, and Nicolas tightened his lips with a nod. Mattias's next words came louder, clearly meant for both of us. "I'll alert the king to our arrival, and both he and your parents will be eager to welcome you in the king's study. You have a moment to clean yourselves first. She's to be placed in the princess suite on the first floor."

Something about that made Nicolas's frown, but he didn't argue. Instead his hand reached to me, and I gladly took hold of the one thing that anchored me to familiarity.

The beauty of the castle now morphed into a warning as we ventured further in, as if reminding me that only perfection was allowed in these walls, and I wasn't allowed to be anything but. Inside tall, oak doors we found a hallway lit from a series of bright stained-glass windows showing monarchs from ages gone by that watched our every step. I clutched my satchel closer to my side, feeling the heaviness of their glass eyes.

"Are you ready for this? We can sneak out the back and leave if you aren't. Stay away for a while." Nicolas paused to hold me in front of him and scan his eyes over me. I wondered what he saw before him. Was it someone who could handle whatever these weeks would bring, or did he see my doubt?

That same doubt lived in his stance now, in the way he shivered though there was no cold and his chest took deeper breaths than necessary. I pulled back my shoulders and vowed to be the strength he needed. "It means a lot that you'd offer, but I'm ready. I'll be fine."

Even as I said those words, my heart was thinking of Elenvérs and the home I wanted to be in, but Nicolas smiled.

"I'll escort you to your room to put away your belongings, then return shortly."

"Sounds perfect."

A few of the castle staff stared at us as we navigated the corridors, but I was too busy memorizing my surroundings to give them much care. The air smelled of freshly plucked flowers and the rug beneath my feet was so thick that each step sank into the cream fabric.

"I swear, this is softer than snow," I whispered under my breath.

It was much brighter than snow, though. Orange appeared to be the theme here, either manifesting in large flowers set up in pale vases atop light brown tables, stitched into the borders of massive tapestries along the walls, or billowing from the curtains draped against windowpanes.

It was bright. It was warm. And it was nothing like the home I came from. My vivid, red hair would not stick out so much in a place such as this.

"This is the downstairs princess suite." Nicolas paused in front of double doors with coral handles to let me in. The hinges didn't squeak as I pushed one door open into a space as large as any of the caves back in Elenvérs. My eyes almost fell to the floor from how wide I opened them.

"I think I might get lost in there." I gaped at the collection of rooms all extending from the center sitting area.

Nicolas laughed. "If you're ever overwhelmed, you may retreat here, and I'll simply tell the castle you couldn't find your way out."

"They might send a search party after me." I grinned at the image.

Nicolas's head tilted to the side. "Then you can hide in mine." He paused to frown and pointed above him. "My chambers are upstairs. There is a princess suite attached, but I don't know why you weren't granted it. I'll speak to the king and sort it out."

"Don't," I answered too quickly then recoiled at the implication that I didn't care to be near him. "I don't want to add anything to the king's mind as he mourns his wife. Things will get sorted for us in due time." I placed a hand on his wrist because it felt like the right thing to do to make my words softer.

He placed a warm hand over mine. "You're too kind."

It wasn't often that someone called me that. Now that I thought of it, that may have been the first time.

He stepped back. "I'll just go drop off my things and be back for you. We will go to my parents together."

My stomach flipped at that sentence, but I bit my lip and watched him go. Then I turned into the mazes of my room alone.

I kept my satchel pinned to my side as I explored the massive area. My actual bedroom sat to the left of the sitting chamber, with fluffy cream pillows and a fuzzy coral blanket spread over the wide bed. A small desk sat next to the bed, barely big enough to fit my satchel if I set it down.

Attached to that room was a closet, with empty shelves and only a few bare hangers. A second door led out from the closet and back to the sitting room. From there I found a second, smaller sitting room in the back with nothing more than a couch along the wall, but a glass door led outside to a small balcony. I left the door open to allow airflow as I explored the final rooms.

I found a bathing room, with a vanity sitting atop a shelved desk and hairbrush calling me to use it. After a few tugs through my hair, I set the brush down and rubbed the dirt from my face before accepting this was as proper as I could make myself look.

The final room appeared to be an entertaining area, with several places for seating, a piano, and a fireplace. I shook my head and returned to the bedroom. I'd grown up with no more than a small room to share with Elis, and now I had three rooms I felt confident I'd never use, along with a bedroom larger than anything I needed.

I finally relinquished my satchel from my shoulder to lay it on the desk beside the bed. My hand reached for the notebook within, and I stroked the leather binding.

The letters Cassian had left for me. My most beloved possession.

Though I itched to read them once more, I put them away just in time for a knock at the door.

"Are you ready?" Nicolas stepped into the front sitting room. He'd changed his outfit into something clean and brushed his hair to the side. With his gold buttons and sharp collar, he looked like a prince instead of the boy I'd been trekking through the kingdoms with. I could only hope that when his parents looked at me, they saw someone half as put together as him.

"Ready."

Chapter Four

THE THICK WOODEN DOOR clawed against the stone floor as Nicolas led me into the king's office, cueing each head to swivel toward us at the same moment. Behind them, sunlight poured through windows as high as the ceiling, bathing my eyes in a light that momentarily blinded me, but as I blinked the glare away, their figures came into view.

First it was the slender frame of a woman bearing a strong resemblance to Nicolas in the way her jaw was set and her cheek bones pulled high near her doe eyes. Her hand perched on the back of a tall chair positioned behind a mahogany desk, as if this were her room and not the king's.

A smile crossed her lips as she took in Nicolas, but it failed to reach her eyes. Instead they turned to rake over me where they flinched ever so slightly. An icy chill pinched my spine.

"The lost son returns!" From the side where they gathered near large sofas, one of the two men stretched out his arms, nearly spilling a red liquid from his tall, golden goblet. A single drop escaped. The other man chuckled but was quick to pry the drink away, setting it down on the window ledge to sit in the sun. Now free from restrictions, the first man barreled toward us, throwing his arms around Nicolas. "You've no idea how happy we are to have you home."

"It's good to be back." Nicolas's hand slid from mine to embrace the large man, whose warm, hazel eyes peeked to me from over Nicolas's shoulder. He winked.

"Rowan, my father." Nicolas stepped back to gesture over the man in front of him, who stuck out his hand to me.

"The girl my son woke with true love's kiss!" His voice carried to the top of the bookshelves and down the hall behind us.

"And this is my mother," Nicolas was quick to go on. The woman had approached us now, though kept her hands at her stomach while she kissed her son's cheeks. These two people intimidated me more than any king I'd come across. Nicolas's parents, Martin and Ava. He'd not spoken much about them, so I couldn't fake familiarity or guess how accepting they'd be of me.

Ava took a deep breath, as if she'd been holding it for quite some time. "Nicolas, thank you for coming back. And the girl is real." She turned to face me, and I straightened myself, now wishing I'd changed into something trimmed with lace instead of dirt. Her eyes seemed to find every imperfection before glancing back to Nicolas. "Is she not a princess?"

My cheeks heated. "I am," I answered for myself. "Princess of Elenvérs when it dwelled in the north. I'm forever grateful to your son for venturing up to wake me. I would have been quite lost without him."

It sounded like a sweet thing to say, and while Martin sighed happily, Ava drummed her fingers against her side as she watched me through slimmed eyes.

"That's our lad, always the hero." The third gentleman kept himself at a distance, and Nicolas coughed.

"Rowan, may I introduce you to King Silas of Thames."

The man before me was not as tall as Nicolas's father, nor bursting with the same energy. Rather, there was a stillness to him—deep and strong—as if a fierce wind couldn't sway him. Though he wore a smile that wrinkled his cheeks, his eyes fell downcast, and the stain of tears marred his skin.

He'd lost his wife, I was abruptly reminded of, and I didn't know what to say to him.

"Your Majesty," I chose, bowing my head.

"It is an honor to have such beauty in our castle," he said, allowing his smile to deepen. Nicolas reached to squeeze my hand, but the way he kept his eye on the king told me he remembered the older man's plight.

"Silas, I'm so sorry about Jezebel. She was a light to this castle, and I was stricken to hear of her passing," Nicolas said, but the king was already waving his hand.

"That's alright my son, I'm just glad to have you home." He came to wrap his hand around Nicolas's in a firm shake, then took a sigh, letting the sadness in his expression fade out like a mist with his breath. In its place sat a gentle smile. "So is there a wedding to look forward to? It might be good for the people to have something to focus on other than this unrest." At this last bit he looked to Nicolas's parents who nodded, though his mother less enthusiastically.

Nicolas straightened beside me, while I stood frozen as marble. "Let's not rush it. But I'd greatly like to hear more about this unrest."

"Another time, another time," King Silas said. "You must be tired from your extensive journey. You could have traveled in carriage if you wanted or stayed with King Nevil. Horseback through the hills must have been tiring."

"For the horses more than us, I'd think," I said. For an uncomfortable moment the three of them looked at me, unsure what to make of my comment, but Nicolas laughed.

"We were fine, truly. The pleasant company made it easy to handle."

I didn't care for the way their eyes shifted between the two of us, trying to analyze our relationship based on these few moments. "I am eager to finally be here, though," I said to keep the silence at bay. "Especially to have good food."

Martin and King Silas chuckled. Ava did not. I shouldn't have expected to win over his mother with a few pretty smiles and kind words, but if she were polite she would at least grin.

Instead, Ava appeared bored by our presence. "You haven't had the proper chance to settle, and we still have much to discuss here. Go; we will speak later." She then whispered to the king, not quietly enough that anyone failed to hear her, "Sire, we really must attend to those matters."

Just like with Mattias, I got the feeling I was being left out of something, but the king turned his back on us and we had no choice but to leave. Ava followed him, but not before she gave another hard look at my dirty clothes, brushing the side of her own silk gown as if she could rub the dirt from my clothes herself.

I opened my mouth to explain we'd just gotten home, but Nicolas's warm fingers slid between mine and he led me from the room.

Just like that, my first meeting with his parents was over, ending with a secure knock of the door swinging shut at our ankles.

"I don't think they fancy me," I said, looking into Nicolas's eyes and hoping not to find disappointment within. "In fact, I think your mother quite disliked me."

There was no disappointment, just a squeeze of my hand and a slight tug on his lips as he chuckled. "My mother doesn't like anyone. She was no more than seventeen when she fought in the war, and it hardened her. Sometimes I wonder if she likes me. She did like the queen, but..." His voice cut off with a cough. "Anyway, my father liked you, I can tell. And Silas must have liked you to suggest we get married so quickly. After all, you'd be queen of his kingdom one day."

"Still," I said, tugging him away from the door where I swore I felt Ava's disapproval radiating off it, the heat of it tingling my skin. "You might have warned me to put on a proper dress, or at least something with less foliage attached." I dusted at my muddy pants.

Nicolas glanced at my attire, as if for the first time noticing how the forest clung to me. But he shook his head. "Would you have liked to wear a stuffy dress for an uncomfortable meeting with my parents?" he asked.

After a moment of thought, I shook my head.

"Then I wouldn't want you to, either. I quite like you just how you are." His eyes didn't waver from mine, even as he spoke with such kindness that my heart pounded against my chest.

I'd given him very little to love, merely a girl mourning for her dead family and feeling lost in a lifetime that wasn't her own. My insides were cavernous, empty remains. Shattered ice within that I feared would take years to put back together.

But when he spoke like that—with such certainty that this thing between us was real, it brought me solace that thawed the ice in my veins. A hundred years of sleep had carved this ice deep, but each day it cracked, soon deep enough that my heart could breathe again.

You don't deserve him, a voice from deep within echoed, clashing against every bone and numbing my mind. *He's too good. Too pure. Too warm for the girl from the ice. Don't break his heart. Leave for Elenvérs and set his gentle spirit free.*

His eyes stayed on me, even as we walked, and I feared he could see the storm roaring inside.

"You mustn't worry about mother, truly," Nicolas spoke, softer this time. I focused on his words, the touch of his hand, not the cruel thoughts in my own head. "She will come to love you."

"I hope so," I said. "I want to belong here."

"You will." Again, such certainty. "Give it time, and I promise to make Thames feel like home."

He didn't know how badly I wanted that, to feel like I had a home.

We'd come back to my door, and he squeezed my hand before letting go. "I'll give you time to rest. Soon I'll take you on a tour so you can see the rest of the castle. There are many hidden beauties here, you'll see."

I thought of the turtles in the stream outside the castle and the orange trees in the courtyard. This castle already proved its beauty, but I was eager to see it through Nicolas's eyes.

He hesitated there, with his hand woven in mine, and I thought he might kiss me goodbye. But he drifted away before I could decide if I wanted him to or not.

I had to determine what I desired, a life here with Nicolas or not. Because it wasn't fair of me to stay if it weren't for forever, and it'd kill me to wound Nicolas with an inevitable departure. He deserved someone who spoke affectionate words with as much confidence as he did, someone who looked at him and knew she was looking at her future.

That's what I searched for, the assurance in my future. Whether it was here, or not, I had to find out.

Chapter Five

A REST SOUNDED WELL-NEEDED, but when I opened the door, my rooms were full of life.

Two women fussed about the large, side sitting room, where the fire now crackled with flames and the curtains were drawn back to let buttery light pour over the yellow rug. One dusted the bookless bookshelf, while the second messed about the sofas, picking at spotless specks. Both had wild and wavy hair like dark rivers running free down their backs. Long, curved brows were set over dark eyes, and their tanned skin matched Nicolas's.

"Imagine, sleeping for a hundred years," one said as she punched at a pillow a few times before propping it along the sofa's side.

"I can imagine," the second replied, her back facing me. "I'd like to sleep for a hundred years."

"If you need more help with Rosalie, I'm happy to assist," the first responded, looking to the other girl. It was then that she noticed me and let out a shrill shriek. "She's here!"

Both girls snapped to attention, throwing themselves closer to the door with smiles that reached their jaws.

"Hello, hello, hello!" A third, cheery voice startled me as an older woman came from the bedroom, a tight apron strung around her generous curves. "You must be Nicolas's sleeping princess."

"Yes," I stammered. "I'm Rowan." I shut the door behind me and stood awkwardly before them.

"It's a pleasure to meet you, my lady. I am Dana, this is my daughter Lucille," she gestured to one of the girls, then to the next. "And my daughter-in-law Isabel."

Dana. Lucille. Isabel. I ran the names through my mind several times.

"If you aren't too busy, we will get you fitted for some clothes. I'll just need a few measurements. I'm sure we have some spare dresses that would fit you in the meantime." She whipped a measuring clothe from her pocket and approached me, holding up the strip to take in my proportions.

An infant's sharp wail cut through the air, directed from the room by the balcony. As I tilted my head, I found the round frame of a bassinet tucked into the corner and a tiny fist flailing in the air in search of something to grab.

"Rosalie is up," Isabel said, hurrying off to fetch her.

"Her daughter," Lucille whispered.

They all moved so naturally through the room as if they lived here. Like we were old friends. I thought I knew the answer, but I had to ask. "I'm sorry, you all are...?"

Lucille's brow furrowed for a moment before nodded in understanding. "Your maids."

ThornHigh had maids. Elenvérs never did. I hadn't thought of the maid Lindy since waking up, and with the reminder came a fresh pang of hurt. I hoped she lived a fine life, filled with joy and happiness. Likely, I'd never know what became of her.

Dana finally finished and rattled off the numbers to herself a few times, while Isabel returned with her daughter bouncing on her hip. The child's wide eyes stared at me.

They all looked at me like I was expected to say something. To give them a task to do or dismiss them. "Forgive me, I'm uncertain what the duties of a maid include. Do you...help me dress?"

A chorus of laughter came from all three. "Goodness no! I assume you can do that by yourself. Help you dress." Dana placed her hands on her belly as it shook. When she'd calmed herself, she wiped tears from her eyes and sighed merrily. "We help with tidying up, seeing that your practical needs are taken care of, providing company through the day. Speaking of, you, my dear, you need a bath. Desperately. Come, there must be some beauty under there, you simply need a honey sugar scrub to find it."

While the concept of 'honey sugar scrub' wasn't one I was familiar with, I agreed that I needed a bath. "Is there a warm spring nearby to bathe in?"

Again came the laughter. "My, how odd things must have been where you lived. No, we will bring the spring to you. You relax for a few minutes while we prepare the water But don't go sitting on the couch, we've just cleaned it and we don't need any of that...my, my is there blood on the hem?"

They each took a step away, and I laughed. "These should probably be burned."

"We can do that." Dana waved a hand over her daughter, who scurred out of the room. Isabel placed Rosalie on the floor where she dragged her small frame to my feet and cooed. I knelt beside her and let her pull at my red hair for several minutes until Lucille returned.

"It's all ready, come come," Lucille replied, ducking her head back out the door. She reminded me of Nicolas in the way that she always seemed in motion.

She led me across the hall. "You'll feel fresh as a sunflower once you've had a nice bath, and the cook prepared fruit compotes that taste splendid over biscuits. I'll sneak us some special wine, too."

When she glanced back, her eyes danced with such delight that I didn't care to say I hadn't the slightest idea what a compote was. It sounded tasty, and I could go for some strong wine.

"Here we are." She opened a thin door. It led to a dusky hallway with a chamber of doors lining each side. She pushed open the first one, and flowery smells hit my nose. "Your bath awaits."

A round window lit the small room, where a marble tub sat beneath the light with bubbles oozing from its side. Scrub brushes sat in wooden holders, a bar of pink soap on a petite plate, and a towel so thick it could serve as a blanket on a cold night.

"Set your clothes outside the door once you've undressed," Lucille instructed. "And that is for when you are done." She pointed to the back of the door, where a long sunny dress hung from a shiny knob.

She backed out of the room but hesitated in the hallway, her words tiptoeing across her tongue like she feared they'd bring insult. "My lady? Take your time in the bath. You quite need it."

I flushed as I nodded. "I will. And Lucille? Could you ask your mother when she goes to make me clothes, that I'd like several pairs of pants as well? And riding clothes?"

She didn't question my request but smiled. "I think I'm going to like you a lot." Then she closed the door between us, leaving me with the smell of violets and lavender and all things clean that my body hadn't encountered in weeks. She needn't have asked me to take my time in the bath. Small strands of steam rose from the water's surface and curled in the light, mixing with the soft fragrances of a garden, welcoming me into the fold where I could happily lie for a hundred more years as the droplets soaked into my skin and cleaned me.

I imagined all my troubles drifting away with the dirt, all my doubts and worries about the future bursting like the bubbles. By the time I was done and dressed, my body was clean and my mind refreshed, and I'd focused on the good that could come from this place. All the happiness this life could bring me. If I stayed on those thoughts, not dwelling on the past that I'd lost or misgivings I had about my future, I felt almost normal.

I ought to take a bath more often if it left me feeling this nice.

Dana actually clapped as I came back into the room. "See? I knew a bath would do you good. Now let's do something about that hair. I know a thing or two about taming wild curls." She kissed Rosalie's head before standing up and ushered me into the bedroom where she sat me before a tall, ivory-stained vanity.

As she combed her fingers through my hair, she peeked into the other rooms where the girls were helping Rosalie walk on unstable feet. "This must be scary for you," she whispered. "Being in a new place with people you don't know. Away from your family."

A gentle smile and light-brown eyes met mine through the vanity's reflection. Her hands moved softly through my hair, tenderly shaping the curls. "We can't replace the family you lost, but we are here for you. Anything you need, any questions you have. Just let me know."

Tears crept to my lids and blurred my vision as I whispered my thanks. She continued to fix me up in the way that a mother would for a daughter. The way that my mother never did for me.

"I do have a question," I spoke to keep myself from crying. "What can you tell me about Nicolas?"

Her eyes brightened. "Boy talk, I love it. I'll tell you everything I know, which isn't much since he's only been around here for a short while. From what I've seen, Nicolas is a splendid young man. He helped my husband get a new position in the castle after he injured his arm in training a year ago. The king wanted to send us off to some countryside, but Nicolas heard our pleas to stay here and got him work as an emissary's assistant. He's quite happy there."

The story made me smile. Nicolas had a kind heart.

"He doesn't talk too much, doesn't get drunk at dinner parties like others." She cast a look to her daughter, almost making me laugh. "And he's respectful of everyone. Perhaps because he wasn't born into nobility, it makes him deserve it even more. He's worthy of you, I guarantee it."

That wasn't what I worried about. It was the opposite—I feared I wasn't worthy of him. If someone had asked anyone in Elenvérs to describe me, would they have smiled like Dana did now? Would they speak to my charity and compassion? Or would they recount my cold exterior and determination to take the throne, no matter what?

"I'm glad to hear he's as good of a man as I thought him to be," I said as she finished with my hair. It was still damp, but the curls weren't as wild as they normally were, and more defined.

Two knocks came against the front door, and Lucille was fast to her feet to answer it. "Perfect," she chirped. An older woman rolled a cart with plates of biscuits and a red, fruity topping into the room. "And the other thing?"

From under the cart, the lady produced a musky bottle of wine.

"Lucille!" Dana crossed her arms and marched into the room. "This is not an hour to be drinking."

Lucille grabbed the wine and ushered the other lady out before she could take back the wine. "Miss Rowan's been sleeping for a hundred years. The girl needs some wine!"

From the floor with Rosalie, Isabel laughed, and I cracked a smile. Lucille was right, I needed wine. Desperately.

Dana huffed, but as Rosalie crawled to her legs, she didn't argue. She shooed her hands at Lucille. "Well then? See that there are glasses under the cart so she can have some. And that better not be from the king's personal stash again."

"Of course not." Lucille grinned, finding glasses to pour generous amounts of deep, opaque red liquid into. She piled a plate high with sweets and presented them both to me. "You can thank me later." She winked, then poured herself an equally full glass.

I was ready to thank her the second the strong wine hit my palate with flavors of cranberry and forest floor. I melted at the flavor, just to melt further when I tasted the compote, which appeared to be plump strawberries soaked in some sort of sugary syrup.

This rivaled the chocolate pudding from home.

A second knock came at the door, bringing all our faces up from our dessert.

"Maybe it's more wine," Lucille spoke through a mouthful of food, wiggling her eyebrows. They looked like worms dancing across her face, as equally mischievous as she was and just as eager to get into trouble.

"Hush now," Dana said, cleaning her mouth on her sleeve. "If it's wine, I'm sending it back."

She swept open the door and straightened. "Your Highness. I certainly can't send you back."

"Erm, hello, Dana. Is Rowan available?" At Nicolas's voice I hoped from my seat, bringing my wine with me.

"I'm here," I said, stepping into the front room. Nicolas's face went slack as he took in the clean hair and new dress.

"Beautiful," he breathed. "Are you ready for that tour?" He held the door wide, tugging on the bottom of his crisp, tan vest. I thought of Dana's story of how he helped her husband and smiled.

I took another large gulp of wine before setting it down on the cart. "I am now."

Chapter Six

THE CASTLE WAS MARVELOUS in every way, with more sunlight trapped inside its walls than we had during an entire summer in Elenvérs. Nicolas was clearly proud of it, practically prancing as he led me through open-roofed halls that smelled of freshly plucked roses and past indoor gardens bursting with color.

Crowds of ladies sat in open chambers with bright dresses and buoyant laughter, greeting Nicolas and I as we neared. They'd whisper as we passed, likely about the girl who was asleep for a hundred years, but I didn't fault them for being curious. I'd whisper, too. Their warm smiles left little room to question their friendliness.

Green Pointe spared no opportunity to charm me, but my favorite part came as Nicolas dropped down a ladder and pushed aside a latch in the ceiling to let down gentle ribbons of wind.

"A garden on the roof," Nicolas explained, holding his hand for me at the top. "It's a special place to me." I climbed to the top and let the latch click shut behind me.

The sun-soaked stone sent warmth through my soft slippers as I took in the view. Flowers of every color bloomed like a rainbow across the patio—reds and oranges on one side bleeding into blues and purples on the other. A circular bench sat in the middle with a path lining the outside.

"It smells so nice," I said. "It's lovely."

"Look at this." Nicolas approached the edge where he leaned over the tall ledge to stare at the world beyond. "You can see the whole castle from here, and the outskirts of the village."

He was right, I could see everything. If I squinted, I could even make out the turtles wading in the moat from afar. Distant laughter echoed through stone to greet us. There seemed to be unending laughter in this kingdom, like one joke continuing forever.

"Is there a story behind the scarves?" I pointed below to the colorful fabric billowing from most of the windows.

Nicolas grinned as he bent over to see them. "They confused me when I first came, too. They add decoration to the castle, which is their primary purpose. But sometimes people send messages through them. If they hang a red one it could mean they are free for the gentlemen to call on them that evening. Or it could mean they are quite livid and wish to be left alone. The court and servants all have different codes for what colors mean what, so others can't guess the meaning."

I wondered what codes were hidden there today, a secret message among a wall of vibrance.

"What messages have you hidden?" I asked him, perhaps appearing too eager to know his secrets.

He leaned back from the wall to balance himself against the ledge, and the light gleaming from his suit buttons brought out the gold flecks in his eyes. "None. I haven't made close enough friends for that. But my manservant has. See this yellow one hanging almost directly below us? Those are my rooms, by the way. Well the yellow is a sign for his love. It means his love for her is as eternal as the sun."

The yellow scarf danced in the breeze, showcasing his promise for all to see. There was something so sweet about that simple little gesture, and I hoped the scarf never moved. "Eternal as the sun," I breathed.

"Have you ever had a sweetheart?" Nicolas asked suddenly, the words spilling from his mouth as if he'd debated them before they burst out. As soon as he spoke, he sucked in his chest and peeked at me through his lashes.

I didn't know how to answer that. Cassian and I developed feelings for each other, but far too late to pursue them. We never held hands, shared tender whispers in the dark, exchanged letters dripping in love promises. I'd never even been kissed.

I should say no, if for no other reason than to spare Nicolas from the thought, but it felt wrong to deny that I had something, so I nodded. "His name was Cassian."

"Cassian?" His brows drew together before shooting halfway up his forehead. "The old man I met?"

He's dead now, I remembered. The man who was once my training partner, friend, and sweetheart is now dead, while my skin still blushed with warm, young blood. That might be the oddest feeling I'd had since awakening. "He wasn't old when I knew him," I reminded Nicolas as much as myself.

"Of course not." He crossed his arms and stared at the flowers, and I could imagine him picturing what the wrinkled man he'd met might have looked like when he was younger. Picturing us together. I couldn't tell if he was being hesitant or thoughtful, but his next words came slower. "Makes sense why he was adamant I save you. So you two were in love?"

There was that word again, the one that brought nothing but confusion to my mind. "Honest answer? I'm not certain. There was something there."

His eyes turned to mine. "Have you never been in love before?" Disbelief rolled from his tone.

"I think I could have been, given the time. But things were quite complicated." It wasn't a proper answer, or anything close, but it was the best I could offer. "Have you been in love?"

My heart tightened a bit as I asked him, an unfamiliar emotion twisting in my chest. Envy, I noted. Envy for whichever girl surly had his heart before me. It was the faintest glimmer that indicated feelings of attraction dwelled within me. Those moments were sparce enough to make me wonder if they were there, but just as I was starting to doubt, I'd get another fluttering and it'd be enough to give me hope.

As I asked the question, Nicolas's withdrew his hand from near mine on the stone banister. "I was. Once. But it was several years ago."

"What was she like?" I couldn't keep myself from asking.

It took him a while to answer, long enough that the wind tousled his hair several times before he chose his answer. "Warm-hearted."

As innocent as his description was, it brought a second pain to my heart. Warm-hearted. Unlike me, the girl from ice. No one would use such a kind term to label me. They would use other words, harsher words, such as *self-centered, power-hungry, cold.* And those would have come from my family. The only ones I'd allowed close to me.

Be careful, my father had once spoke to Cassian while I listened in. *Power can corrupt the purest hearts.*

My heart had certainly been corrupted in Elenvérs, and if I wasn't careful, it'd ruin me again.

I wouldn't allow that to happen here. I twisted nearer to Nicolas until the sun aligned behind his head, casting its golden glow across the roof. "What happened with her? Unless you were also separated by a sleeping curse," I joked.

He grinned. "No. Nothing quite as extravagant as that. It was a few years ago, and she decided she didn't want me, so she left."

It was the barest bones of the story, but I didn't mind. He'd been so considerate with me, giving me space where I needed it. I wouldn't push him, either.

"But it's all for the best, because now I get the chance to pursue you."

I became keenly aware of the way his eyes held mine unwaveringly, and how small of a space stood between us. I wondered if he might close it, or if he knew that I wanted him to. He hadn't kissed me since Elenvérs, and a kiss while we were both conscious sounded nice.

He and I both had pasts, but somehow, we'd come together, and nothing else mattered than that. Perhaps it was the romantic rooftop garden with the setting sun behind us, or perhaps the wine Lucille gave me was stronger than I thought.

But in this moment, I believed that I could have a future here. A happy one.

His hand inched forward, moving slow along the warm stone. I reached to meet it and waited in eager anticipation for what might come next.

I expected the warmth of a kiss. Not the sharp sting of an arrow tearing across the skin of my arm.

It sunk into the wooden box of soil beside us with a thud, and we stared in shock for a moment. Nicolas reacted first, hurling himself over me to pin us to the ground.

An arrow, I thought wildly. *Was that an arrow?*

"Don't move, you'll be safe," Nicolas's voice rasped into my ear.

Poor timing, for at the next moment another arrow came, shot at a higher angle so it tipped in the air and dropped back toward us. It hit the other end of the tower, but I guessed the archer would adjust quickly. The next shot could very well pierce us.

My arm tingled with pain, but nothing bad enough that I feared significant blood loss. I didn't look at my wound as I searched for the trap door.

Shouting came a moment later from the east, and Nicolas bent his head down to mine. "That's our guards. It's going to be okay."

I nodded, but still braced myself for another arrow. None came.

We stayed in that position—my body against the ground and Nicolas braced above me, until the shouting ceased and the air sat still. Then Nicolas eased himself to the railing to peer over. I was terrified he'd get an arrow to the face, but a moment later he pulled back and shrugged. "I don't see anything."

Mattias crawled onto the roof a moment later, making us both jump. "At ease." He put up his hands. "Everything is safe now. Though I recommend staying inside for a while."

"Who was that?" Nicolas asked.

"That," Mattias said, "was the unrest I had told you about. You should speak with the king urgently."

"But what do they want?" Nicolas pressed. "I don't know why there'd be unrest." He glanced at me as if I might have the answer, but I was too busy controlling my heart rate to shake my head.

The other man sighed heavily. "Their problem, it would appear, is you."

Chapter Seven

"YOU SHOULD NEVER HAVE been on the roof," Ava scolded, as if us being shot at was our fault. Or, from the way she was ignoring me, my fault. I wanted to say something to defend us or give her a sharp reply which she richly deserved, but I held my tongue.

"The unrest," Nicolas looked directly to King Silas who rubbed his temples while leaning back in the chair behind his desk. "What is it over?"

"There are so many things that people can get upset about," the king said in a voice that sounded practiced. "Tariffs, living conditions, not enough festivals, it's quite difficult to keep them happy all the time."

"Mattias told me it was because of me," Nicolas said. He didn't waver from his stance in front of the closed door, keeping his arms crossed over his chest and head squared in determination to get his answer. I kept one hand wrapped around my arm to still the bleeding and hide my wound. Nicolas didn't need to worry over me right now.

"He should not have told you that," Ava grumbled.

Martin glanced between the other two before coughing. "Here's the deal, son. Some feel the way you acquired the throne is...unfair. After all, you were third in line and no one expected you to claim the title. But you did. Some claim you orchestrated that, but that can't be proven."

"Because it's false."

"Yes, yes. But if you can come to the throne, a mere son of a sea merchant with the barest relation to the king, then other's feel they have a claim as well. Now, multiple eligible families are stepping forward with why their son deserves to be the next king and are gaining some support."

Nicolas stepped back, pain stricken. "They doubt me?"

"Well you've been gone for quite some time," Ava commented with a sharp look at me. That woman did not mask her feelings. "But we will right this. You needn't have been bothered." Now she cast a displeasing look upon Martin.

Now I could be useful. I could show them I was more than a girl who took a really long nap. "So send Nicolas out to these regions to regain the support of his people. Prove that not only is he the one with the strongest rightful claim to the throne, but the best one to have it."

Ava gasped. "You want to send my son into the wild to get shot?"

I resisted rolling my eyes. "Surely you have more faith in your knights than that?"

"You will find that I have faith in very little, except for that the fight for a throne can be a bloody one."

"It's not a bad idea," Nicolas said.

King Silas scratched his head. "There's no way to guarantee you'd win their favor. Some people are very loyal to the sons from their regions."

"Then find a way to discredit these sons," I suggested. Martin smiled while the king looked at me as if for the first time. Sizing me up. Seeing what I might be capable of.

"We don't expect you to solve this. We have our advisors on it."

"I like her ideas," Nicolas, faithful as ever, spoke up. Then he fell silent again. His chin tucked into his chest as he stared at the ground, his eyes darting from one stone to the next as if he saw the puzzle on the ground and he could sort it there, but with each moment his brows only drew tighter together.

I straightened my shoulders and mimicked my father's face as he would speak to his council. "I am happy to join these advisors. I was well trained by my father to run my kingdom, and don't wish to waste my talents."

Ava's head tipped back to look down her nose at me. "Were you? Interesting."

"Elenvérs was well respected for it's smart leaders and ability to strategize," I informed her.

"If I recall correctly," Ava glanced at her husband and the king. "Elenvérs fell."

Her words stabbed my chest as sharp as any iron-tipped sword, and my emotions threatened to bleed on the floor for all to see. Guilt. Shame. Pain over what had happened to my country. I kept my jaw clenched and spoke through my teeth. "Elenvérs was saved. They thrive in the south, do they not?"

"Hm," she replied. The corners of her lips tightened as she turned to stroll about the room in a casual demeanor. She paused by the window and stared out at the night, and it was hard to tell if she was lost in thought or free of thoughts completely.

Nicolas had brought his hands to his chin and breathed into them. "Something has to be done. What if Your Majesty accompanies me to the eligible sons' homes? Be certain that a crowd follows us. Show them official documents stating that I'm next in line and see who still protests. They may grumble against me, but it takes a bold man to disagree with his king."

King Silas and Martin exchanged glances. While I was impressed with the idea, their frowns didn't appear convinced. "We fear for your safety if you travel in such a manner. It wouldn't be wise for you both to leave the castle together," Martin said.

"Besides, we are beyond that. What started as whispers has turned to roars. The people are no longer quiet about their desires to put their own bloodline on the throne. Families who, forgive me for saying so," King Silas glanced to Ava, "deserve the right just as much as your family."

Nicolas spoke with determination. "Then we let one of them have it."

The entire room silenced.

"Let them," he went on. "I've never cared to be king, and if they do, they should have the chance."

King Silas drew his lips into a long, thin line. "It won't do good. We give it to one, the others will still want it. And while their families may be deserving, I know the sons they are putting forward. They would not rule as well as you. Ultimately it would bring great ruin to Thames."

Nicolas opened his mouth to say more, but Ava pulled away from the window. "May I propose a new idea? Refusing them will only brew more strife. So we entertain them. They think they deserve the throne, so we give them a chance at it."

Though she paused here, the room remained silent, each of us squinting our eyes or tilting our heads to guess at her meaning. It sounded like what Nicolas had just said.

"Those boys aren't worthy," King Silas repeated.

Ava grinned in the confusion, allowing herself to dwell in it as if she basked in the idea of being the only one with some knowledge.

Finally, after Nicolas pressed for her to go on, she spoke again.

"Nicolas won't lose his right. But we allow eligible families to send their picks, their *female* picks, to compete for the place of queen."

She grinned at me, as if this idea brought her great joy. As if the idea of getting rid of me was as appealing as squashing the unrest in the kingdom. As if I was as much of a threat to Thames as anything.

All I could do was stare back, suddenly realizing what form of opponent she may turn out to be.

"Absolutely not," Nicolas was quick to shake his head. "No. I have my queen." His hand found mine, but the unspoken words between us screamed louder than his remark. We were not in love. We were not planning a wedding. At the moment, we were little more than friends who were attempting to find the spark in our relationship.

And if he could find that spark with someone else and save his kingdom, who was I to stand in the way?

"The kingdom knows of Rowan. They know Nicolas went to find his bride. We can't erase that."

Ava shrugged. "We don't have to. Let us put on games to find our queen. Competitions the girls must partake in to see who is the worthiest. If the other girls fall short in these tests while Rowan excels, then it will be no one's fault when she is crowned. The people get a good sport out of it, they are given a fair opportunity at the throne, and it will be made clear that should their girls lose, further squabbles will be dealt with most harshly."

King Silas brought a hand to his chin.

"We can create a contract they must sign before sending a girl," Ava went on, "saying they'll agree to the outcome of the competition. They may send one delegate to watch to be certain it is a fair ruling."

"No," Nicolas protested further, and his father backed him up, but the king took a deep sigh. This was his kingdom, and he likely cared very little about which girl Nicolas ended up with. If this crazy plan would settle the unrest, he wouldn't give me another thought.

Seeing his hesitation, Ava nudged, "At the very least, it buys us more time. A lot more time. If the future of Thames is important to us, then this is the smartest plan."

She was intelligent. I'd been put into a position where I couldn't argue without appearing as if I didn't care for Thames, but if I didn't say something then it appeared like I didn't care for Nicolas.

"We would be giving them what they want—a chance at the throne," King Silas stroked his short, brown beard, "and in an environment where we could control the outcome."

"Exactly," Ava said.

"And when none of their daughters win? It'll be obvious this was a scheme," Martin spoke up.

Ava gave her husband a look. "It won't. We will make the competitions difficult enough that the girls might even send themselves home. But who knows? Perhaps one of them will win us all over in the end."

My jaw clenched together. She didn't look my way.

"I'll have to talk this over with my advisors," King Silas said. "But I approve of the plan, and I say we start as soon as possible. A competition for the crown prince's hand, we will call it."

"No," Nicolas laughed like this must be some joke. He looked from between his parents and the king. "No. Never. I'll pick Rowan at the end of it; I won't play with her like that."

King Silas stepped forward, determination brewing in his eyes. The sort of determination that wouldn't be quelled. His decision was made, and with it, my position in his plan established. Not even Nicolas could stop this from happening. "For your country, you will do anything. You will condone this competition, you will be nice to the contestants, and you will allow Rowan to prove herself."

He brushed past us to open the door. "You fought to wake this girl. Now it's time to see if she will fight for you."

Chapter Eight

THE KING WALKED OUT, and I only waited a few moments before following, my voice caught in my throat and frustration steaming in my bones. Nicolas grabbed my hand before I crossed the doorway. "You can't change his mind," he said. To his credit, disappointment simmered behind his warm eyes, along with a dash of hopelessness as he searched mine.

"I'm not trying to change his mind," I said, spinning to see him and pulling my arm free. "I'm going to my room. It's late, I'm tired, and I've been shot."

I released my blood-coated hand from on my other arm, where for the first time they all noticed the cut from the arrow. It wasn't deep, but the time that I'd allowed it to go untended had resulted in a fair amount of smudged blood that made it appear worse, especially when a drop spilled from my fingers.

It landed on the stone floor, inches from the perfectly clean carpet.

"Was that from the roof?" Nicolas stared. "Why didn't you say something?"

"Because it seemed others had more important things to say. If you'll excuse me."

Nicolas was always so good about giving me space, but this time he trailed after me. His mother called for him to let me go, but he didn't listen. "Rowan, let me take you to the hospital wing." He stopped me in the hallway. "That should be washed."

The night had settled around us, and with it, the first hint of stillness the palace had offered me. There were no ladies in the corridor to exchange jokes or stare at me when I passed, no curious maids scurrying by with their odd-looking hats tied under their chins. There was only Nicolas and me, and a feeling that I'd become trapped in something I couldn't avoid.

It was a feeling I knew well. I'd been trapped in a curse my whole life. I didn't escape that, either.

I longed for freedom. I longed for a home. I longed for a sense of control over my life. But as I yearned for these things, the air grew thinner around me, threatening to never give me these things that came so easily to others.

"I just want to go to bed," I said, curling my arms by my side, using the back of my hand to prevent the wound from bloodying my nice dress. "It's been such a long day, and now

I'm being asked to fight for something that, I just don't know..."

My voice trailed. He took a step back.

"You don't know if you want this enough to compete," he finished the line for me.

That wasn't what I planned to say, but it might as well have been. The truth of the situation burned into me, reminding me of all the reasons why I should walk away.

"We're not in love," I whispered, aware of his parents lingering in the room behind him. "We don't share a history together or have a collection of fond memories to get us through this. I'd be no different than any of the other girls to you, except they'd be coming in with far more determination and seduction than I could fake right now."

He planted his feet on the floor and ran his hand through his long hair. "You don't want to try anymore."

"I didn't say that. I said I don't know."

"I didn't trudge through the frozen north for them. I didn't devote years to finding them. I didn't promise myself to them. I've done those things for you, Rowan. You. And through these few months together I've proved that I am in this, no matter how complicated it may be. But it's splendid to know where you stand right now. No one is forcing you to stay. I meant it when I said you can leave at any time; and if staying and helping me fight for my kingdom isn't what you desire, then you are welcome to leave."

He'd been so patient and caring over the months. But he'd finally snapped.

Nicolas was offering the freedom I pinned for, but why did it only bring further pain?

We stood facing each other, and it felt very much like the beginning of a match, one that I didn't see a way for us to both win. "We need sleep," I said finally.

"Good night, then." Nicolas strode past me. "Don't forget to clean your arm. It could get infected."

As he walked away, I couldn't help but feel that I'd broken something that was never perfect to begin with. A crack marred our relationship, and now we were like one of the scarves hanging from the windows—barely hanging on and prone to drift whichever way the wind blew us.

I could only hope we were both in one piece when the wind settled.

My room was cloaked in darkness as I crept in. Only a lone candle flickered beside a velvet chair where Dana perched with fabric draped over her leg and a silver needle in her fingers. She set these aside to greet me. "Good evening, Rowan. Rosalie is asleep in the back, so don't be too loud." Her eyes trailed to my arm. "Can we expect to find blood on you every time you walk through that door?"

I smiled, despite myself. "Let's hope not."

Isabel peeked from the side room, where Lucille was fast asleep on one of the couches behind her. Her eyes bulged when she saw my arm. "You're going to be a handful, aren't you?"

"It would appear that way," I whispered, glancing to my arm. Blood from the small wound had been smeared to my elbow, coating a quarter of my arm. Isabel went into my bedroom before coming back with a wooden basin and dark rag hanging over the side.

"Wash it," she ordered, setting it on the floor with a grunt. "I'll find something to tie around it so you don't get blood on the freshly cleaned sheets. Dana, you go on to bed. I've got this here."

Dana stroked her daughter-in-law's hair. "Thank you, dear. I'll be back as the sun rises."

"Don't rush," I whispered over my shoulder. "I expect to be asleep long after that."

With a nod, she gently closed the door behind her, and I settled on the floor beside Isabel. "You don't have to bother with that," I said, taking the rag from her hand before she could clean my arm. "I'll take care of myself."

She didn't protest as she handed it over, but she hesitated before moving. "Should I ask why you're in a sour mood? Your face is tight, and if you push your lips any closer together, they might crack."

I hadn't realized I was pursing my lips. I sighed and relaxed my face. "It's nothing. Merely politics that I greatly desire to not be a part of."

"Hmm." She nodded as if she understood completely. I wished she did. I wished she could tell me what to do. The confidence I once had in Elenvérs now felt out of reach, trapped in a chasm that I couldn't access, crumbled along with the rest of my home. Leaving pieces of myself that I couldn't recognize.

Isabel did have one piece of advice. "Then don't be a part of them."

It sounded too easy. "I don't think that's an option."

She scrunched her face in apology as she wiped her wet hands on her sleeves. "I wish I were more help."

"You're married, right?" I asked before she trailed back to bed.

Her head tilted, like the very thought of it warmed her heart. Her fingers went to the delicate copper link around her neck. "I am. To Dana's son." Her voice was softer as she spoke, the fondness radiating off every syllable.

I thought before pressing. "How did you know when you were in love?"

"When I wanted to be around him all the time," she said without delay. Her eyes twinkled like stars. I set down my rag to listen, hoping to catch a piece of her relationship and transfer it to my own heart, like her love could summon the feelings from inside me. "It brought peace to my heart, and even when we'd have an argument, I still knew he was the right one for me. It was a certainty I'd never experienced before."

I had anything but certainty.

At my face, she smiled. "I can tell by your expression that I've cleared things up for you. Don't worry, Rowan. Love takes time. I didn't like Mateo at all when I met him."

That part soothed my worries more than she could know. At least I liked Nicolas, that wasn't in question. Perhaps all I needed was more time. And after a while, maybe my face would shine when someone mentioned Nicolas just like Isabel's did. Then one day I'd look back on this queen competition as how we fell in love, not how I was forced into something I didn't want.

"Thank you, Isabel. That helps a lot."

"Then I've done my job for the night. I'll be in the other room if you need me."

My feelings for Nicolas refused to be sorted out tonight, but one thing settled over me with absolute clarity. If Ava wanted to test me, I would prove myself to her, and to this country, as a woman they could not trifle with. And hopefully I'd find my place along the way.

A knock on the door awoke me as Lucille picked up her skirts to go answer it. The sun broke through the thin curtains as tiny shards that hung in the air, and a small loaf of bread accompanied by a jar of honey sat beside my bed.

I reached for the bread, but stopped short when Lucille cried out, "Are you decent?"

"Yes," I replied after a quick glance.

Nicolas stepped into the sitting room. I sat up straighter.

He brought himself to the threshold of the bedroom, where he cleared his throat. His fingers trifled with the hem of his dark green suit, and his olive shoes tapped in a jittery motion. "I'm so sorry, Rowan. I tried to stop them. I went to the advisor's meeting this morning, but they approved the idea of a queen competition."

Lucille's face crunched into confusion at the term, while my shoulders sunk. It was too late to stop this from happening now.

"When?" I breathed.

He sighed. "The invitations have already been sent out. The girls will arrive in two weeks."

Chapter Nine

I SPENT THE MORNING in my room, holed up with the bread and honey, with Cassian's journal and paintings sprawled out on the bed. It was the first time I could examine them in such a way, so openly without fear of mud tarnishing them or offending Nicolas at how obsessed I was over them.

My parent's faces stared back at me, aging from one image to the next. Cassian had drawn himself as well, along with a picture depicting each of his children. Compassion, or it might have been pity, led him to leave his wife out of the drawings, so I didn't have to stare at the girl who had his heart after I did.

The entries began as soon as they settled into their new home after my wish took them south. Cassian wrote about what the land was like, their struggles forming relationships with the neighbors, and the process of rebuilding from the ruins of old. He spoke of our family's tears as they left not one, but two daughters behind. One to sleep and one to rule an enemy kingdom.

Elis was never mentioned again, so I could only assume their relationship never repaired.

From there, the entries were short and spaced out by many years. Cassian's coronation, his first child, handing the throne over. Some of my parent's travels, and a vineyard they grew together in retirement. He recounted the few times he traveled to see me, as well as the one time he brought my parents along with him. The path was treacherous, and he knew my parents wouldn't fare well. Sure enough, just as I remembered from when I was asleep, my parents died outside the walls of Elenvérs.

The final entry described meeting Nicolas, and his hope that this boy would one day wake me.

Then he signed off with these final words,

Because of your selflessness and bravery, Elenvérs thrives. You are forever a queen, and forever have a piece of my heart.

With love,

Cassian

I folded the note back up. After asking Nicolas to wake me when Nicolas was no more than the child of a sea merchant, Cassian couldn't have known I'd have a chance to be a queen again someday. He couldn't know what would become of me. But he chose to use his final words to me as a reminder that I am a queen, even if no one sees it.

It was different words than my mother might have left me, or my father. They would say I'd fought well, and to enjoy my new life. That Elenvérs was safe and I could lay down my arms. To love and be happy.

I no longer urged to be queen. Cassian would be shocked to know that. All I desired was some sort of happiness in this life.

"My lady."

I looked up, surprised by the formality as much as I was about the sudden voice. Lucille stood in the doorway wearing a deep red dress and straight face.

"What is it?" I set the notebook aside to stand. Some of the yellowed drawings drifted off the bedspread to graze my toes.

Lucille kept her back as straight as a broadsword as she folded her thin hands in front of her body. "Lady Ava would like to meet with you."

I frowned. "You know, I must tell you Isabel. That lady is not—"

"Lady Ava, may I present Princess Rowan!" Lucille rushed to speak, stepping to the side to allow Nicolas's mother to step from around the corner. My cheeks flushed red.

"Ava. I wasn't expecting you."

Her hair was a curtain of silk around her shoulders, with the softest curls gracing the tips. She wore a simple, button up dress, a band of gold on each wrist, and most interestingly, a smile.

I could only fear what I'd done for her to wear a face of false pleasure.

"I hope I'm not disturbing you this morning," she said, her voice dripping with all the sugar of the land. "Yesterday did not go well, and I'm here to mend that."

I wondered if she meant when she met me, or when she declared she'd be bringing other women into the castle to take my place. I'd no experience in meeting a sweetheart's parents, but that might be the worst that the day could have gone.

Either way I kept my hands clasped together in polite stillness as she slithered nearer. Her eye's fell to the papers on my bed and I wanted to tear them away or pull a blanket over my possessions because her looking at them somehow left her mark on them.

She looked back to me. "Nicolas has spoken quite fondly of you all day. My husband seems just as in love as he is. I realized I didn't take the chance to get to know you as I ought to."

Because she doesn't love me, too. Because she can't fathom what her son sees in me. I didn't say those things out loud but donned a smile of my own. "That'd be lovely."

Lucille remained in the sitting room busying herself, but she peeked into the room to see how it was going. I wanted to make a face, but there was nothing I could do without Ava's gaze catching me.

Ava sighed, as if we had much to discuss. "First, let's speak of this queen competition. Nicolas showed me how my actions could lead you to believe I don't want you here. That is not the intention. In fact, I think we could work together to assure you win, without leaving a trace for the public to see."

"That's the trick, isn't it?" I asked, settling on the corner of my bed to gather the papers. "Making the competition appear real when no one can truly win. A king might hope his people were smarter than that."

"Smart people do not need to be led," Ava flashed back. "Or else they'd have no use of their king."

She might be right, but so was I. They could force me to compete, but I could never win. Not as a pawn under her thumb.

I stayed on the bed after my papers were stacked away, appreciating both the comfort of it and how my appearing at ease gave me slightly more control. "The other girls should still win something. Places on the council, ranks among the knights, land for their family. So none can say they wasted their time," I suggested.

She tilted her head at me. "Wise advice. What of the actual competitions? What are your strengths? Weaknesses?"

"I'm good at archery," I answered without thinking, then snapped my mouth shut.

Her eyes gleamed like opals, and her mouth was set in a smile that appeared friendly. But she leaned forward in a way that indicated intense focus, like she waited for me to slip up. To reveal some secret.

My strengths and weaknesses. These would be considered as she planned the competitions. And if she planned them around my weaknesses, I would be sure to lose.

It was a game, and I suspected her of playing it well.

"I'm terrible at swordplay, however. And dancing. And navigating the stars." I dropped lie after lie, hoping none could trap me. She couldn't know the lessons I'd been given growing up that taught me each of these skills well. If she used any of these weaknesses as a theme in the competition, I would do fine.

"Go on," she urged.

"I'm decent at horseback riding," I continued to fib. I could lead a horse through snow-capped mountains, but that was about it. "I'm fond of embroidery and have always had a natural ability to cook desserts."

With each thing I said, her smile deepened, and her head nodded. "Good, good," she said, and clasped her hands together once I finished speaking. "We can use those. Perfect. If you'll excuse me, there is much preparation to do."

"May I help with anything?" I asked. The more control I had over these competitions, the better.

She clicked her tongue. "I'm afraid not. We mustn't appear to show favoritism toward you. For the sake of appearances and all," she added with a nonchalant gesture and wink, like the two of us shared in a grand joke.

"Of course."

Her answer didn't surprise me. How could they not appear to show me favoritism when I lived in the castle with them already? When Nicolas woke me with true love's kiss? If I were any of the other girls, I'd be intimidated by challenging me for the place as Nicolas's queen.

I could use that. They needn't know that Nicolas and I were struggling to fall in love. They needn't know that his heart might be easily won by another. I could make them believe we were inseparable, and that even if they could win this competition, they'd never have his affection.

If I wanted, I could scare them away. It'd certainly come more naturally to me than charming them.

"My lady?" Lucille's soft voice drew Ava's attention. A short, thin man with a tri-colored vest and striking blue eyes stood at her side with his arms folded before him.

"Chancley, thank you for finding me." Ava rushed from my bedroom and into the sitting room to greet the man with a kiss on both cheeks.

"You said it was urgent," he said between her kisses.

"Quite. Take this," she produced a stark-white envelope with orange markings on the front from the sides of her flowy jacket, "and hurry. There can be no delays."

He glanced to the front, and a brow raised. He opened his mouth, but Ava put up a hand. "Go."

With the slightest hesitation in his step, he bowed out.

She watched him depart before glancing to me. "I'll see you later, my dear." Her footsteps echoed long after the door shut between us.

I took my first deep breath since she'd arrived, and Lucille chuckled. "Your dislike is curious. She's never proven to be anything other than kind."

The closed door stared at me, challenging me. I could open it, undo what I'd just done. Confess my real strengths and weaknesses and trust she'd use the information the way I intended. But with each moment that passed my decision became final. At the first competition I'd either struggle because of my lies or be proven right by excelling. Either way I feared I'd just made an enemy.

"Let us hope you are wrong," I said. "Or else I just made a terrible mistake."

Chapter Ten

MOST OF THE WINDOWS in the castle were open, allowing a gentle breeze to dance through the wide halls, prompting me to pair a long-sleeved sweater with my dress. It was the warmest I'd dressed since arriving here, but as the afternoon turned to evening, it would only get colder, and the additional layer would be appreciated.

Nicolas had told me the yellow scarf from his manservant was from his rooms, so using that as a guide led me to his hallway, where a helpful servant pointed me to the right door. It sat slightly ajar, allowing two voices to stream out.

"...fifteen families," Nicolas's voice was the first to become clear.

The second let out a low whistle. "That's a lot of girls who are about to be in the castle."

Fifteen. I hadn't known that. I couldn't decide if that number felt high or low.

"If they all arrive. Many are already promised to another," Nicolas said.

I brought my hand to the level of my chest to knock as the other man replied, "Still. You think you'll find one you like more than Rowan?"

I should knock. They should know that I'm here. But my hand stilled in the air, and I held my breath for the reply.

It didn't come right away. But finally Nicolas answered, "I don't. I really don't."

"So you love Rowan?"

Knock. Raise your hand and knock on the door.

My body refused to listen to anything other than their voices. "Not yet. But I like her quite a bit. She's smart, I can tell. And fearless. Has a taste for adventure. She's more than those witless daughters of diplomats who visit sometimes who only know how to laugh and swat my arm with their fans. Honestly, my arm is red by the end of the night. I've got half a mind to take those ridiculous fans away."

I made a mental note to never swat his arm with a fan.

"I hope she deserves you, sire. That is all."

Desire stirred within me, a desire to be the woman Nicolas thought I was. To be someone who deserved him. To remove my walls and know what it felt like to be loved by someone I could trust.

My heart ached. When someone asked how he felt about me, I wanted there to be no doubt in his reply.

I retreated several paces back down the hallway, then exaggerated the volume of my steps leading back to the door, where I knocked loudly. "Nicolas?"

A different gentleman appeared, one with a full, black beard and gray garments stretched over a large frame.

"Rowan," Nicolas stepped into view with haphazard hair and the sleeves of his maroon jacket rolled carelessly by his elbows. He pushed back the chair by his desk and crossed to us with a gesture to the man before me. "This is my manservant and friend, Giermo."

Giermo gave a slight bow, only flickering his eyes from me for a moment.

"It's great to meet you," I told him in an even tone. Unsure if he cared for me or hated me by the intense look in his eye.

"Likewise." His gaze trailed over me similar to Mattias's when he first met me. Calculating. Curious. Wondering about the girl Nicolas woke from the northern ice palace and who she might turn out to be.

"I'll leave you two alone." Giermo offered another bow, to Nicolas this time, before closing the door behind him. He left us alone with the snap of fire by a marble hearth and the rustle of silky curtains prancing with each new breeze.

Nicolas stepped closer and put a hand over his chest. "Rowan, I'm sorry about how things went yesterday. Trust me,

I've been thinking of introducing you to my parents since long before I awoke you, and never did I consider you being shot by an arrow or my mom suggesting a competition for your place."

The way he said it now sounded almost funny. As if decisions hadn't been made that still affected us.

He glanced to my arm where Isabel helped me wrap new bandages. They weren't necessary now; it was more to keep prying eyes from staring at a long cut. I attracted enough stares as it was.

"My arm is fine," I informed him. "As for the Queen's Competition—we'll figure it out. But I shouldn't have spoken out like that yesterday."

His brows went up slightly and shoulders relaxed, as if he'd been ready for an argument. I offered a small smile to show him I brought none with me, and he grinned back.

"Please, always speak your mind with me. I must say, you sound more," he searched for the word as he led me to the hearth where two heavily cushioned chairs basked in the warmth, "hopeful than you did last night. Has something changed?"

I sighed, half from exhaustion and half from the satisfaction of settling into such a soft chair. We didn't have extravagance like this in Elenvérs. My mind searched for words to describe how I felt without repeating the harshness of last night.

My hands rested on my lap. "I'm unsure of anything at the moment, so I ought to adopt a flexible attitude while we navigate something that is new to both of us. Lashing out at you isn't fair when you've been generous in giving me time to find my place." Those words were clear enough that I remained uncertain about my position here, but they promised I'd try to figure it out, and be civil as I did so.

"Thank you," he said through a smile.

I pinched my skirts between my fingers to fumble with as I went on. "But I wanted to talk to you about something first."

"Anything." Nicolas leaned forward on his elbows while the flames sent orange hues gamboling over his skin. He looked handsome in the woods with dirt trapped in his hair and hunting knife in his hand, but here in his castle, bathed and dressed in finery, he was classy and confident. Handsome in a more regal sort of way. And he *smelled* fantastic.

To forget how he smelled and focus on what needed to be said, I required a second deep breath. "All of this is an attempt to heal the divide in your kingdom. It's an offering for one of the nobles to rise to power in Thames. Clearly I am not helpful in doing that." Nicolas frowned while I hurried to finish. "It might make sense for you to consider one of the other girls."

He stood from his seat. "Is this having a flexible attitude? Asking me to choose another?"

I straightened. "This is me trying to help."

He looked at me like I was insane. "No. I'm doing my best not to be hurt by your obvious lack of desire to get to know me better. It's a real blow to my pride, I'll tell you that. But I am only interested in pursuing you."

Pain cracked across his face as his brows bent together and lips curved toward his chin. He didn't move to sit by me again, so I stood to be near him.

I smiled so he'd see some of my heart. "I want to get to know you better. I want to see if we can have a life together. But I don't want to be the fall of your kingdom. All I'm asking is that you go into this with an open mind. Meet the other girls first. If you still decide that you want me, then I promise to fight for you with equal fervor."

The frown on his face didn't pull as deep anymore, and it flattened as I took his hand in mine. His large hands dwarfed mine, and the hairs on his forearm tickled when I stepped closer.

I stared into his caramel eyes, hoping he'd understand me. "For now, I want to be here. But I saw my kingdom fall, and in my mind, it wasn't that long ago. I won't be the collapse of another."

"You won't." His breath caressed my forehead, warm and tinged with mint. "Rowan, I intend for you to be the jewel of the kingdom, and together, we will make it strong. You will bring nothing but joy to us all."

The image of that sent sparks rushing through my veins. We could have a marvelous future together. "I hope so."

His chest took its time to rise and fall. "Now, if we are quite done speaking of me picking a new bride after I went through quite the ordeal to find you, there was something I wanted to talk about as well. You were right when you said our relationship doesn't have much to stand on right now. We need memories of our own. There are two weeks before the other girls get here, so let's use that to our advantage. Those two weeks are for you and me."

"Agreed."

His face scrunched together. "Right after today. I have a full day of meetings that I can't get out of. But tomorrow?"

I gave a small smile. "Tomorrow."

Chapter Eleven

ISABEL SET ROSALIE ON her lap where the child alternated between sucking on her thumb and the mass of knitted blanket around them. Their hair matched today—frizzy coils that didn't stand a chance against this humidity. It hung in the air like a stubborn pond that refused to settle on the ground, thick enough that I was convinced all I needed to do was stick out my tongue and I'd get a drink. Lucille opened the windows to give us a cool breeze, but I wondered if I'd ever feel something as cold as the mountains in Elenvérs again.

"So what is a Queen's Competition?" Isabel asked. Her voice was as soothing as a mother's ought to be, and little Rosalie tilted her head up at the sound.

"It's every bit as awful as it sounds," I said, curling my legs beneath me. "A competition for the place of queen."

Lucille and Isabel exchanged looks, while Dana set down the towels to raise a brow. "King Silas seeking a bride?"

"I wish," I said. "That would be fine. In fact, I think I should suggest that very thing. But no, not Silas."

They gave understanding nods. "Nicolas?"

"Nicolas."

Isabel tore a strand of her hair from Rosalie's tight grasp. "But he has you."

"He also has his mother," I groaned. "And a kingdom in unrest. Apparently, many of the local lords are offering their eligible sons to take Nicolas's place, and King Silas is instead suggesting they offer their eligible daughters to compete for the place of future queen of Thames."

Lucille fastened the curtain away from the window before joining us. "Normally this would excite me. But what does that mean for you?"

I shrugged. "I have to compete."

"But Nicolas already chose you," Lucille argued.

"Doesn't matter. The competition isn't up to Nicolas. He won't have a say in who wins. He could say he wants me all day long, but unless I prove myself in these competitions, it won't matter." Not to mention that I doubted Nicolas would fight for me if I didn't fight myself. Last night he made it decently clear that he was coming to the end of his patience.

It was fair. But it was terrifying that he'd need an answer soon. Be his queen or walk away.

"I bet you'll excel in the competitions," Dana said helpfully.

"If they are all fighting, then yes. But truthfully, I don't know how to be queen of a country that I know so little about. If they ask one question about Thames' history, I'll look like a fool."

"Everyone knows your story," Isabel said. "You'll be given grace."

Perhaps. But a queen shouldn't need grace. The other girls would have a significant advantage coming in. They knew Thames much better than I. And odds were, they knew Nicolas about as well as I did, too.

"Luckily, I have two weeks to prepare. So I can absorb as much history during that time as possible," I suggested.

Lucille nudged Isabel. "Perhaps Rowan should go to the library now to study."

I frowned. "I don't need to start right this hour."

Lucille coughed and nudged Isabel again. The older girl knit her brows together. "Why right now?" She glanced to the clock. "Oh, you know what, now would be a splendid time."

"I appreciate your enthusiasm for me to win, but I'm quite famished. Could I study later."

"No," the girls said in unison. Lucille practically dragged me off the lounger. "Come now, the library is practically vacant at this hour. Plus, mama always told me not to put things off."

"That's right I did," Dana replied with a knowing smile. I cast her a helpless look, but she shooed me on. "Go on now. It'll give me a proper chance to tidy this place up."

I couldn't argue with Dana. I allowed Lucille to lead me down the hallway and down a narrow set of stairs. The cobblestones grew dustier and the walls shorter as we descended the spiraling case. Our footsteps echoed loudly. Lucille glanced back once to be certain I followed, and she was grinning from ear to ear.

"I didn't know you were so excited about libraries," I mumbled. As she descended further underground, I stopped. "Thames keeps their library below ground? Why?"

Lucille waved her hand in the air. "You know, the sun...the temperature...the location. I'm not certain. No more questions."

She stopped at a wooden door and gave three knocks. The door was narrow and weathered and the latch flimsy enough that the lock wasn't worth locking. Books must not be prized treasures here.

I'd just opened my mouth to comment on it when the door opened. Nicolas stood inside.

Lucille bowed and scurried off before I had time to respond.

"This isn't the library," I said dumbly.

He laughed. "No, it isn't." He opened the door further. There was no window, but approximately fifty candles lit the small room, ledged on crooked tables and old chairs. Rows of blue fabric hung from the walls and draped along the ceilings, and sheer silk layered overtop until the entire room was transformed into shades of shimmering blue and silver.

Most impressively, snowflakes cut from parchment hung on string.

He'd created winter.

"What is this?" I asked breathlessly.

He held out his hand for me. "Until this place feels like a home for you, I brought your home to you."

I put my hand over my mouth. He'd even set up bucket of ice in the corners to combat this heat. "This must have taken ages."

"I had help," he admitted. "And the best part is," he gestured to one of the tables where two bowls sat, "I got chocolate pudding."

An indistinguishable sound came from my throat. "You know me so well."

He laughed at my expression. "Not as well as I'd like to. I thought it'd be nice to hear more about what Elenvérs was like." He led us to cushions on the floor beside the pudding where cut out snowflakes were scattered on the ground.

As I sat down, one thought ran over and over through my mind. *I don't deserve this.*

He remined me of Elis's suitor, Briggs, when they were first together. My sister was about as romantic as I, but Briggs had more romantic bones in his body than not, and he used everyone to pursue her. Once he'd sent her on a scavenger hunt through the mountains to collect items through a grand hunt: the hooves of wild dear. Antlers of a moose. Fur of a bear. When she returned, he'd had the entire court cheer for her like a returning hero. It'd been exactly the sort of thing that Elis loved.

Even with only knowing me for a few months, Nicolas knew what I loved. My home country and chocolate pudding.

Nicolas dished a spoonful of the dessert into his mouth. He lifted his bowl to look at it. "I haven't had this in years but it's delightful. I don't indulge my sweet tooth as often as I should."

"I can help with that," I said between bites. "Your country has desserts that rival this. Elenvérs was limited on food options, so this was the best we had." The flavor wasn't exactly the same as I was used to, this one was sweeter and thicker, but still good enough to eat the entire bowl.

"You can have as many sweets as the kingdom offers if you decide to stay," Nicolas said.

The Queen's Competition was forefront in my mind, as it must have been in his. But neither of us mentioned it. He'd gone through all this work to do a nice thing for me, and it'd be ruined by talk of what the next few weeks would bring.

"Tell me," Nicolas said, "about what Elenvérs was like."

"Cold," I answered. "Very cold. But at night, the moon hit the ice palace and the color was just like this." I gestured to the silks on the wall. "And suddenly it didn't feel cold anymore. Just beautiful."

"It hardly gets cold here, even in the winter," Nicolas admitted. "Tell me more."

"We made wool blankets and dyed them colors, then hung them over the mouth of caves to make homes. The entire kingdom lived in caves built in the mountainside, and we used to walk through them and explore where the caves led. It was a never-ending tunnel of homes, but sometimes we'd stumble on a new path and find gems in the rocks."

Elis and I had always been so proud to mine the few stones and bring them home like we'd personally saved the kingdom from starvation with our little gems. Her parents had made us feel so special every time.

"My sister used to eat this with me," I said suddenly.

He perked up. "You haven't mentioned a sister."

"She wasn't really my sister." My spoon traced circles in the bottom of the bowl. I hadn't meant to crack open that chasm, but he waited patiently for the words to come out. Elis was more than my sister, she was my best friend. My only friend. The one who loved me more than any, and who hurt me more than I thought someone could.

If he wanted to know who I was, her story was tangled with mine.

Nicolas set his bowl aside to turn himself and face me. He rested on his arm while candles flickered at his feet.

"Her name was Elis. She was the daughter of the nobles who raised me."

And the story came out. He didn't say a word, but his fingers laced through mine and his eye never let go of my gaze. I cringed as I told him about Tarion and how I thought he'd fancied me until realizing it was my sister all along.

"The worst part is, I can't even be mad at her," I said at the end. "She fell in love, and she chased that love at all costs. I can't hate her for that. It just ended so suddenly, and I was left to remember the pain of losing her for one hundred years."

"Were you aware during that time?" Nicolas asked.

I nodded. "I thought of her often. I'll never get to know how her story ended."

Nicolas rubbed his chin thoughtfully. "I don't have a sibling, so I can't know the pain of losing one, but your feelings are perfectly valid. She fell in love, but she betrayed you, and anyone would feel hurt over that."

I gave his hand a squeeze. "Thank you. I just wish I could have spoken to her one more time."

Instead, the last memory I have of her is choosing Tarion over me, and later Tarion coming to kill me because Elis wasn't strong enough to do it herself. I feared I'd never get over that betrayal.

A horrifying thought came to mind.

"I'm caught in the past," I realized.

Nicolas looked at me. "What do you mean?"

"I mean, I'm obsessed with it." I breathed deep. "I think about it all the time—my home, my family, what life was like and what it could have been. I'm constantly comparing this kingdom to Elenvérs and thinking about those who I left behind. I have been around for over a hundred years, but I'm still stuck in that lifetime."

Nicolas watched me. Here before me was a perfectly delightful gentleman, one who knew both how to survive in the woods and how to rule a kingdom. One who took time to make me feel cherished and was patient with my feelings. But I was so trapped in my past that I couldn't enjoy my present.

"If I don't let go, I'll never be happy."

"Tell me how to help you let go," Nicolas said. "Because I want a life with you now."

I wish it could be so simple. I searched for what would help me put my past behind me. Time would be the best remedy for that, and we didn't have unlimited time.

"Kiss me," I said. "And just for a second, let me forget everything else."

He leaned forward without hesitation to cup my neck with his hand. Ever so gently, he brought his lips to mine.

It worked. That kiss was more than I could hope for. It was a reminder that this right here was real. That I had someone who valued me more than I deserved, and that I had something in this life worth living for.

I hooked my arm behind his back to pull myself closer to him. This was a kiss worth waiting a hundred years for.

I pulled back. "Thank you," I whispered.

"Anytime," he said back. "I mean that. I quite like kissing you."

I studied the room with the touch of his kiss lingering on my lips. Elenvérs didn't make men like him. He was one of a kind. If I waited too long to decide what I wanted, I'd lose him.

"I don't need this anymore," I said looking around. The blue and the ice and the snow weren't a part of my life anymore, and I couldn't spend my years mourning for them. I have something new now, and something beautiful. "I don't need Elenvérs. It's time for me to move on."

Nicolas brushed a strand of my red curls away from my face. "You were lost. You woke up to a land where you knew no one and had lost everything. You have every right to be confused."

He was so gracious, but I hated the person who I'd been the past few months. Stumbling through the days with no real direction. Not feeling like I belonged anywhere. More than that, I hated who I was before I fell asleep, too. I didn't want to be that girl anymore. I wanted to be like Nicolas: kind and thoughtful. Selfless for no reason.

I reached up to him. "I'm done being lost. I'm ready to find myself again, and I'm ready to see if I can have a life with you." And just as his face broke into a wide smile, I kissed him again.

He broke away for a moment to whisper. "There's a traveling carnival coming through the villages tonight. Let's sneak out after dark and go."

"Is that allowed?" I asked. My arm tingled where it'd been shot with an arrow, and my body shivered at the thought of how exposed we'd be in town for any rebels to hunt us.

Adventure danced in his eye. "Let's not ask. They'll throw guards at us, or worse, force us to isolate ourselves within these walls. We'll dress as servants and sneak out after dinner to get some time together before the girls arrive." He bounced on his heels like an excited boy. "Are you in?"

I couldn't deny him when he looked so happy. An adventure would do us good. I grinned. "So in."

That night, I found a parchment on my vanity. Nicolas's writing was inside.

I recognized the name when you said it, but I needed to be certain. King Tarion and Queen Elis ruled ThornHigh for thirty-six years. Elis was a beloved queen, who helped expand their kingdom through the mountains and improve relationships with other countries. Without her, ThornHigh would have fallen. She is their most beloved monarch.

Their daughter took over the throne when they stepped down. That daughter's full name was Constance Elaina Rowan Mereed. She gave her first-born daughter your name.

I put a hand to my chest and read it over twice. Elis must have loved me to give her child my name, and Tarion must have loved her to let her.

We never got the chance to make amends, but that knowledge sealed over my pain like a scab, and the bleeding stopped.

"Thank you, Nicolas," I whispered into the silent night, "for knowing exactly what I needed."

Chapter Twelve

THE SLIVERED MOON SPARED enough light to see the courtyard by, and through the shadows a figure moved. My hand instinctively went to the hilt of my sword which Nicolas had insisted be brought. We knew little of what dangers lurked in the tall woods between the castle and the villages, but we had to assume there could be some. Someone who wanted the throne, and an unaccompanied prince would be easy for the reaping.

My feet jittered as I waited for Nicolas. I'd dressed in one of Isabel's simple flax chemises and thin overcoat to mask my sharpened weapons. To hide my one recognizable feature, my stark red hair was pinned at the nape of my neck, and every so often it itched fiercely.

It itched now, but I resisted scratching to watch the figure move. It took the shape of Nicolas, but it wasn't until he shifted from the wall toward the bent hickory tree that his face came into view. He waved to me, indicating I wasn't hidden as well as I'd thought.

"Ready?" I whispered, stepping from the shadows.

He nodded. He wore garments similar to what he had on during our travels from Elenvérs—a simple shirt with laced up collar, long jacket, buckled brown shoes, and daggers at his waist.

"No sword?" I asked.

"Couldn't find a way to hide it. I'm more comfortable with the dagger anyhow, but I bet we won't need it." Still, his eyes traced the stone walls around us, on alert for an intruder in his own home. Or perhaps checking for guards which could halt our midnight escapade.

We'd chosen a courtyard near the back that offered a rear exit. This took us on a longer path through the forest, one riddled with fallen down trees and weepy branches whose leaves kissed the uneven dirt trail that threatened to trip us in the dark night. Broken shards of moonlight occasionally curved through the thick overhang, putting much faith in our ability to maneuver through territory that was unfamiliar to me.

Nicolas fared better, but even he wasn't spared from the occasional branch in the face.

"That one will leave a mark," he grunted, ducking under the thick branch that he'd unexpectedly strolled into.

The dim light made it impossible to see any marring on his cheek. From the slight sting on my skin, I carried a few scratches of my own, but a long-sleeved dress would hide them well. "You can tell your parents that you fell from your bed and they'll think nothing of it," I said.

Nicolas laughed, the first loud sound we'd allowed to carry through the night. He spoke with more hush, "Quite. I fell, and the flat ground carved a scratch into my cheek. They'll be convinced."

I laughed along with him.

Now far enough from the castle and with limited possibility of being caught, Nicolas took my hand and sighed. "How do you like Thames so far? My emotionless mother and the Queen's Competition aside."

Those things didn't feel as big now that I was removed from them. Even Ava seemed less of a threat as I breathed in the cool air and felt Nicolas's hand squeeze mine. I stumbled over unpredictable ground, but his hold on me never wavered.

"I love the colors of the castle. And the warmth. And how the windows are always open, and the moat that's filled with tiny turtles. The wine is sweet, and my maids are sweeter. It's a beautiful place," I told him. "Quite different from the ice walls, narrow hallways, and stony landscape of Elenvérs."

I added that last part to be nice, though despite their differences, I'd always find Elenvérs beautiful. A different sort of beauty than Thames, but no less magnificent. Still, despite what I'd said, my heart fluttered as Nicolas said, "I thought Elenvérs was glorious."

I tightened my grip on his hand, and he smiled down at me. "I'm glad you're enjoying Thames though; it could be a nice home for the two of us. One of my first missions is to convince my parents to move back home to the seaside manor so we can have some peace, but they have taken a strong liking to the castle and it might be hard to compel them away."

"Or we could move to the manor. Any chance the king will let you take over rulership from there?" I asked.

Nicolas tilted back his head and closed his eyes. "I wish. The beauty of Thames is nothing compared to the charming simplicity of my childhood home. The frothing waters lapping against the cliffs in the morning, the footprints left in sand by the causeway, the smell of salt lingering in the evening air— you'd love it. It's impossible not to."

His voice changed as he spoke. It fell deeper and carried a hint of softness to it like his very soul were whispering the words. The longing bled through the tone.

I paused in my steps for a moment to take both his hands. "Then move back there. You shouldn't be forced to stay here, no matter how cute the turtles are."

I made out a hint of a smile, but also the presence of disappointment in the way his chest fell. "I can't. I have a duty here."

"Are you certain it's true what King Silas said? That any of the other lads asking for the throne would only bring destruction? Surely there must be a decent option somewhere." I found it hard to believe that in all the kingdom, there was not one eligible chap with a good head on his shoulders who could lead Thames well. From what I'd seen of Nicolas, he'd do a splendid job, but one could never fully flourish in a place when their heart dwelled in another. He may lead well, but he'd always be trapped by the thoughts of what his life could be like at the seaside manor.

It was a feeling forever anchored to my mind—wondering what my life might have been if I'd escaped the curse. Nicolas shouldn't be bound to the same fate. I'd do anything to spare him from it.

"If you don't want to rule, you shouldn't have to," I added.

He groaned. "I don't. I no longer think I'll hate it, though I doubt I'll ever love the job as I ought to. But I investigated the other men asking for the throne, and Silas might be right. One's family is famous for violence, another's known only for being drunk at all hours, one's a cheat, all of them power hungry and no more gentleman than the next. In an interesting find, one of them runs a household prone to disappearing servants, and it's suspected he kills them in anger. Silas chooses to ignore this due to the amount of wealth he brings to the country, but I plan to make a different decision in my rule. Anyway," he sighed, "it's hopeless. It seems the only decent men were those in line before me, and they are dead now."

As was the queen. The number of persons close to the crown who were now dead was alarming.

"Well," I said, "you never wanted to rule, but I did. Hopefully, I can show you some of the beauty in it."

His thumb traced slow circles on the back of my hand. "If you're a part of it, it's already become beautiful."

Comments like that made my heart tremble. It wasn't used to such kind sentiments, however simple they were.

Just as the terrain had faded from castle to forest, it changed again. Light twinkled through the thickets. The moon was no longer alone in brightening the night, but torches set atop stakes had begun to take over the sky.

"We are almost there," Nicolas said.

The trees thinned out, and hints of a village came to view. Homes were set low in the valley, while large tents decorated the hills. Soft music floated like a cloud through the smoky air, gentle enough that children sleeping in the town below wouldn't be bothered, but enough to set the mood of the carnival.

And what a splendid mood that was.

The largest of the tents sat in the middle ablaze with light and laughter as performers in white and crimson face paint loomed near the front inviting people in to see the fun. Not many guests roamed about, but the performers acted as if the whole kingdom were there to witness their glory. Elephants marched in wide circles around the perimeter with jewels hanging from their ears and guests on their large backs, jugglers threw fire into the sky and caught it with their mouths, and daring folk walked on thin ropes tied from peaks of tents.

"Nothing like a lighthearted carnival to help us escape the stress of the castle," Nicolas whispered in my ear.

"I had no idea elephants were so large," I said back, and he laughed.

The light of the flames seeped into his face until his expression was lit with pleasure. I forgot about an attacker finding us or guards coming after us but instead marveled in the beauty of the night and the feeling of experiencing it with Nicolas.

He'd been right, this was exactly what we needed. Memories of our own. This night could be everything I was looking for.

Chapter Thirteen

"COME FOR THE FUN, eh?" A mouth hidden behind a twirled mustache called to us from behind a striped desk where a man wearing a tall hat leaned back in his seat. "Welcome to the carnival. Who have we here?"

"Merely a candlemaker and his wife," Nicolas replied, pulling me closer. "Fee?"

"One copper each," the man nodded, looking pleased Nicolas asked.

I hadn't thought to bring money. I was about to tell Nicolas when he produced a small sack from his side and allowed two small coins to drop into the other man's hand.

"Off ye go! You're a tad late, but the fun never ends here—till the sun rises, that is." He winked as we walked away.

"Candlemaker and his wife?" I whispered into Nicolas's shoulder as we took a stony path down the bend.

He grinned. "I could be a candlemaker. Biggest thing they have to worry about is wax dripping on their shirt." He pulled at the end of his shift which carried enough stains to it that candlewax wouldn't make much difference.

The stones beneath our feet turned to soft dirt as others had smoothened the trail for us, opening into a large maze of directions we could take, each leading one way and the next, always winding back to the main attraction—the glowing tent in the middle. That tent intrigued me, offering the chance to get lost in a sea of people with Nicolas, laughing at nonsense and marveling at wonderous acts.

But staying discreet meant staying out of the light. My wounded arm was a reminder of the dangers some wished upon the monarchy.

"Would it be better if we kept to back tents and avoided exposure?" I tugged Nicolas's sleeve to stop him from advancing forward.

He frowned. "Maybe. To be safe. I'd hate for you to get attacked every time you're with me."

I grinned. "At least being with you isn't boring."

"I wouldn't want to bore you." He scanned the area. "What of those small tents along the side? Shall we investigate?" His gaze led to numerous dim tents dotted on the hills, quietly playing music and staying vacant from most wandering visitors.

I couldn't imagine what excitement we'd find there, but the purpose was to spend time with Nicolas, and that could be accomplished anywhere.

Horses neighed as we passed a stable to travel toward the outer tents. "Come, see the excitement from the main tent! We have fire dancers today!" some would say as we passed, draping their hands toward the excitement which we walked away from. We'd shake our heads and keep our faces tilted low, keeping to ourselves.

"Can you imagine dancing with fire?" Nicolas asked as we passed another who tried to lure us their direction.

I honestly couldn't. "My world was one of icicles and snow, not fire."

"Fair enough." We stumbled down the path as it grew narrower, and entertainers no longer called out to us. We were far from the action now, but the peaceful night attracted me more than a loud fair could.

"I couldn't dance with fire," Nicolas said. "You'll find I'm not a skilled dancer. But I could juggle."

"You think so?" I asked. I'd tried once, but even the fairies' gifts bestowed upon me as a child couldn't help me manage juggling.

The image of Nicolas juggling was difficult to conjure. Though he was far more laid-back than I and his smiles came freely, all I'd seen of him so far was helping us survive in the woods and dealing with his parents while here. I hadn't gotten to see him carefree.

But he winked at me now, as if no weight rested upon his shoulders. As if all that mattered right now was this magical night, the low notes of the music coming from tents around us, and me by his side. "I could. It's a hidden talent of mine." He broke his gaze to scan the shadows. "Let me see...splendid! Watch."

He darted off the path, and I followed toward plump pine trees that stretched to the sky. Nicolas crouched beneath their hanging branches to ruffle through the thick grasses, one by one picking up three pinecones. A few tents sat there, but they were dark and silent, most likely sleeping arrangements for the performers. Their vibrant canvases flapped in subtle breezes, watching us as we tiptoed through tall weeds.

The festival lived on, but we were so far from the activity now that no one would guess we came for it. It made the night more special somehow, as if we were two lovers who would rather be with each other than anyone else. I let myself pretend we'd snuck away to the outskirts of the town to steal a few kisses, too caught up in our feelings to care of the spectacles behind us. Too bewitched by our own love to care for the charlatan magicians of the carnival.

When he'd found what he searched for, he tossed me a giddy look and prepared to show me his skill. He maneuvered back through the grass, finding ground that was flat beneath his feet near one of the empty tents.

He nodded to me, and I extended my arms in an open gesture, beckoning him to show me this juggling he claimed to do.

His hands lifted to throw, then they froze.

An odd expression crossed his face, one of interest that morphed to confusion. By the time he let all three pinecones drop to the soft dirt, it was one of pure horror.

His hands flew to his face as a single finger crossed over his lips. His eyes warned me. I nodded, promising my silence as he dipped his fingers to his palm. Beckoning me closer.

I picked up my skirts to slink near, and he shifted closer to the tent, leading with his ear.

Someone spoke within.

Now aware of it, I ought to have heard it sooner. While they didn't shout, they obviously cared little of whispering in a place so far from the other tents. No one had reason to venture near enough to hear them, and in their confidence, they didn't lower their tones.

"I understand that, but this provides a new opportunity. All we need is a girl."

"And hope she wins?" A man with a deep voice asked. He barked a laugh, but it carried no humor in it. "I don't leave my plans to hope. Let that silly competition go on. It'll be our own man who takes the throne, and perhaps keeps the girl who wins as a prize."

My blood shivered beneath my skin. Nicolas's hand rested on my arm, and it trembled.

"They were careless on the rooftop. Next time I can get a better shot."

Nicolas's hand froze, as did I. The man who shot as us was inside, perhaps an arm's reach away, unaware that his targets stood so close.

And that they were almost defenseless.

"Not necessary," Deep Voice said. "Nicolas will never be king. It is Silas who we will kill. And I haven't seen him frolicking on rooftops recently."

Silas. A selfish part of me exhaled at that, relieved that Nicolas wasn't their main target. That meant that even if things went the rioter's way, Nicolas could be spared. Freed, even. But I knew many blood-thirsty men in my time, and they wouldn't hesitate to kill Nicolas to secure the throne.

"Silas? I was told Nicolas," the man who shot us said.

"It changed. We don't want to wait to take over or fight for eligibility. We take out the king, allow the kingdom to further fall to chaos, then provide the answer the people need. If Nicolas dies in the process, better for us."

It didn't sound like a clear plan to me, but it left no confusion on their goal. They planned to take the throne.

And right now, that was a threat to me as well.

My chest tightened. This was something Nicolas and I had yet to go through together. Our romantic getaway suddenly morphed into something far more dangerous. But we'd just heard a threat to the kingdom, and from someone who sounded like they had power, leaving the smartest move right now to be taking them both out. Eliminate some of our enemies and let the rest struggle in their absence.

How could I ask Nicolas to help me kill someone?

Fighting required trust—trust that they would watch your back, trust that they could hold their own in a fight, trust that they wouldn't die. We didn't know each other's fighting style yet, and the only weapons between us were my sword and his long dagger.

They could be unarmed, but they might have a whole rack of sharp weapons in there.

"How do we kill the king?" The one man asked the important question.

A hard noise came from inside, jolting us both. But it was nothing more than something hard being set down somewhere. I leaned forward to catch the other's response.

"The betrayal has already begun."

I placed a hand on Nicolas's chest, leaning to whisper, but he spoke first, "We need to stop them."

I nodded. "You don't have a sword, so stay here. I don't want you to be hurt." I said back.

We were taking a risk speaking at all, and I wouldn't give the men an opportunity to find us before I got to them. As soon as I uttered the words, I spun away, turning for the opening.

Nicolas reached for my wrist after I pulled away. He hissed my name, but I was already at the front of the tent and could finish this quickly without endangering Nicolas's life.

This was to protect him.

The familiar weight of cold steel in my palm lit the fire within me, and I burst through the thick tent with a roar. The space was large enough to allow two humans to lay in a row both directions, though a dark wood table with engraved legs took up most of the space. The two men stood on either side of it, hands on the table, bent over as if maps lay on the surface though only cups lay there. They both whipped their heads up to reveal wild eyes and jaw-dropped mouths.

They didn't get much time to react before my sword rose and slashed at the nearest man, one with wavy, dark hair reaching his shoulders. He yelped and dove to the ground in time to avoid the block but didn't roll fast enough to dodge when my blade sliced down, carving a decent line through his calf.

His howl echoed into the night, a high-pitched shrill that tore through my ears.

The sound identified him. This was the man who'd shot me.

With one man wounded, I spun for Deep Voice, but he'd recovered from his shock and a table stood in our way. Worse—he was armed. A long, fine tipped sword pointed toward me, as sharp as the look in his eye.

He opened his mouth but wasn't given an opportunity to speak. Nicolas charged in after me, bearing his dagger as a shield to push against the sword as he threw his entire body against the man, slamming them both into the ground.

A hand grabbed my leg, and we were all taken down.

From beneath the table Nicolas struggled against Deep Voice, blocking the sword with his dagger and wrestling with the other arm. "You shouldn't have come," I cried out, kicking at the other man while he reached for my weapon. At least one was without a blade.

"Too...precious to...lose," Nicolas's words came in grunts as Deep Voice clocked him with a punch to the face. His head hung at a sickening angle before he recovered, just to receive a second punch.

The other man had lost a lot of blood, much of it pooling under my own knees. His eyelids fluttered.

You're too weak to kill anyone. Cassian once told me that. I'd believed him.

But Nicolas's life was at stake, and that gave me the strength to close my eyes and drive my blade through the man on the ground beside me. I blacked out against everything that followed until my sword was out and he was still on the ground.

My stomach lurched, but I bit down against it.

"Run, Rowan," Nicolas pleaded with me. He summoned enough energy to push Deep Voice away, sending his head knocking against the table. Deep Voice swung at Nicolas, but he twisted his blade in such a way that the sword sliced in front of him, not piercing his skin.

Nicolas fared well with his dagger, but Deep Voice would be no match against two of us.

I slid my sword against Deep Voice's throat to pin him where he sat against the table. His dark eyes narrowed and he growled, but he didn't move. His sword fell from his hands.

"Do we kill him or use him for information?" I asked. My shallow breaths rasped in my throat, and the other man's blood felt like fire against my skin.

Nicolas lowered his dagger. "Information. I'd very much like to know more of his plans." Sweat gathered at his brow, but he wiped it away.

"Are you okay?" I checked in. He nodded.

That moment between us was my first mistake. My old mentor had taught me many things through the years, but the first lesson I remembered came at the price of a bruised rib.

"Why did you do that?" I had rubbed my side as the chill of snow seeped into my riding pants. My fallen blade sat beside me, and the ache throbbed where Gen had driven her weapon against my helpless frame.

"You were distracted," Gen had said. She offered a hand to help me up, and I groaned at the dull pain that came with movement.

"Tell Cassian to let me train in quiet." I had glared Cassian's way, where he sat in the shade hollering anything that would catch my attention. He had roared with laughter as I'd fallen like the victory belonged to him.

Gen drove the tip of the polearm into the ground to lean on the weight. "He's helping you. You need to learn to fight when distracted." She beckoned Cassian to our side where he jabbed me once in the injured side. I snarled. "When you two are in a battle," Gen said with a warning look to Cassian, "you must remain alert. You'll want to search the fighters for your loved ones, but if you let down your guard, you will be easily overtaken. You two will fight with each other, trust each other, and never lose your focus."

"Yes, Gen," we had said.

"Focus," she had repeated. "Focus on the battle until all else fades away. You can worry over your loved ones later."

As Cassian left, I'd grunted how I wouldn't fight by him, I'd fight by my sister. Gen had planted herself in front of me and put a hand on my polearm. "Why do you think you two train together?" she had asked.

"Because we are the same age?"

"No. It's because you are chosen as his protector, and he is reliant upon you. The two of you will guard each other through every fight." At my frown, her expression hardened. "It's a serious matter, Rowan. To Cassian, you are more important than any guard. It is your mission to protect the king."

I'd let her down now. Here in this dark tent with the copper taste of blood in the air and the heat blazing against my skin, I held a blade to a man's throat. But when the fight wasn't fully over, I let my attention falter to check on Nicolas. My care for him lowered my guard, and I forgot my mission. To protect my king.

My second mistake was not holding the sword tighter as the man bit against it, driving it down with his wrist, and kicking me out of the way.

Deep Voice grabbed Nicolas's dagger. He turned it against him. My body chilled as he plunged it into his body.

Nicolas's scream haunted me. He placed both palms against his blade to tear it out and pushed back against Deep Voice.

Deep Voice just lost his ticket to life. My sword had been ripped from my hands, and I scampered to retrieve it, grinding my teeth together. Nicolas fell to the ground. The dagger pressed under his hands.

The triumphant man turned to me. I closed my fist around my sword. He kicked at the ground, bringing the hilt of his own sword up to his hands in a fancy move that might cost me my life.

But it wasn't my blade that attacked him.

From behind, Nicolas had risen enough to drive the dagger into the back of Deep Voice, sending him to his grave. He collapsed on the floor between us.

Nicolas swayed on his feet. "Never boring," he grumbled. Then he dropped back to his knees.

I threw myself at his side, pressing my hand to his chest.

"It didn't...go in all the way," he struggled to speak. "I'll recover." But his skin was paling fast, and his body trembled.

"Stay with me," I begged him. Sticky blood covered my hand. "Breathe. You'll be fine." My words whimpered far too much to sound convincing. "Stay with me. Don't die."

Breath escaped his lips in a slow hiss. "We need," he coughed, "we need to get back to the castle."

How he could travel in this state, I had no idea. The walk back would take half an hour, and I hadn't the strength to carry him when his legs gave out.

"Stay here," I told him. "We need to put pressure on that."

I didn't like it, but I stripped Deep Voice of his shirt and wrapped the sleeves tightly around Nicolas's chest, pulling as hard as I could to seal the wound. Blood seeped through the fabric, but it wasn't as fast of a pace as before.

"I'll be right back."

With my heart torn in two, I fled the tent.

I'd seen horses at the carnival, and that was our only hope of getting Nicolas home alive.

I tore across the hillside, wildly searching for someone nearby. "Help me," I cried out. "Someone help me." I raced back toward the stables we'd passed before, shouting for anyone who'd listen.

A fellow with plum-colored pants and a feathered hat peeked from around a tent. "Ello there? Can I help you?" He paused at the sight of me. Bloodied dress, red-stained hands, tears marring my cheeks, and a desperate plea upon my lips.

"You must help me. I need a horse. It's for the crown," I begged, almost falling to my knees in desperation.

He froze, and I yelled again. "Do you hear me? I need a horse now. Your prince needs a horse or he will die and I swear I will bring the full wrath of Thames upon you for not helping me."

He jumped and ran to the side, disappearing into the shadows.

"Ahh!" I threw back my head and yelled into the night. Where were those blasted stables? "Someone help me!"

"Alright, alright, I'm coming!" the man yelled back. I threw myself his direction just as he came out from the darkness with a horse in tow. "Wouldn't want the wrath of Thames upon me. Now where is this fellow who might die?"

I couldn't show my gratefulness enough. "Come with me." I took off at a sprint back for Nicolas.

He'd dragged himself out from the tent, panting.

"You weren't supposed to move." I dropped beside him and grasped his hands. "Nicolas, you're going to be okay. I'll get you home."

He nodded but didn't speak. His jaw clenched and eyes squeezed tight while his grip on my hand stiffened.

"Hurry," I shouted behind me. The horse complained as he was led down the hillside, but the man tugged harder. He let out a slew of curse words upon seeing Nicolas sprawled on the grass.

"Let's get him up." He steadied the horse beside us and pulled Nicolas's arm over his head. "Ready?"

Together, we set him over the back of the horse, allowing him to lean on the beast's mane. The man helped me up behind him, and I wrapped my arms around Nicolas's sides to hold the reins.

"Thank you," I hurried to speak. "I don't have money to pay you, but I'll see the horse is returned."

I couldn't wait for his reply. With a sharp jab to the side, we took off into the night.

As the jovial music of the carnival faded behind us, we were left with nothing but the sound of hooves, Nicolas's strained breathing, and my own sniffs as tears fell to his shoulders. The forest consumed us, and every second felt like eternity. If I lost Nicolas tonight, I'd lose the only thing anchoring me to this lifetime. He was all I had left.

"Please don't die," I whispered. "I need you."

Chapter Fourteen

WE REACHED THE SHADOW-COVERED rear of the castle as the moon hit its peak in the sky, illuminating every drop of blood down Nicolas's shirt. His skin was ghost-like, and his frame leaned against the horse as if it held no strength of its own.

"Stay with me," I whispered, easing him off the horse. He fell into me, and it took all my strength to keep us upright.

I started toward the door, but Nicolas's feet refused to follow. "You have to try. I need you to give me something," I commanded, grunting under his weight. "One foot in front of the other, Nicolas. We are almost there."

My hand trembled as it grabbed the doorknob and yanked it open. Nicolas's head slumped to the side, his eyes closed and his mouth slightly open.

"Please Nicolas." I couldn't keep the whimper from my voice. "Don't die." It took all my focus not to stare at the dark blood tarnishing his tunic. He said the blade didn't go in far, but he acted as if upon death's door.

"Don't take me to the hospital wing." That was the most certain his voice had sounded since the blade struck him, but it didn't make sense.

"You need help."

"Not the hospital wing. They can't know we snuck out. Your maids can sew, right?" He coughed, and his words died out.

I paled as I realized what he wanted. My lips drew in a line, but his whole body shook, and arguing with him would cost precious time. "This is a bad idea. You're dangerously wounded. If that blade went in further than you think it did, you could easily die."

"Just need stitches." His words were breathless. "If we're caught, they could do more than lock us inside. They could limit our interactions, seeing as you're a bad influence on me."

"I'm nothing of the sort," I choked on my laugh, my throat still tight with worry.

Nicolas tried to straighten, but most of his weight still fell to me. "They won't take chances. Keeping me safe is a priority. I'm quite special, you know." The sly grin on his face told me his humor seeped out, though an enormous amount of his blood also had.

Still, the thought of the king keeping Nicolas and I apart, save for guarded interactions, numbed me. I couldn't know what measures they'd take to keep Nicolas safe, but tonight proved I wasn't capable of protecting him on my own. I should have swung my blade faster; I should have been merciless in my killing. I should have kept him safe.

"Fine. I'll take you to my maids."

He carried half of his own weight, leaving me to drag the other half through the quiet halls as the castle slept around us. Hopefully none woke early to light fires or prep the kitchen, or else they'd get quite a fright upon seeing us. If spotted, it'd be impossible to keep word from spreading.

"I can't." Nicolas's voice was mostly strained breathing, with hints of desperation leaking through. "I can't."

"You have to." My voice cracked. "Because I cannot lose you, you hear me? You have to be okay. Come on." I pulled again, finally seeing my doorway in the distance.

Each step took too long, each strained movement sending flickers of pain across his face, each breath shallower than the one before, until at last we reached my door. I pushed through it as my tears fell to the floor and eased Nicolas inside.

"Help me." I shut the door and spoke louder this time. "Help me. Please. Isabel, Lucille, please wake up."

Nicolas collapsed to the ground just as figures stirred from the side room. The fireplace cracked with flashes of light.

"What's going on?" Isabel's voice whispered. She grabbed a shawl from the back of the couch and took a step closer. Her mouth fell open.

I raised a bloody hand to my mouth to keep the crying at bay. "He was stabbed. He's been bleeding for a while."

The tears came freely now, while Nicolas remained unmoving at my feet.

"I can't lose him. I can't," I stuttered. "Don't let him die. I can't lose him. Please."

They were a flurry of action now, coming to our side and stripping Nicolas of the shirt I'd tied around him.

"Go get your mama," Isabel ordered. Lucille nodded and sprinted out the door. "Was the blade that struck him clean?" She glanced to me. Her figure was blurry behind my river of tears.

"I don't know. I don't know what to do."

Her voice remained steady. "It's fine. Go to the wash bin and dampen a rag. Bring it to me." I took off, plunging my hands into the water and watching it turn red before pulling the cloth back out and rushing to Nicolas's side.

"Help me with his shirt." Isabel guided me to steer Nicolas's shirt over his head. He grimaced but shifted to allow the sticky shirt to peel upward, streaking blood up with it. The wound beneath was dark as merlot, carved into his chest near his right armpit. His hands trembled at his sides while both of us froze for a moment. Isabel broke free first, picking up the rag and dabbing the wound.

I closed a hand over Nicolas's. "You're going to be fine," I said, though uncertainty still consumed me.

He tipped his head my way and peeked through wet lashes. "You're hurting me."

I let go of his hand. "I'm so sorry." I retook it but kept it on my lap and offered slow strokes with my thumb instead of a bone-crushing squeeze.

Dana and Lucille slid through the door. Neither hesitated before offering help. Dana brought a small, amethyst box with gold trim and a narrow latch, which she flipped open with a small click to rummage through the contents. She pulled out black thread and a small, silver needle which she wiped on her side. I gulped.

"You'll be fine," I stroked his hand more fervently. At this point I was convincing myself as much as consoling him.

Lucille held an orange-tinted round tin, though it may have been the firelight casting that color. She unscrewed the lid and dipped her fingers inside, smothering his wound with a thick, opaque substance.

From her pocket, Dana handed me a sash. "To bite," she said when I gave her a look. "I have nothing more to offer than that."

I folded it once before sliding it into Nicolas's mouth, then I squeezed his hand, giving him permission to squeeze back if needed.

Isabel finished cleaning trickles of blood from Nicolas's chest, and she stepped back. "Alright. He's ready."

"I'm going to be sick," Nicolas spoke through the sash.

"Please pass out," I whispered. "Please don't feel this."

Dana offered me a pitied look before beginning. Nicolas's jaw clenched so hard his veins throbbed, and a low growl came from his throat.

"Slow breaths," Dana reminded him, but a moment later his face relaxed, and his breaths no longer strained through his nose.

Dana nodded. "He's unconscious. That'll make this easier."

I had to close my own eyes, or else the sight of her pulling the thread through his flesh would have sent me unconscious as well.

"I take it because you came to us instead of the doctors, you don't want word of this spreading to anyone." Dana didn't phrase it as a question and kept her eyes on her work. "I can agree to that, if you promise me it was not you who stabbed him."

"No," the word spilled from my lips. "Of course not. We were at a carnival and got into a bit of a fight with rebels when he got stabbed."

She nodded. "Very well then. I'm finished. Let's find a sheet to tear into bandages, then get him wrapped and settled into the bed. Keep a cool cloth on his forehead. I'll be back to check on him in the morning."

"Thank you." I could cry again.

"Certainly, my dear. Your prince will be fine. Perhaps no more...carnivals in the future?"

I promised, and she bowed to leave.

We wrapped Nicolas up, laid him in my bed, and folded a rag across his head. His chest moved more steadily now with rhythmic breathing, and his eyelids fluttered softly in sleep. With the blankets pulled to his chest and the peaceful look upon his face, I wouldn't guess at the wound that lay beneath, or that minutes ago he was fighting for his life.

"Are you alright?" Isabel whispered.

"I am now. You can both go to sleep; I'll take care of him."

They gave Nicolas one last look before heading back to the sitting room to curl up on the couches.

I sat next to Nicolas to watch him breathe, contented with the mere sight of each breath, knowing it meant life. His hand no longer felt cold as my own wrapped around it and the color crept back to his skin. Somehow, we'd made it from the dirty, carnival tent to the warm bed, and he was alive.

If I'd lost Nicolas tonight, I would have lost everything. I had no family in this lifetime, no true friends yet, and no one to take care of or to care for me. Nicolas was more than just the boy who'd awoken me from my sleep—right now he was my entire world. Everything I was doing here was for him.

Tonight proved more than ever that without him I'd be lost, and the slightest of winds could blow me away. I stared at his face in the dim firelight, wondering when he'd become so important to me, and thanking every star I knew that he was still with me.

As the night turned into morning I remained at his side, just to be certain he made it to see the sunrise again.

Chapter Fifteen

NICOLAS'S HAND ON MY arm woke me. Somewhere in the morning I must have drifted to sleep.

"I'm so sorry." I sprang up in the bed, immediately fussing over him. I checked the rag, surprised to find it still damp, and peeked at his bandages. "How do you feel? Is everything alright?"

Rosalie played with rattle toys in the sitting room while Lucille guarded the fireplace from her, and Isabel scrubbed the flagstone floor where we'd cared for Nicolas last night. Nicolas sat in the bed, briefly closing his eyes to lean against the backboard and take a deep breath. "I feel fine. Now would be a good time to tell you that I hate the sight of blood. I might have overreacted a bit last night. Anything more than a papercut sends me into a frenzy."

I stared at him for a moment before laughing. All the tight emotions from last night let themselves out in that sound. "That would have been splendid to know. But I'm glad you're safe now."

He groaned. "Safe as long as none come looking for me. We'd cause quite the scandal should I be found in your bedchambers in the early morning. And under your covers, no less. These are quite soft by the way; if you aren't careful, I'm going to steal them from you."

He patted the covers, showing no signs of worry or pain.

"I'm willing to fight you for them," I grinned. "Do you need help getting back to your room?"

He shook his head. "Dana is bringing me, oh there she is! Perfect, thank you. This fresh shirt was all I required. Now," he groaned again as he slid from the bed and pulled the shirt over his head. He threaded his arm through the sleeves carefully, then pulled it over his torso. "None will be the wiser."

"Be gentle, or else you'll pull the stiches. No heavy lifting or drunk fighting for you." She wagged a finger at him.

"There go my plans for the night," Nicolas chuckled. "Thank you, Dana. I'll be careful."

"See that you are. Go clean yourself up, both of you. I've been informed that today Rowan is to be presented to the court officially."

Nicolas and I exchanged glances. After the excitement of last night, the last thing I wanted was interaction with other people, let alone the entire court. I'd rather spend the day with Nicolas, being certain he was fine and talking about what we'd overheard last night. But Dana flitted into the closet to rummage through dresses, and Nicolas took a deep sigh.

"Very well then. I'll see you later."

He lifted my hand, still generously stained with his blood, and pressed a kiss to my skin. We'd still yet to have a proper kiss since he woke me. Soon there'd be other girls here to compete for my place as the future queen, no doubt thinking they'd be the ones to someday earn his kisses. Though we competed not for Nicolas, but to prove ourselves as queens, it was impossible not to know that Nicolas came with that position.

Queen was the furthest thing from what I looked like right now. Flax frocks dipped in blood, wild hair, tear stained eyes. We had work to do if I was to be seen before the court.

"I'll see you soon," I promised, then watched as Nicolas slipped out, covering his chest with one hand.

"Alright," I turned to my helpful maids who deserved every good thing in life for how they'd helped me last night. "I'll go take a bath. When I get back, I want to know every bit of gossip about the court members, and anything that could help me win favor in their eyes. If I'm to win this Queen's Competition as planned, then I'll need their support."

After I was scrubbed until my skin turned red as a tomato and my hair was brushed until it polished like sea glass, they presented a heavy, layered dress the shade of orchid with glossy pearls stitched into the bodice.

"No corset?" I asked as I put it on.

Lucille laughed in her throat. "We have a corset, if you want your organs squished together." She paused from lacing the violet strings in the back to raise a brow at me.

"No," I rushed to reply. "I merely thought it was traditional. My mother always wore them."

Lucille's gaze softened at the mention of my deceased mother. "Women don't wear those as often anymore. But I can get you one if you wish to remember her."

"It's alright." My voice was softer this time. "Thank you, though."

Isabel's arm pointed to the chair. Rosalie settled on my lap as her mother stacked my curls high on my head, allowing one free to rest over my shoulder. I searched for my mother in my face, but the makeup here was different and the clothing style new, and as much as I searched, I couldn't find a trace of her.

It'd once been a blessing that I didn't bear a strong resemblance to my parents, as we attempted to hide my heritage. Now it felt like a curse.

My mother would win over the court easily. She'd been more lovable than I.

Rosalie giggled as I bounced her on my knee, her bright eyes knowing nothing of the worries in my own. I wished I could enter the court as Rosalie was: innocent, pure, and soft-hearted, with a laugh to make any fall in love with her.

"Can you teach me to be as sweet as you are?" I asked, tickling her belly. "Teach me your cute ways."

"She said she will, if you teach her to sleep through the night," Isabel said, placing a string of pearls in my hair.

I laughed, and Rosalie mimicked the sound. "Sleeping happens to be a talent of mine."

With a smile, Isabel stepped back. Her eyes trailed over me, and she nodded. "You're ready to meet the court. Remember, they'll treat you as a queen if you act like one."

Little did she know, I'd been pretending I was queen since I was a girl. That wouldn't be the problem.

Chapter Sixteen

IN SPIRIT OF ACTING like queen, I knocked only twice on the tall, mahogany doors before pushing the golden knob forward to allow myself in. Chirps of conversation bubbled in the air, mixed with the scents of polished wood and citrus. A massive, arched ceiling covered overhead with a pristine chandelier draping like an ornament, sending dashes of light to the furthest corners of the room.

The throne room was dressed in bright colors: maidens in sunflower yellows, gentlemen in dashing cerulean, cream and orange handkerchiefs, and polished, golden shoes.

"Princess Rowan." King Silas stood on a dais, descending it to acknowledge me. "Welcome to Thames court."

Applause followed, not the thunderous kind that pounded on eardrums, but still eager, the claps coming at a rapid pace from smiling figures. They bowed to me as admiration dripped from their gazes. Many were familiar faces from passings in the corridors where we'd exchange a polite greeting as I attempted to remember names. None had ever swept me into their conversations; it was always a simple hello, then returning to their companions. But none turned away this time. They only gazed upon me.

In all my time at Elenvérs, I'd never been recognized in such a manner. Never welcomed in such a fond ceremony. Never even known as their princess.

Princess Rowan. The name rolled off the king's tongue as if the most natural thing in the world.

That was the first thing that felt unfamiliar in this. The second was the warmth in the room. The friendliness. Though I searched for a strained smile, a calculating look, an eye watching for my weakness, I found nothing but sincere smiles, even from the older generation. I'd known them to be sinister folk in my time who were more eager to strategize than make friends, but this generation seemed to hold none of the sort.

I curtsied as their applause continued. Was that all? Was there nothing they expected from me other than a smile and a bow? I breathed deeper at the lack of scrutiny the occasion held. Perhaps my mother's charisma or Rosalie's innocence weren't required to win over the court.

"Princess Rowan comes from Elenvérs, from a time when it was located in the Northern Mountains." King Silas addressed the room while holding out a hand to usher me forward.

I crossed to him, taking a place at the foot of the dais where Nicolas bled from the crowd to find my side. He moved with a slowness disguised as grace to cover the wound he claimed caused him no pain this morning.

I slid my hand through his arm and gave a gentle squeeze, soaking in strength from his presence as the king continued.

"Our very own Nicolas braved the long journey and the crippling cold to find her, asleep in her abandoned castle, where he woke her with true love's kiss. And now we are the lucky ones, to have such a beauty within our home."

He ended with a wink at me.

My cheeks ached from the smile pinned to my face, my back was tense from pulling my shoulders so straight, and my toes pinched from the pointed shoes upon my feet. But the room applauded again, and only quieted by the king's raised hand.

"As many of you know, we are holding a Queen's Competition very soon." Nods came from across the room. "This is not because we don't welcome Rowan into our home, but because we want to be certain we are giving this kingdom the best queen possible to rule beside our Nicolas."

Though the smile didn't leave my face, the floor fell from beneath me. *They didn't know this was all a façade. They didn't know I was the intended winner of the competition.* To them, the competitions were very real, giving them no reason to accept me until it was official that I'd be staying.

I couldn't help it—I peeked at Nicolas to see if he knew this. He kept his face still, but his arm stiffened beneath my touch, and he gulped. Uncomfortable, but it wasn't clear enough of an answer.

The speech went on. "The girls will be arriving shortly, and then the games will begin. But until then, let's welcome Princess Rowan to the kingdom of Thames!"

He wove through the crowd as they gave a final applause, though it felt less welcoming this time. More demeaning. As if I was an act for them to watch, a pet to do clever tricks. Some show they could watch and decide at the end if they liked me or not. Not a queen to be respected, but entertainment to be enjoyed.

A cold and calculating court would be more desirable at this point, for at least that was something easy to work with. I knew little of earning hearts and more of obtaining respect.

I was a queen, not a jester.

"They do not know that I will be their future queen no matter what?" I whispered to Nicolas.

He turned his face to me and searched my eyes. "To be fair, do you even know that? Do you know that you want to stay with me?"

I shut my mouth, for I had no confident answer to that.

He returned his gaze to the court. "The kingdom needs something to distract them right now. Let them fall in love with you while you decide if you'll love me."

Still, no words tasted right on my tongue. *I want to be with you, but I might change my mind later.*

"Come," Nicolas tugged on my arm. "The court's favors are easy to win, but easily swayed. You have an advantage by being here before the other girls, and I say we take it."

No sooner than his words left his mouth did the towering doors open again, this time without a knock to announce themselves. A lithe girl with sunshine in her long hair and muscular guards at her feet waltzed into the room, not stopping until she reached the center where all could admire her.

I didn't recognize her from the castle, and the family crest on her guard's tunics verified she wasn't from here.

A deep red dress with a bold neckline hugged her body while a diamond as large as her eyes sat on her open chest. Her lips curled into a smile, and she turned her head slowly back and forth to inspect the whispering room as we waited for someone to speak.

I hated it, but the first thought that came to mind was how this girl looked like a queen.

The second thought was not as pretty. I could guess why she was here.

"Nadine, you have arrived already." King Silas was the first to step forward with arms stretched to welcome the young woman. "We weren't expecting anyone for at least a week."

"I know, I know." Her voice reeked of sugar and fake pleasantries. "I just couldn't wait to come. It's not a problem, is it?" She tilted her head, and I resisted scowling.

"Certainly not. You are always welcome at my court. We will get your rooms prepared right away." King Silas waved a hand to a guard, who pried his eyes from Nadine to obey.

"Good." She grinned. She spotted Nicolas, and even though my arm remained laced in his, she winked. "I can't wait for the games to begin."

My grip on him tightened.

"So," I hissed under my breath as she melted seamlessly into the court, who molded themselves around her. "It seems the other girls are arriving. There's really no escaping it now."

Chapter Seventeen

THE GIRLS ARRIVED LIKE a storm after that, trickling in one moment before suddenly we were caught in a downpour of satin ribbons, lace rosette trains, lavender perfume, ruby-painted lips, and smiles sharp as daggers. It was a hurricane of colors, names, formalities, and sun-lit afternoons with the court. It seemed all guessed winning favors from the court could increase their odds of winning, and all appeared more adept at accruing approval than I could pretend to be.

"It's endless," I recounted to Lucille, who poured more wine as she allowed me my string of complaints from the couch. "The competitions haven't even begun and I'm ready for them to go home. I swear, Lucille, I like people less and less every day."

She filled my glass to the brim before easing it to me. "You sound like you'd be a wonderful queen," she mocked.

"And I can't escape them," I went on, ignoring her. "Whether I'm practicing archery, swordplay, or jousting--they are there, too. Even when I went for a ride, who should be in the stable when I return but Nadine." The name curled from my tongue like poison.

"I hear she rides as if one with the beast," Lucille said. As my lethal look, she burst to laughter, nearly spilling the red wine over the cream couch.

She recovered, holding the precious wine close to her body as she shot me a grin. "You are too tense. You know you will win, and you know Nicolas loves you. So stop fussing over them and breathe before your face turns as rosy as your hair."

I took a long inhale, followed by a heavy intake of the wine, which would calm me more than a deep breath could. Perhaps some courage would seep into my blood along with the alcohol. Or at least tolerance to survive these next few months with the other girls before I had the peace of the castle back to myself.

This state of panic wasn't familiar to me. The jealously pulsing under my skin as I caught the girls speaking of Nicolas, or the fear that somehow the competition would tip from my favor, it was all confusing. Try as I might to order my emotions to remain calm or to still my nervous heart, nothing kept me from worrying over what this month could bring.

Even the bloody curse hadn't bothered me as much as these girls did.

I had more to lose than any of them. I had Nicolas. I'd fought for my place as queen once, but never before was my heart on the line. I would not see it shattered.

"I think I'm starting to care for Nicolas," I admitted, running a finger along the brim of my glass.

Lucille snorted. "It's about time. Every girl fell in love with him within a day of him arriving. We thought you were going for some sort of record."

There it was again. That pang as I thought of other girls vying for his attention. What was happening to me?

This was the feeling that caused men to give up everything for a woman. The feeling that drove sane people to do ludicrous things. This was why I would compete in these challenges—all to keep the one who made my heart flutter close by.

The emotions inside weren't as overpowering as love yet—more deep infatuation and overwhelming curiosity to see what could become—and yet I was already willing to bring a kingdom to its knees to keep Nicolas. Or in this case, take on a flurry of women.

I couldn't decide which I'd prefer.

Nicolas hadn't formally met the other ladies yet. Since officially the competition was more about proving their worth as queen than winning his hand, he would only see them in passing and at the competitions before a winner was chosen. Due to this, he and I were ordered to keep our interactions private so not to alert suspicion that the competition was rigged.

"Secret rendezvous," Lucille had said when I explained it to her. "Sounds scandalous."

Nicolas didn't ask me what the girls were like, but I wondered if Giermo was bringing him information about them, tiny bits of detail of the ladies who stayed in his home and fought for his crown. Which were the prettiest, or who the court liked so far. Which ones boasted the most powerful families.

"And that's another thing." I sat up straight and stretched out my arms. "Have you seen how many guards Nadine has with her? It's like she's expecting an ambush. Why? What's the purpose of that? I don't understand why she needs a flank of men at her side when the other girls brought no more than ten attendants."

Lucille tucked an arm under her head. "Her father is very protective of her. His manor must be practically empty with how many he's sent with Nadine. He has a fair army under his control, though."

My lips tightened. "Where I come from, the king commanded the armies of Elenvérs, not various nobles." Just another reminder of how different this world was, and how difficult it would be for me to reign over a kingdom so unlike my own.

"You're doing it again, stop it." Lucille tugged my hand away from my face. "Mama worked so hard to get your natural curls looking nice, and it'll do you no good to pull on them."

I sank into my seat. "Fine. You know what I need? Pudding. Or more of those fruit compotes from the other day."

She laughed, setting her glass down on the marble end table. "There's some in the kitchens, but could you fetch it? Mama will have a fit if she gets back and I haven't polished the mantle."

My brow arched as I looked over the slick marble. "It looks polished to me."

A sound rumbled from deep in her throat. "Don't get me started."

I'd been right to spend the afternoon with Lucille. She calmed me as much as slaying a straw statue with a sword ever did. I brought my wine with me to the door, sliding my feet in fuzzy, peach slippers before slipping out the door to find some good food.

Laughter bit my ears. Another reason I preferred to stay in my room—the girls had been placed in rooms right by mine and I had little escape from their presence.

A light breeze drifted through the bright halls, bringing with them the scent of candle wax and roses. I paused at one of the windows to stare across the courtyard, searching for the bright yellow scarf under Nicolas's window. It danced in the wind, same as always.

A love as eternal as the sun.

The sentiment still melted me. One day, Nicolas and I might have a love like that, one as everlasting as the lights in the sky, and then I'd have someone to hang my own scarves for.

A heavy influx of laughter turned my ear, and I spun on my heel to find the kitchens, return to my room, and be free of their noise. But a new sound stopped me, the familiar roll of my own name coming from their lips.

"I hear she's uneducated. That she can't even say a sentence without tumbling over her words," one girl said.

"I've heard that, too. And that she's enormously unpleasant to be around. That's why we hardly see her—King Silas keeps her tucked away to not humiliate the kingdom."

Three voices laughed while I fumed. How dare these girls, whom I'd been nothing but cordial to, speak of me in such a manner? While I had my own rakish thoughts of them, I had the decency to keep them from floating freely through the corridors.

"It's no wonder Nicolas doesn't care for her. She should have been left to freeze in the ice."

A kinder woman might've walked away. A gentler lass could have ignored the insult and allowed them their petty gossip. The Fates knew I was neither those things.

I grabbed a fistful of my skirt in one hand, raised my wine in the other, and marched to the doorway where I stood like a bear, taking up space with my fury.

"That's funny, because I heard she's the favorite of the court," I snapped.

Three girls, Bella, Cathleen, and Tia froze on the bed, staring wide eyed at me. I savored their panic.

That would have been one opportunity to walk away. I didn't take it. My tongue rambled on, drunk on the feeling of courage coursing through my bones. They knew who I was, and they knew they'd been caught speaking wrongly of me. Their shifting eyes spoke as much to their discomfort as how their hands fumbled with the sheets beneath them.

"And the reason you don't see her often isn't because she's tucked away in a room by herself, but rather because she's hiding with Prince Nicolas, exchanging kisses sweeter than sugar."

That might have been too far, and not in the spirit of 'keeping our relationship quiet,' but it felt too good to say. What was better was how their mouths dropped open, one by one.

"Ahem."

With a slow turn, I found Nicolas's man servant, Giermo, lurking behind me with a smug smile under his bushy, black mustache, and a crisply-folded envelope in his hand.

I flushed; certain this little story would find its way to Nicolas's ears. His reaction to my outburst could go either way—proud that I'd stood up for myself or appalled at the rumor I'd just started of the two of us, one that would no doubt circulate through the kingdom by nightfall.

I'd just given the impression that we spent our days locked in a room together, unable to keep our hands off one another.

"For you." Giermo handed the note out to me. A hint of amusement rested amidst the twitch in his eye.

I kept my head high. I was in too far to feign embarrassment now. "Thank you," I plucked it from his hand, then turned to the girls. "And thank you." I took off, hoping the speed at which I walked would create a breeze strong enough to cool the heat from my cheeks. Mocking snickers didn't follow.

Where was that kitchen? Chocolate pudding was exactly what I needed right now. Lucille would have a proper laugh when she heard of the spectacle I'd just made of myself, and perhaps laughing about it with her would erase the grating sting that the other girls' words had brought.

She should have been left to freeze in the ice.

Such words bit colder than any winter's frost, even ones spoken in jealousy.

The only thing I could do to prove them wrong was win these competitions and prove that I had something of worth to give this kingdom.

I had value to Nicolas. His letter weighed in my hand, and suddenly I didn't want to wait to read it. I pulled myself into a corner to devour his words.

Rowan,

We must find time to meet again, and soon. These matters of a betrayal we heard at the carnival are weighing on me heavily, and I can't sort through them. If the king is at risk, then so am I, and through that, you are. I fear I should have taken you directly to my seaside manor instead of getting you trapped in all of this. We could be getting lost in the frothing waves instead of drowning in royal politics.

I'll be sending a glass of your favorite wine to your room tonight to ease your worries for the competitions beginning tomorrow. Though the details of the competition are hidden from me, I have no doubt you'll do splendid. I'll be cheering you on, but not too loudly because I have been warned repeatedly against doing so.

With all my heart,

Nicolas

P.S. If you feel like holding this close to your heart to feel close to me, I won't judge you. I know you must miss me dreadfully.

A laugh rippled out. I could picture the lopsided smile as he winked.

Running off to the seaside manor with Nicolas would be a dream, and it killed me that I couldn't think of a way to give that to him. But I could try my hardest to win the first competition tomorrow to reassure to him and the court that I was the best choice for queen, and from there I'd do all I could to bear the stress of the crown for him.

"You made it; I thought you must have died with how long that took," Lucille teased when I came back to the room with a platter of pudding and Nicolas's note tucked into my pocket. The room was full now. Isabel sat on the floor with Rosalie while Dana pressed the laundry until it was as crisp as a fine morning.

"I got a tad distracted," I admitted, using my foot to close the door behind me until it clicked.

As I set the food down, Dana and Isabel exchanged a look, one filled with worry and heaviness. Their twitching eyes slid to Lucille, who painted a smile on as she reached for the plate. "I truly appreciate that you have no respect for proper meals, Rowan," she said while shoveling pudding into her mouth.

The tension between Dana and Isabel didn't simmer, and I studied them as I picked up my own crystal goblet with pudding. I took the first bite slowly, not removing my eyes from the two of them, until finally Lucille huffed.

"You two." She set down her spoon with great harrumph. "I swear I'm never telling you any secrets. Alright then, out with it, if you won't let her enjoy delicious food first."

Isabel tucked the end of her long braid into her mouth to mumble through. "We have bad news."

My hand tightened on the goblet until it could crack. "Alright. Today was feeling too easy."

Dana set aside the laundry and planted her hands on her wide hips. "Here's the situation, love. Isabel's husband returned from outer towns. They've been pulling more soldiers in to be fully prepared during these competitions. He uncovered the premise for the competition tomorrow."

With each word, her voice grew further saturated with unease.

My brows shot up. Knowing what the competition was should give me a huge advantage, but that wouldn't give reason for the tight look upon Dana's face now. I almost stopped breathing as I waited for their answer, but first they paused to exchange another uncertain glance.

"Stop that; just tell me what it is."

"It seems either Ava believed you, or she saw through your trick and hopes to dismantle you. The first competition is to be stitching a fine blanket. You have no chance to win."

My brows curled together. "Why? Why would they make us do that? What does that prove?"

Dana swept her hair behind her ear before returning to her laundry. "Actually, the queen is responsible for creating a certain amount of blankets and clothes per year to keep the kingdom dressed. It's an honor that the late queen took quite seriously. Unfortunately, that doesn't happen to be a skill of yours."

It wasn't. I couldn't even fake skill at this.

I drummed my fingers against my glass, focusing on the clinking noise it made instead of the unrest bubbling through my blood. "Why would they do this?" I asked. "Clearly Ava wants me to fail."

"She could have thought you were serious when you told her it was a strength of yours."

I grunted, taking a bite of pudding. "She knew. It's clear she doesn't want me to win this competition. But why would she put the fate of the kingdom to such a test? If I don't win, it could be any of the other girls, and I doubt they could rule a kingdom well. Blast. I have to learn how to make clothes."

Now it was Lucille who tossed her sister-in-law a shifty glance, but Isabel shook her head.

"It will work!" Lucille didn't wait for me to ask. "I have an idea, and it's going to be great."

Dana rolled her lip between her teeth but didn't argue. "It's risky."

"I like risky," I said. "What is it?"

Rosalie skirted among us with bliss, unaware of how the adults in the room were fretting over tomorrow's events. Once again, I envied her.

"It's simple," Lucille said, picking back up her pudding and speaking through a mouthful. She waved the gold-tinted spoon through the air as she spoke. "You'll be escorted to a room with the supplies to make blankets. Whoever makes the most beautiful blanket wins. But," she put emphasis on this word and gave her mother a sneaky grin, "we could stitch a blanket into the skirt of your dress tomorrow, and then all you must do is pull it free and you have your blanket."

Her words hung in the air, waiting for how I would absorb them. Lucille shrugged, dipping her spoon back in her pudding. Isabel chewed more heavily on the end of her braid, while Dana knitted her forehead into all sorts of knots, her fingers crawling to redo some of the laundry, though it was perfectly fine.

Without cheating, I'd lose. If caught cheating, Ava could discredit me in front of the entire kingdom and both my and my maid's positions here at the castle would be in danger.

It was dishonest, and it was risky. But it was for the sake of winning these competitions and for Nicolas. For that reason, I obliged.

"Let's do it."

Chapter Eighteen

The First Test

THE AIR TASTED OF patchouli, cedarwood, and uncertainty. The thickness of the blanket stitched into my gown made my thighs perspire, and the nerves running through my veins made my hands perspire even more.

A voice commanded the skies, bringing the entire pavilion to a hush. Even children quieted and leaned forward in their mother's arms to get a peek of the twelve girls lined upon the wooden dais in the late morning.

"Today we will witness the first test in our Queen's Competition!"

Hands applauded, but they stilled almost as soon as they began, not wanting to miss a word.

A few girls fidgeted, but I kept my back tall as a pine tree and just as rigid, letting my eyes dance around the crowd. Every so often I'd catch someone's eye, and I allowed myself a small smile. It was how a queen should appear—comfortable in face of uncertainty, and kind in the eyes of her subjects.

It was how I always saw my mother.

A few of the other girls did the same. Nadine, most notably. She dressed in a gown of rouge with dainty daisies woven into her long braid, and her stance didn't waver as she stood before the crowd. For a moment I cared little for beating the other girls, so long as I bested her.

Her slender eyes darted to me, fast enough that I might have missed it had I not been looking at her. She must have done as I had—right away we'd singled each other out as our greatest competition.

The delegates had all arrived to witness the competitions. If they approved of the winner chosen, then the nobles would be bound by contract to agree to the winner, at the penalty of their titles and lands. As much as we needed to prove to the people that we were worthy, we had to prove it to the delegates even more.

They sat near the king in fine clothes and stiff expressions.

When the king continued, we all looked back to him.

"There will be three tests the girls will go through, each one proving their ability as a queen." King Silas stood upon a tall platform on the left, one adorned with gold sparrow-tailed banners and a jewel-decorated throne. Nicolas stood at his side, wearing a buttoned-up suit the same warm color as his eyes, tight enough to see his arm muscles underneath. A sparkling crown rested on his brow, momentarily taking my breath away. The crown was unlike any I'd ever seen, braided with intricate leaves and complex vines, sometimes twirling up to form peaks around the band, and it made Nicolas look more handsome than ever before. With that crown combined with his curled, dark hair, his tan skin, and his full lips, he looked more like a god banished to the land than a humble lord from a small seaside town.

He should have worn that when he woke me. I would have fallen in love in an instant.

Nicolas found my eye and winked. I winked back, but he'd already returned to his still position with face directed at the people gathered behind the gates.

King Silas delivered the prepared speech.

"Today, the competition will test the girls' skill, for we cannot have an incompetent queen. It will test their attention to detail, for being queen requires an ability to focus on many little matters at once. And it will test their heart for their people, for what is a queen without generosity to others?"

The audience murmured and nodded, captivated by the fancy speech. A few called out a certain girl's name and waved, throwing their favors in their direction. They were publicly announcing who they'd want as their next ruler.

My name didn't get called. They didn't know me yet, and I wasn't from their towns, so I didn't let the matter wound my pride.

Ava's slicing stare found me as her hands folded over the skirt of her beige dress and a smile arched on her lips, like a ring master taking pride in his performers. A greedy look, hungry for the events to unfold. For a horrifying moment, the idea that she's\d tricked my maids into believing what the competition was crossed my mind, sending a shiver down my spine that was difficult to conceal.

I forced my attention forward again, to the eager faces of young children and innocent audience as they waited for the first test to begin.

"For the first competition to find our new queen," King Silas allowed a moment of anticipation, appearing as an eager boy on holiday, "each girl will be locked in a room with fabric and thread where they are to create a beautiful, intricate blanket. As you know, my late wife used to make blankets for all those in town. This is a tradition we wish our next queen to carry on."

I let out an unstoppable sigh of relief. The soft fabric of the blanket brushed my legs, reminding me that I'd already finished the challenge. All there was to do was peel the blanket off and wait for the competition to be finished.

But then the king said these words, "To validate their ability, we wish the girls to stitch a rose in the corner of the blanket."

No. We hadn't done that.

"The rose holds a special meaning to this competition," he went on as my face paled. "It is a symbol of our kingdom, and of what we are accomplishing these next few weeks. Through these tests, we will find a girl fit enough to rule. Like the rose, she will be pure, strong, and enchanting. A queen of roses."

The girl standing beside me wore a red dress stitched with lace rosettes, and she straightened, no doubt feeling she'd accomplished something great by correctly wearing roses. My own dress was a shade of light purple, once again paying homage to my birthright as a queen. The symbolism didn't feel as valuable now compared to the roses.

Roses were a rarity in Elenvérs, but their worth was famous and their beauty renowned. The term 'a queen of roses' painted a clear image for me, and one not similar to myself.

If I was a rose, I was more thorns than beauty.

But if I could stitch a rose into the corner of the blanket, I still had a chance to win.

"The girls will now be escorted to their rooms in the tower." King Silas motioned to the tower to his right. "They have one hour to complete the task, then will be escorted back here for the inspection. So ladies," With a swoop of his arm he pointed us to large, double doors that swung open at his command, where two serious-looking guards in crisp suits stood at attention on either side. A long, golden carpet ran from the dais to the doors. The crowd cheered loud enough that I almost didn't catch his final words.

"May we find our queen of roses."

With fistfuls of skirts, anticipation in our steps, and thunderous applause leading our way, each of us twelve girls crossed the path to the looming doors that welcomed us into our first competition. Our smiles that greeted the crowds only a moment before turned downcast, one by one, as we left the light of day and entered the bitter darkness of the tower. The door locked and the cheering faded. We took one last look at each other before the guards motioned for us to follow them up a spiral staircase.

There was no laughter now. No friendly smiles exchanged. Starting now, we were in competition with each other, and there could be but one queen standing at the end.

Nadine took the first step, and I followed behind her. Step by step we ascended, stopping shortly at a narrow door where a heavily-clad guard inserted a delicate key.

"The first girl," he ordered. Nadine stepped in without hesitation, and the door snapped shut behind her.

We paused again ten paces later. The guard glanced to where I stood at the front of the group, and I stepped into the next chamber. With a low creak and a sharp bang, I was trapped in a room alone.

The soft pattering of slippers chorused behind me, and whispers of the audience outside slipped through the closed window, but none of that mattered now. I had one hour to stitch a fine rose on the corner of the blanket and make it look as if I meant for it to be there all along.

The room was small; I could walk only five paces one way before meeting a dulled, gray stone wall with slivers of cracks imprinted on their surface, some deep enough to stick my smallest finger through. A heavy air clouded the room, thick and moist, filling my nose with a hint of cedarwood, likely coming from the fireplace along the curved, outer wall.

A shuffle came outside the door, like shifting of feet against the wall. A guard must be stationed there.

Sweat pricked my skin, but I wiped it away. The other girls must make an entire blanket, while I only needed one rose.

The idea occurred to me that if they truly wanted me to be the obvious winner, the king might have included a fine blanket in the room, one so intricate and magnificent that none could deny my talent. I ruffled through the belongings, but all I found was a heap of bright fabric, some thread, and silver needle for stitching.

For Nicolas, I would stitch the finest rose there ever was.

First, I glanced out the window until I found the warm color of Nicolas's curls, where he now sat in the shade next to the king, heads bent together in discussion. Perhaps he was warning him of the plot we overheard.

That's the problem I wanted to deal with. Give me a sword and let me seek out those who plot against the king. Let me strategize how to keep the control. Let another stitch blankets.

"I need to begin," I spoke into the small room.

The chair creaked as I leaned into it, and the fabric slid between my fingers like any fine silk would. There were thicker cloths here as well, ones perfect for keeping warm in winter, if they got anything close to winter here. There were seven colors to choose from, all ranging shades of reds and yellows and oranges. A flurry of fire at my fingertips.

Isabel's husband had been able to predict these colors. He hadn't predicted the rose-twist.

I'd only need the red thread to stitch the flower and complete the blanket. My back turned to the door, blocking the view as I pulled up my skirts and got to work removing the blanket underneath. We held it up with several pins this morning, and it took several minutes to free the thick, yellow blanket from my dress. At last, the final corner slid free and fell to a bundle at my feet.

A rose didn't sound complicated, but it took five frustrating attempts to stitch something resembling the delicate flower, and still the petals were lopsided and the details minimum. Dana had stitched an image of a queen handing out blankets to the town across the front of the blanket, and it'd look spectacular with a rose friar at the bottom, as if we were watching the image from behind the thorns, but after the one rose, I gave up with the elaborate plan and convinced myself it was good enough.

It might not be the best blanket, but it only needed to be good enough that the king could say it was better than the other girls' were. And who else could have stitched such a complex design in merely an hour?

"This is the best it will get," I mumbled, putting the needle down next to the tall racks of cloth.

The tall, *full* racks of cloth. Curses flew from my mouth. They'd know I cheated when not one stich of fabric was used to make this blanket. It wouldn't be possible. The fabric must look used, or else an innocent guard could ruin the entire plan.

How could I use the extra fabric without ruining the blanket? Any alterations to the cloth would make it look worse than it did now, and Dana would have a fit that I messed with her masterpiece.

As if knowing I needed its saving flames, the fire crackled beside me, sending sparks of embers and hope toward me.

I could burn the extra cloth.

There wasn't a way to know how much time was left, but the guard outside the door shuffled again. I froze in place until certain he wasn't going to open the door, then frantically unwound the yellow cloth from the spool, carrying it to the flames, and folding it into their hot embrace. They curled over it, devouring the cloth with their thirsty licks, until it was charred remains scattered over the firewood.

Next, I took the orange thread, the same color that Dana had used for the embroidery and fed it to the fire.

The last of the thread had just fallen from my fingers when the door moaned behind me and the guard poked his head into the room.

"Time is up, m'lady. I hope you are finished because the crowd is waiting to find their winner."

Chapter Nineteen

"FINALLY," I SAID WITH a wide smile and smoothing of my skirts. "I've been done for ages." I returned to the stool, gathered the blanket in my arms, and stepped back into the narrow hallway.

The other girls trailed around me, each one holding the blanket close as if their ideas might be stolen. I tried not to pry, but I couldn't help myself from trying to get a look at the other bundles to see what mine was up against.

I squinted against the harsh light as we were paraded back outside while the audience came to life at our appearance. They crowded back against the fence to reach through the bars to wave and call out the names of their favorites. King Silas and Nicolas stood.

We weren't brought back to our dais, but rather to the feet of the king. He looked at each of us as we approached, his eye holding mine for a moment longer. I thought a hint of sparkle appeared in his gaze but couldn't be certain.

"Let us see the blankets," King Silas spoke. A guard ushered the first girl forward, a girl by the name of Blaire with a petite nose and mouth but large eyes. She floated forward and knelt, holding up her blanket.

King Silas took the deep red fabric and held it up for the audience. Roses covered it, starting thick at the top and falling like rain toward the bottom. Blaire grinned as the crowd's cheers grew louder. With a nod, the king set the blanket back and nodded his head.

The delegates leaned forward on the bench to see it better. The group of them exchanged glances and whispers but kept still faces that were difficult to read.

"Very good. Next?"

With a frown, Blaire withdrew back in line while the next girl stepped forward.

In a direct violation of our orders to keep our close relationship secret, Nicolas caught my eye and grinned before slicing his eye back forward. That one grin was enough to even my rushing heartbeat. How lucky was I to have someone who'd risk the wrath of the king to make me feel treasured? Worse, he risked the wrath of his mother.

You could love him, my heart seemed to tell me. *He would be easy to love.*

The king's commanding voice drew back my attention. "Next."

Nadine stepped forward and offered her blanket. With the soft oranges and ruffled edges, it was pretty, but not as pretty as Blaire's.

One by one the eleven blankets were offered, until only I remained.

"Princess Rowan?"

I was the only girl he beckoned by name. I bowed as I handed the blanket to the king, noting how Nicolas beamed at its sight. In honor of honesty I'd have to tell him later that I couldn't actually stitch something so beautiful.

King Silas's wide smile faltered slightly as he inspected the rose, and he peeked at me. Though my knees shivered, I kept my shoulders strong and lips in a tight smile. He glanced once to Nicolas, then once to the audience.

"Your Majesty?" A short guard came near. He held his arms out for the blankets.

The king cleared his throat. "No, take the blankets back inside. We can distribute them with the next load of clothes."

The guard shifted on his feet. "Sire? We were to put them on the gate to be admired." He glanced to the audience who stood almost close enough to hear his words.

"And yet," King Silas smiled again, but it wasn't as natural as before. "I am king and I've asked them to go back inside. Please." His last word broke with the weight of desperation, and the guard nodded. He scooped up the blankets and carried them back to the tower while the other guards exchanged glances.

Something wasn't right. King Silas stood too rigid and was silent for too long. Nicolas gestured with his hand, though it took me a moment to comprehend. I still stood by myself in front of the other girls, drawing attention in this moment of confusion. I withdrew and waited for the announcement of the winner.

As King Silas pondered, his weary eye fell to me, and his head shook ever so slightly. I held my breath as his mouth opened.

"The winner of the first competition in our quest to find our queen," he began.

The entire kingdom fell quiet.

"Is Lady Blaire."

My teeth gnawed together. I'd failed. The crowd cheered, sounding like mockery. Nicolas swung his head to look at the king, but his focus was ignored. King Silas only looked at me.

He spoke again. "Followed closely by Princess Rowan."

But the crowd didn't care. They had their winner, and my name could hardly be heard over their adorning praise. Blaire flushed and swept into the most elegant curtsy ever seen, flitting to the gate to greet the audience.

The other girls stood stiff with dull claps, accepting the disappointment with little display of emotion. I mimicked them, but instead of watching Blaire I turned to Ava.

She smiled. She'd gotten her way.

"You are dismissed," King Silas said, but his voice was difficult to hear by now. Some of the girls trickled back inside, others turning to complain amongst each other, while I headed straight after the king.

He slipped into the tower, and I followed a moment after.

"Sire," I asked. A few guards stepped forward.

"The winner is not to be argued about," they said. "The king is to judge however he seems fit."

King Silas turned with a sigh. "It is fine; give us a moment," he said. Though they frowned, they bowed and took their leave.

Nicolas entered a moment later, shutting the door behind him.

"What happened? Her blanket was beautiful. She is supposed to win every competition," he said, crossing his arms.

"And you are to keep your voice down and your relationship quiet," King Silas snapped. "Don't think I didn't see your wink. This competition is fragile enough as it is, but one wrong move from you can bring it crumbling down. And you," he turned to me with the same fire in his eyes. "If you are caught cheating, the situation may be out of my hands. The blanket was clearly designed by someone other than you. The rose was childlike in comparison to the rest of it. Had I allowed those blankets to go straight to the people, you'd be called a fraud before the sun had set."

I shook my head in fury. "Then next time plan a competition that I can excel at. Stitching a beautiful blanket does not make a great queen. My rose might not have looked as beautiful as the other girls, but I gave everything I had trying to make it look nice, just as I am willing to give everything I have to this kingdom. But you couldn't tell that from this absurd test."

I turned to Nicolas, who wore a shocked expression. "I am willing to fight for you and for Thames. But that won't be seen if we are locked in a tower during the tests. Next time put me in front of the people and give us a test that proves our heart, not our skill with a needle. And tell me the competition beforehand so I can prepare better." I gave the king a last look before brushing past him, but he caught my arm.

"You weren't told the competition beforehand?"

I hesitated. Genuine curiosity covered his face. "No. I wasn't. My maids found out last night and helped me prepare that blanket, but they put themselves at a great risk doing so."

He ran his hands down his face, stretching the skin with exhaustion. "I see. Ava oversees these tests, and she was to tell you days in advance so you could be ready."

Nicolas and I groaned at the same moment.

"It seems," Nicolas said, "that my mother is being more difficult than usual." To my surprise, he cursed right there in front of the king.

"Next time Rowan will be better prepared. We only have two tests left to prove to the kingdom that she is the right queen for me, and I won't let my mother ruin this."

King Silas nodded and took off, mumbling to himself as he did so. His frame disappeared down the dark hallway. As soon as he was gone, Nicolas closed the gap between us.

"I'm sorry," he whispered, resting his forehead on mine. The edges of his brilliant crown tilted against me. "I'll speak to my mother about this, and I promise to fix things. I'd banish her from the land if I could."

I laughed. My anger subsided at his touch. "I can handle one tricky mother. I'll be alright."

I closed my eyes and pretended it was only us in the entire castle, that there weren't eleven other girls outside who'd been tossing him looks, hoping he glanced their way. Like there wasn't a crowd outside whose distant voices seeped under the door, reminding me that they didn't care who I was.

Like there wasn't a competition to compete in to distract a kingdom in unrest.

The guards came back, but at the sight of Nicolas and I together, they slowly backed out again.

This would only fuel the rumors that Nicolas and I were hopelessly in love. Still, I didn't part from him.

"Do you think these tests are helping ease the rebellious people?" I asked. From the conversation we'd overheard at the carnival, they didn't care about the test at all. I hated wasting time in a competition if it would mean nothing at the end. This was only to save Nicolas, but I found it difficult to believe it was distracting the kingdom from their worries over the next ruler.

Nicolas's mouth twitched. "Silas thinks so. Riots have stopped as people are consumed over which girl will win the place of the future queen of Thames. I'm not convinced the unrest will settle down, but it gives us time."

"I'm not convinced either, but as long as I'm helping."

He nodded. "You are. If you could track down the rest of the ones plotting to kill me and Silas, that'd help even more."

"I'll get right on it. I'll use my stitching needle to stab them all, since I can't use it to make a decent rose," I said in a serious tone, and he chuckled.

That was the part that made this competition feel silly to me. It may help those who argue against Nicolas's claim to the throne, but it won't stop the ones who are planning to kill him. Those people are already too far filled by hate to be quelled with a simple competition.

Against those, I was terribly useless.

While worries filled me, Nicolas kept close and a content sound rumbled in his throat. It seemed plots against the throne were the furthest thing on his mind as he played with a lock of my hair.

"Did you mean what you said," he asked. "About fighting for me? Does that mean you've decided you want to stay?" He dropped the piece of hair and moved his hands to my own, where his thumb rubbed hopefully.

I opened my mouth, but the words I wanted to say clawed themselves in my throat, not allowing me to free them. With Nicolas here, holding my hand tight and breathing as if I made him more at peace than anything in the world, it was easy to say I wanted this for forever. Especially with him looking like he did today.

He woke me. He was supposed to be my true love. I could love him.

But as I thought of Ava and of the pressure of being Thames's queen—a country that didn't know me and didn't love me—and of a lifetime of struggling to gain people's approval, a part of me ached. If I said yes to forever, there'd be no escaping that.

"You make me want to say yes," I admitted.

His chest sunk. "But you're not there yet."

"Not yet."

To give him some hope, I drew nearer to him, resting my head against his chest and wrapping my arms around his back. His bandages could be felt through his shirt, reminding me of how we'd snuck away together and how he'd fought beside me. Of how in front of twelve girls, he acted like he only saw me. Of how he'd never given me reason to doubt his dedication to our relationship.

I'd never had that before, and perhaps that was why this scared me. Because what if that was the reason I liked him—because he liked me?

I'd spent so many years hiding behind curtains in meetings and behind a false title. I was asked to conceal myself so no one saw the truth. But now someone saw me, and it felt so good to be seen. To not have to hide anything.

I needed to be certain that I liked Nicolas because of who he was, and not just because he was the first person to see me. Not because he was the first person to make me think I'd found my forever.

Forever was too long of a time to agree to without being certain the feeling in my heart would last.

But as his arms tightened around mine, and his nose traced a line on my forehead, I wanted nothing more than to give in and let him have every piece of my heart.

This was what adoration felt like, and it was a feeling I'd easily become drunk on. Even being queen couldn't make me feel this complete.

With a gentle kiss on my hairline, Nicolas whispered, "I'm yours for however long you want me. Together, we could be as eternal as the sun."

Chapter Twenty

"ROWAN." LUCILLE SHOOK ME from my content slumber. "You have to get up."

Darkness loomed outside the window, and I groaned. "You must not have met me before. I'm a person who sleeps in. Even the turtles in the moat aren't up yet," I complained.

"The sun has already peeked over the hills," Lucille countered. She peeked out the window. "And the turtles are up."

I glanced at the window, where I'd previously missed a hint of light. Perhaps she was right, but it still didn't make it an acceptable time to roll from the comfortable bed.

"The blankets are so warm." I drew out the last word to enunciate my disapproval.

The familiar creak of the front door pierced the air. "Is she here?" Nicolas's voice woke me faster than Lucille ever could.

"Nicolas?"

He poked his head to the room. I slid my feet over the bed and into my slippers.

"You are needed in the throne room," he said. He wore a thick, teal jacket and pointed shoes, with his hair ruffled and bags under his eyes.

"What's going on?" I asked at the same time that Lucille pushed me into the closet to get dressed.

"I don't know," Nicolas called through the door. I slipped from my nightgown and into a simple day dress the color of peaches with a laced bodice. It was long enough to conceal my slippers, which I kept on my feet.

I pushed open the closet door and ran my hands through my wild curls. "You don't know? Is this the second competition?"

He shook his head and shrugged. "I don't know." Worry filled his tone and his hand fiddled with the doorknob. "I only know you are supposed to go to the throne room immediately. I don't see any of the other girls."

My interest was piqued.

"King Silas is going to announce to the court that I am their future queen, and we can be done with these silly competitions," I wished. "This will be wonderful. I'm ready."

Lucille gave me a look, but I feigned a confident stance to ease some of Nicolas's fidgeting. He kept a tight brow as he offered an arm to me.

We strolled through the morning halls as an early sunrise pushed orange light through open windows, and outside the bluebirds sang of blessings and joy. The air was as crisp as apple pie, which it also smelled of, and I silently promised myself I'd investigate later to find the dessert. Perhaps I could sneak some to Nicolas's room and we could enjoy it together—a fine way to soothe the tension in his arm.

He looked straight ahead, gnawing on his lip with each step until it might bleed.

"I'm sure it will be fine," I whispered to him. He ducked his head to smile at me, but his eyes didn't soften.

"It's my mother I'm worried about. She was too happy this morning. I never trust someone who is that happy so early in the morning." He paused. "Are you wearing slippers?"

The tip of my slippers peeked out from under my dress to wiggle at him. "Yes I am. Maybe that's why I'm in a better mood than you," I said with a nod to his own stuffy shoes.

"Maybe. Just be on guard. This may have something to do with the competition, and after the last one..."

He didn't have to finish the sentence. After the last one, I needed a win.

We paused at the door, and I raised a hand to his cheek. "It'll be fine," I said one last time, before alert guards gruffly opened the looming doors.

The court wasn't there, making the room look far hallower than the last time, more like a pristine prison built with marble and drafty wind rather than a gathering haven for friends and spiced wine.

But the room wasn't empty.

King Silas sat in his throne, the first time I'd seen him do as such, with a towering crown shining atop his head in a manner that dared any to forget he was the king. The golden throne sat void to his left with a crown of daisies adorning its seat. A tribute to the fallen queen.

Martin and Ava stood in attention nearby at the foot of the dais, both dressed in sharp, evening clothes and holding their hands respectfully in front of them, tipping their heads in acknowledgment as we entered.

A line of guards stood at both sides, but they didn't wear the Thames crest. Rather, it was an ice blue lion's head, with icicles for a mane. The swirled figure of an E lay faded overtop.

"Princess Rowan, thank you for coming on such a short notice." King Silas didn't rise from his place, but he held his hand out to me. Nicolas placed a hand at my back, and I followed the movement to the feet of the king where I bowed.

"Sire. Can I be of service?" I stood once more and scanned the guards.

It was then that a man stepped forward from the line, one wearing a guard's livery but a humble band around his head marking him as nobility.

Now that I saw him, I wondered how I didn't see him sooner.

My knees bent together and chest filled with a gasp of air. The light appeared to bend from the windows until everything led to him, this man standing before me. The guards disappeared, the king dulled behind me, and the only sound was my blood rushing in my ears.

There was only him. Cassian.

The one I'd grown up with.

The one I'd pledged myself to as a spy to save Elenvérs a hundred years ago.

The one I'd fallen for, before the kingdom fell.

"How can this be?" I whispered under my breath. The man whom I'd cared for before I fell asleep should have died long ago. He couldn't have survived the hundred-year curse, he ought to be a pile of bones beneath the dirt. Yet he stood here with pink tinging his cheeks and muscles moving as he lowered himself into a bow, removing his crown in my presence.

"Princess Rowan," he spoke. "I am King Edric of Elenvérs, and I'm here to bring you home."

The illusion shattered with his sentence. This wasn't Cassian, this was his grandson. I ought to have recognized him from the drawings in Cassian's book.

His nose wasn't as bent, his hair not quite as dark, and his stance not as wide as Cassian's usually was. His eyes didn't sparkle as he spoke, and there was no recognition within them.

I took a shaky breath to compose myself. "I wasn't aware Elenvérs knew of my presence," I said.

"We weren't," he confessed. "Until we received a letter informing us of the girl who'd been awoken from our previous home in the northern mountains. Now seeing you, it's clear you bear the mark of our late queen Marigold. It is my deepest apology that I did not come myself to wake you."

Nicolas stood behind him with skin white as cake and still as stone. He stared at me, but his eyes seemed to look through me, as if he wasn't there at all.

"It seems you have more of a claim to our throne than I do," King Edric went on. He took a few more steps and bent to his knees again to place the crown on the floor. "As it is, I've been without a wife for my entire rule. It would be an honor to bring you home as my bride if you'll have me."

Nicolas stumbled forward on his feet, looking rather drunk in his shocked state. "Well that's rather bold of you, chap," he said. His words were no more than a breathless whisper, but they caught the king's attention all the same.

King Edric rose to his feet to look over Nicolas. "I mean no disrespect by it. Elenvérs would be glad to have their queen returned, and I'd be glad to have a bride. If not, we would still love to have Rowan home where she belongs."

"Where she belongs?" Nicolas barked a laugh. King Silas placed a heavy hand on my shoulder.

"The decision is yours," he spoke in a tone soft enough that it might have just been for me. "It seems two kingdoms wish you to be their queen."

King Edric looked to me, and for another moment he looked exactly like Cassian. This was why Cassian hadn't told his own kingdom of their sleeping princess. Because then they would have sent his grandson to wake me, and that was something neither of us could bear. He was too similar. It struck too close to the wound in my heart of a love I never got to have.

Once, all I wanted was to rule Elenvérs. Even now I could go back and take it, fight King Edric for the claim and rule on my own. I could have the throne I deserved by birthright. But that land was not mine, and those people already had a king. As I tested my answer out on my heart, it stopped beating with such ferocity and the room stopped spinning around me.

My exact path was uncertain, but this was not it.

"I am not Elenvérs' rightful queen anymore," I said. While a part of that broke me, it also carried the certainty I'd been looking for. With a firm lip, I spoke, "I am not destined to rule with you. I choose to stay here."

Nicolas threw his head back with a deep breath, while King Edric calmly bent down to retrieve his crown.

"As you desire, m'lady. If you change your mind, you always have a home at Elenvérs."

Ava's knuckles whitened and her jaw clenched, but she kept it snapped shut as the guard led their king out. The same guards that were prepared to lead me out with him and defend me as their queen. Not one of them gave me a second glance, and soon the door closed and their ice blue tunics were gone from sight.

"You better know what you're doing." The words slid from Ava's mouth like a curtain of ice, cold enough to chill my bones. Her mouth curled in a sour frown, and any similarity she once bore to Nicolas vanished. "You just gave up a kingdom."

My gaze sliced to her where it hardened. There was no doubt in my mind who'd sent the letter telling them to come retrieve their forgotten queen. "I know what I am doing, and I haven't lost anything today. Elenvérs is no longer the kingdom I fight for." I glanced back to the king. "May I have my leave?"

"You may. Be prepared for the brunch with the other contestants shortly."

Beneath his stoic expression rested a soft smile and pride in his eyes.

Giving Ava one final look, I said, "I await the instructions for the next competition soon. I trust there will be no further oversights on your part."

Her lips drew in a thin line.

"Very well. I'm off to find some pie."

Chapter Twenty-One

NICOLAS DIDN'T UTTER A single word. He clung to my hand like an anchor, either tethering us together or pinning himself to the world through me. Either way, I held tight, letting comfort flow through our touch.

I'm here. I'm not going anywhere, silly boy.

He pushed through the door to his room and went straight to the window where he leaned out. A breeze ruffled his hair, but other than that he was still. Frozen in time or frozen in fear.

We ought to get prepared for the official brunch with the other girls, but he didn't move to unbutton his jacket or open his closet. The door gently closed and my breath was the only thing to be heard, though if I strained, I swore I heard the nervous tap of his fingertips against the sill.

Seeing Cassian's grandson shook him more than it did me.

At last, he leaned against the wall and put a hand over his chest. His dark lashes fluttered as his eyes closed, and his voice, heavily clad in relief, spilled from his lips. "The pompous king has left."

"Nicolas, are you okay?" I approached the window to be near him. The light brought out golden flecks in his eyes, but also illuminated the tiny quivers that sparked under his skin—first a tremor in his knee, then his arm, then his chin. Signs of disquiet overtook him, pulsing out with each breath. My nearness didn't seem to quell it.

When he spoke, his tone was soft, as if it came from a place deep in his chest rather than his lips. "I thought I'd lost you. Right there, I thought you were gone. That king was going to take you away and I'd lose the most important thing to me."

My reaction to his pain should have been compassion, but instead bliss whirled within. The mere thought of losing me put a weight on his shoulders that he looked like he could crack under.

Someone cared enough to break for me.

Hopefully, my words could piece him back together. "I will always love Elenvérs," I said, resisting taking one last look at King Edric as he left the kingdom, taking with him my ability to change my mind. Had I said yes, it would have given me an entirely different life. But I suspected it would have been far less adventurous than the one with Nicolas. "That's not where I belong now. I belong with the man who braved the harsh mountains and my harsher personality to be with me."

He smiled, and that small act felt like a win.

"Your personality isn't harsh." With a sigh he ran his hands through his hair, then pulled at the bridge of his nose between his eyes. The heaviness began to lighten in his voice. "I wouldn't quite call it delicate though." He relaxed. "I was so worried. I would have dueled him right then and there for you."

I laughed at the image. "You would have lost."

When he put on an appalled expression, I clarified. "You're wounded! You would have ripped your stitches, then we would have been forced to explain how you got stabbed in the chest. It would have been a mess."

"It'd be worth it to save you." His hand went to his injury. "I ended up telling Silas because he ought to know what we overheard. His life is at stake, though I fear for my own should my mother learn we snuck out." He straightened. "Still, I could have clobbered him."

I doubted it, but it wasn't polite to say such a thing twice.

"We should get ready for the brunch," I said with a sideways glance to the door. "I think the king likes me, but he'd still be mad if I ruined this competition for him. Besides, it'll look scandalous if neither you nor I turn up."

Nicolas made no move for the door. Instead he wrapped his strong arms around me, buried his face into my shoulder until his hair tickled my ears, and shook his head. "Never. Let's stay here all day and pretend we were kidnapped."

"You're going to get me in trouble." I could practically see the girls patiently waiting at the table for me and Nicolas to appear, King Silas making a polite excuse as to our tardiness, the court exchanging vivid whispers, and Ava fiercely glaring a hole through the dining room door. Martin, bless his kind soul, would be helping himself to food, abandoning all cares of the world. Nicolas's father had built a good life by the sea, but he wasn't made for court politics.

I tried to pry Nicolas from my body, but he held tight.

"Sorry m'lady. You're stuck with me."

My laugh was light as the wind, taking ribbons of stress with it, letting them float out like the scarves draping from the windows. I checked for Giermo's scarf, the yellow fabric symbolizing his everlasting love, but Nicolas's window was empty. "The scarf!"

"Ah yes," Nicolas peeled away and peeked to the empty windowsill. "That. It seems Giermo and his love are in a little tiff at the moment and he didn't think she deserved the scarf anymore."

My mouth fell open. That scarf had brought me more happiness than I could say. It'd been a symbol of what I chased after, and a beacon of hope as I stumbled about the castle in confusion, looking for my place. I sought something as fierce as an everlasting love, and when that scarf touched the sky, it reminded me of the hope within these walls.

Now that hope had been taken down.

"Eternal as the sun! Not eternal as their current happiness! If their love isn't strong enough, than what hope does anyone else have?" I looked over again, as if the scarf might suddenly appear where it should be.

Nicolas chuckled. "Did you even know his maiden?"

I ducked my head as heat rose to my cheeks. "No. But there was something about the sentiment that I might have become obsessed with. It sounded so romantic—a token of his affection fluttering in the wind for all to see." I sighed. "I'll get over it."

He still watched me as if I were mad, but at least his mind didn't appear consumed by the possibility of me being whisked away by the Elenvérs king.

"I suspect they will patch matters up, if that makes you feel better." A tinge of mockery played in Nicolas's voice and in the wiggle of his forehead.

I allowed him his laugh. "I hope so. For romance's sake."

He crossed his arms as he leaned his head back against the wall, flattening the haphazard curls against the dull-gray stone. "For romance's sake?" A sly smile crossed his face. "I heard a little romantic story of my own recently. Apparently, things between you and I are in quite the passionate state. Rumor of the court is that we spend our days locked in my room unable to leave each other's side. I believe there was mention of kissing."

I'd almost forgotten that I'd said that. My face flushed and hands turned sweaty, but when I met Nicolas's eye there was nothing but humor within. His cheeks cracked with his wide smile.

"Did Giermo tell you that?" Suddenly I wasn't as worried about that man's love life. "Because you can't trust rumors. Never reliable. Truly, you should just forget you heard it."

Nicolas broke into a rich laugh. "I heard you were the start of such talk, as well as the giver of a harsh word to the other girls."

At least he wasn't mad.

"You should have heard those girls," I said. "They needed a harsh word. For the rumor though, I will apologize. It seemed like a good idea at the time."

"Ah I see." He wrapped his arms around me once more. "I don't mind at all. I like the sound of losing count of the days with you. Ordering food to be brought to the room, heaps of dry wines and caramel chocolates, sharing secrets and sweet kisses."

His nose traced mine. "I wouldn't mind an entire day of kissing you."

Breathing suddenly became very difficult, as I'd forgotten how. All I knew was how he smelled like lemon verbena, how his arms felt as they flexed under me, how his warm breath coiled over my lips, and how his dark lashes drifted closed.

As our noses brushed each other, he paused outside my lips and took his time to breathe me in. His grasp tightened until I was placed between the wall and him, leaving me covered and protected. In a kingdom that was never my own, he was my safety.

My heart pounded against my chest hard enough that he must have felt it. I traced my hand up his back to encourage him, and his head dropped closer.

At last came the faintest brush against my lips, a whisper of a promise between us. But before the rest of the kiss followed, the door swung open behind Nicolas.

There was a loud cough. Nicolas groaned and dropped his head over my shoulder.

I didn't care who was at the door. I'd kill them.

King Silas stood with arms crossed and a fire blazing in his eye. "Do you two wish to bring this kingdom down?"

Blast. I couldn't kill him.

Nicolas removed himself from me with another groan. "No, sire." It was the first time he'd addressed the king by something other than his first name.

"Good. Do you not realize that this competition is fixing the illegitimate claims to the throne? Restoring a bit of harmony to the kingdom? Bringing me a sliver of peace that I have not had since my beloved wife died?"

I took a few uncomfortable steps away from Nicolas, who bowed his head. "Yes, sire."

King Silas's voice remained level, but the aggravation grew. His eyes bore into us. "And do you not realize that for these tests to work, this competition for your future queen, you need to be present? *Both* of you?"

"Yes, sire," Nicolas and I spoke in unison.

The king straightened his crisp, brocade jacket and put on a smile. "Splendid. For a moment I thought you'd prefer necking as my kingdom fell. I expect to see you at the brunch promptly."

His sharp footsteps retreated, but he left the door open. I breathed for the first time in two minutes.

"I knew you'd get me in trouble," I told Nicolas. "The entire court will think I'm a bad influence on you."

He spun on his heel to face me. "Silly girl," he said. "When will you realize I don't care about them. I only care about you."

He crossed the distance and kissed me fiercely. There was no hesitation, no lingering to savor each moment. There was only the relentless kiss that devoured my entire being.

I wouldn't mind an entire day of kissing you, he'd said. I could spend a lifetime kissing him and never get enough.

"We should go." He pulled back, a devious smile on his face as I instinctively leaned back toward him. "I wouldn't want to get you in further trouble," he mocked me.

"I don't care anymore. I like trouble." My words came as a rasp.

He chuckled, extending a hand for me to grab. "Good. Because I predict a lot more trouble in our future."

Chapter Twenty-Two

WHILE NICOLAS HEADED DIRECTLY to the brunch, I diverted to my room to change from my simple dress into something fitting for brunch with the court. I almost tripped several times as my mind refused to think of anything except the kiss, but at last I made it to my chambers.

I pushed the door open with a happy sigh. "Good morning, Lucille."

She waved a rag at me from where she polished the wood trimming. Then she gave me a second look.

"Why are you so happy? You were ready to murder me an hour ago."

The smile refused to be pushed from my face, so instead I shrugged and meandered to the closet.

Lucille followed me. "Isabel, come look at Rowan. Something's wrong. She's inexplicably happy."

"Stop it," I laughed. "This is merely what I look like. I am a happy person."

"I say this because I care for you." Lucille put a hand over her chest. "You are not a naturally happy person. You are quite intolerant."

Isabel peeked from the back room with Rosalie on her hip. Her braid fell over her shoulder as she looked me up and down. I rolled my eyes sarcastically. "She does look happy. And a bit flushed." Isabel gasped. "I know what that means."

I ducked into the closet just as Lucille called out, "Mama come quick! Rowan's been kissing!"

Suddenly I was flocked by three grown women with bright eyes and eager ears, all prying for information. They paid little mind to my undressing while I tried to fend them off the best that I could.

"It was nothing. If you don't let me through, I'll be late to the brunch." They needn't know I was already entirely late, but as I tried to push through, they bunched together in a wall of mischievous smiles.

"You kissed him, and we want to know about it." Lucille pointed a finger. "Or else you're never going to that brunch."

I threw up my hands, but it warmed my heart to have them here, even if they were intruding on my moment. It didn't feel like prying maids scourging for gossip, but a family anxious for news. Even little Rosalie clapped her hands in glee.

I relented. "One question. That's what you get."

"How was it?" Lucille blurted out.

"Are you in love?" Isabel asked next. Dana only smiled and waited for my reply.

The word to describe the kiss didn't exist. Something between divine and flawless and romantic, all in one. I settled on, "Consuming," and they all sighed. "And not the first time it's happened."

They all gasped.

"My question now. Are you in love?" Isabel repeated before Lucille could get another question in.

At the thought, my smile stretched wider, and they squealed. Even Dana laughed.

"I don't know, I don't know." I hushed them. "I think I could be getting there. He's just so thoughtful and everything with him is easy, and he makes me all smiley inside." My cheeks were tender from smiling.

"Rowan's in love," Lucille cooed.

"Rowan is also going to be in a lot of trouble if she doesn't go now," I said, slipping past them. This time they let me through. "I have a dull brunch to attend."

"Go get your prince." They wiggled their brows at me.

As I rushed to the dining room, the thought of love enraptured my mind as much as the exquisite kiss, until my skin was on fire with the overpowering feelings. I wanted to see Nicolas again, see if his cheeks were still flushed and chest raising rapidly.

I was so close. I stood on the brink of love, ready to dive in and experience everything with Nicolas.

The guards opened the door for me, and I strolled in with little care to how late I was. Even Ava's disapproving shake of the head wouldn't diminish my spirits. Nicolas sat at the right hand of the king, already halfway through his plate, but his eyes hardly left mine as I slid into my place between Blaire and Nadine.

"Took you long enough to get here," Blaire snorted. She'd never spoken to me in such a manner before. Winning the first competition must have made her bold.

I gave little more than a shrug as I reached for the gold-crusted platter of sugar-coated fruits and raspberry jam covered tartlets, piling them onto my plate as my stomach grumbled.

Nadine, ever the lady, paid me no mind as she went on nibbling her poached eggs, but Blaire watched as I dug into the sweet meal. "You'll get fat if you eat all that."

I set my fork down with a clank. "Blaire, can I help you with something? Or do you have little else to do than bother me?"

Her darling blue eyes widened, as if she were an angel that couldn't understand what she'd done to upset me. Her dainty hand rested over her chest. "I am only trying to help you. You so clearly need it."

"Because I eat a lot? At least I am strong enough to throw a spear, while I suspect you'd struggle to open the door if the guards didn't help you."

Nadine choked on a laugh. Blaire's eyes narrowed, and she turned back to huff over her empty plate. I continued with my meal, my mood only somewhat dampened by the other girls' presence. A few glanced our way but they kept their conversations to themselves.

Only two more tests, then we'd be rid of them.

After that, it'd be only me and Nicolas, and the start of our lives together.

That thought would have frightened me a week ago, but between sneaking out with Nicolas, competing to be his queen, and sharing kisses, I'd started to want this. And not just a little, I wanted this a lot. I could see a future with him so clearly that I'd be willing to fight to keep it.

Somewhere along the way, I got the clarity I needed. I knew what I wanted, now I just had to fight for it.

"She'll never forgive you for that, you know," Nadine whispered to me. She didn't turn her head, only spoke through the curtain of her silky hair. "Blaire has a vicious memory."

The lithe girl to my left didn't frighten me. But before I could say so, the large, double doors opened again.

Four guards clad in red marched in with stiff arms at their sides and grim looks on their faces, halting after only a few paces to separate themselves. A girl stood in the middle with one hand on the hip of her pure, white dress, which billowed out as a cloud which she floated upon.

"She looks ready for her wedding," Blaire commented, this time her frown pointed at the girl.

"At least I wasn't the only one late to brunch," I said. The other girls whispered around the table as well, each focused on the brunette beauty with the pointed nose and tilted eyes.

Ava stood with arms spread as wide as her smile. Her chipper voice carried from the walls to the towering ceiling. "Lady Celeste, welcome my dear."

Celeste clasped her hands together. "I'm so sorry to be late." Her gaze landed at the head of the table, where she smirked. "Nicolas."

He stumbled out of his seat to uncertain feet, his skin pale and hand trembling. "Celeste, what are you doing here?" His breathy words wavered as much as his feet. If he weren't holding his chair with a white-knuckled grip, he would be a puddle on the floor.

Celeste, still commanding the room, threw her head back in a vibrant laugh. "I'm competing to be your queen. There's a fair amount of people back home who think I'd be excellent at it, unless you've forgotten?"

My chest tightened as Nicolas struggled to find his words. Only a minute ago I wished his cheeks would flush at the thought of me, but it was another girl who made him weak in the knees.

Celeste waved her guards to the side of the room as she came to find a seat across the table from me. The two competitors at her sides, Cathleen and Tia, shifted and straightened their backs.

"You're very late," Nadine said. She was the only one who didn't look intimidated by the newcomer. "We've already competed in the first test."

"I've been given permission to take the test tonight," Celeste said as she cut into a honey-glazed sausage link. "I'm sure Nicolas won't mind." Her wily smile made my stomach churn.

"Is there history there?" I blurted out. The king's table sat far enough away that they couldn't hear our conversation, or else I might not have been bold enough to ask such a thing. Celeste's smile deepened, as if she'd been hoping someone would ask.

The other girls leaned in at my question.

Celeste played with her food for a moment before replying. "Yes. His family and mine have long been connected. Generations ago when his family was given the rights to the throne, my family was the second in contention. Many thought we deserved it over his. We've never bickered over it, but our family has remained close to the throne ever since."

Was that all? My nerves calmed. That wasn't the history that she made it appear to be by her mysterious entrance. Just as all the girls settled back in their seats, Celeste sighed dramatically. "Plus, we were once lovers."

There was no sound but the click of her fork on her plate as she savored our jaws dropping in unison.

Nicolas had told me there was a girl before who'd broken his heart. This must've been her.

I filled my lungs with air, hoping that as I exhaled, all of this would disappear. But when I opened them, Celeste still sat with her little smile on her face, the other girls with their frowns and whispers, and Nicolas pulling at his sleeves with shifty eyes darting between Celeste and me.

When he caught my eye, he perked up, but I couldn't keep his gaze. This wasn't his fault, but I'd never forget how he trembled in her presence. Whatever his heart felt, it wasn't over her.

There was an excellent person I could blame for this. Ava picked at her meal with renewed energy, glancing up to see how we responded. As our eyes met, her lips turned in a wicked smile.

She'd pulled the rug from under me twice today. First by bringing someone here with an offer of proposal to me, then by bringing someone to interfere with Nicolas's heart. She pulled at strings that weren't hers to touch and did so with a guiltless grace.

Ava played a dangerous game.

I wouldn't play this one. I wouldn't sit in front of Celeste and cower at what she and Nicolas once had. With rough hands, I pushed from the table and stood. "Your Majesty, I am feeling quite unwell. I hope you'll excuse my presence, but it's really best that I stay in my room."

Celeste tipped her head back to study me but my emotions stayed far from my facial expression. King Silas nodded. I'd given a proper excuse to my absence, both earlier and now, so he could have little reason to be upset.

Nicolas rose but I shook my head and brushed by, unwilling to share my heart with him. This was unfamiliar to me, and I'd been naïve. While I knew how to fight with foes, I was utterly unprepared to fight for my own heart. Skill with the blade could not help me here.

The sole desire left in me was to survive this month without becoming entirely undone.

Chapter Twenty-Three

The Second Test

SHARPEN YOUR BLADE, GIRL. You're going to need it. - Ava

Lucille read the plum-trimmed note out loud in a voice that copied Ava. She mastered the way Ava dropped her tone at the end of sentences to make everything more dramatic, then she waved the note under my nose.

"Looks like you're fighting in this next challenge."

At last, a bit of good news. I took the note to read it over. "That is something I won't need help with. I'll win this one easily."

"I hope so," Dana said from the chair where she pulled a needle through a new blanket she'd been working on. The other two girls didn't reply.

"I'm sorry." I crossed my arms. "That was where you say 'yes Rowan, you'll win this for sure. No doubt in my mind. You're so talented.' Anyone?"

Lucille chuckled, but also shrugged. "I don't know, some of those other girls are fierce."

"Mateo could work on drills with you this morning if you want?" Isabel offered.

"Is your husband well experienced?" I asked.

She lit up. "He is. He's resting now but I'll go fetch him if you want."

I folded the note and tossed it on the armoire. "No need. I don't want to be tired before the test this afternoon. Everything is going to be fine."

It's the exact thing I'd told Nicolas before King Edric showed up and before Celeste waltzed in. Nicolas knocked on my door last night, but I was already asleep. It took all my energy this morning to keep from wondering where he'd been all day that he couldn't come until night.

"You'll be great." Dana offered the encouragement I searched for. "Just remember, some of those girls have a killer instinct. They might not play fair. Don't be afraid to throw in your sword to save your life."

They turned away to leave me to prepare.

Dana's words shouldn't haunt me so, but they played on repeat all morning as I prepared myself for the afternoon competition, like a never-ending warning coursing through my veins, the words tingling my skin until I genuinely feared one of the girls might attempt to kill me.

Nadine might do it. She was poised, but that girl could bring down an army with the fire in her eyes.

Blaire was nearing vicious in how she acted toward me yesterday. If put up to it, she might pull a hidden dagger and aim for my neck.

Then there was Celeste. After my exit yesterday, she might have asked around about me and discovered my close relationship with Nicolas. She wouldn't have to look too hard to find out I'm the girl he woke from the ice, making me his true love. If she loved him, that might be reason enough to kill me.

My morning tea suddenly looked suspicious. A little too...green.

"I'm losing my mind." I buried my head into my lap. "All I needed was positive energy from you all, is that too much to ask?" I waved over the three maids who'd been peeking at me all morning with disturbed expressions. "You're looking at me as if I'm dressed for my own funeral."

Lucille blew into her cheeks and reset her face. With an elaborated appearance, she said, "You're going to be great! The best there is! All will quake at your presence."

After that they were a flurry of compliments.

I clapped. "Much better, thank you."

A knock on the door sobered all our moods. "Princess Rowan?" A rough voice came. Dana opened the door for a wide man with pale hair and jittery feet. "I'm here to escort the lady to the arena for the second test."

I stepped forward, tightening the brown belt around my gray tunic. "Ready."

He held out a covered sword for me. "Here is your weapon." The steel hilt balanced well as he dropped it in my hand and was similar enough to my usual one that it wouldn't feel different when I wielded it. A smile crept to my face.

The other girls weren't prepared for what they'd see today.

My tall, leather boots sank into the mud with each step that led us to the gated arena where the atmosphere was alive with the audience. Again they held signs for their favorites. Nadine's name was there many times, as was Blaire's. My name didn't jump out among the chaos.

Word must have gotten out that Celeste had joined the competition, because her name flooded the crowd from one side to the next. Almost half the audience was there for her.

Even the delegates straightened and pointed when she was brought out, while the crowd jumped from their seats to roar her name.

Celeste might be a more formidable foe than Nadine if the delegates favored her. The only section that remained seated was Nadine's large company of guards.

Celeste kept a simple smile and polite wave to greet them, then stood in line with her head held high. She looked every bit as a queen with her curled hair pinned at the nape of her neck, her high-collared button up shirt, and her pants tucked in to golden-laced boots. Even her sword had a gold hilt.

King Silas sat under a canopy with his sparkling crown and a knowing look in his eye. He nodded as I came in. Don't mess this up, I could almost hear him say. I nodded back, tightening my grip on my sword.

Nicolas stared at me, and I gave a timid smile back. His shoulders relaxed under his thin, navy shirt. He'd, too, skipped the formal clothes and wore a more casual top with short sleeves that left his forearms bare. He mouthed something to me, though I couldn't make out what it was.

Most of the other girls were there already, lined in the center of the arena clad for battle. We'd all traded in our elaborate skirts from the first test in favor of cuffed tunics and tights, with belts draped at their waists to carry their weapons. A tall rack of weapons sat at the back wall, leaning against the wooden planks keeping us in. The crowd banged against the top of these planks in frenzied excitement. My guard left me standing beside Cathleen and retreated from the arena to climb the stairs to watch.

Two more girls were brought in after me. I peeked down the row to count. Still missing one.

King Silas drummed his fingers over his knee.

"Blaire is late," Cathleen whispered.

"Late seems to be the style now," Nadine said with an unmistakable side-glance to me, then over Cathleen's shoulder to Celeste. We both ignored her. Further down the line, Tia quivered so hard she might fall over, and I silently hoped I'd be paired against her.

A win in front of all these people would be good for me, and I was eager to prove my skill with the blade. A queen who could wield a sword was tremendously more valuable than a queen who could sew.

My feet dug into my shoes, eager to begin.

"We will have to start without one competitor," Ava's voice bit the air. She climbed next to King Silas and addressed the crowd, who hushed to hear her words. She didn't dress in fine silks or wear her hair down as she usually did. Today, her hair was pinned atop her head and her curves were decorated in a simple tunic, wide belt, and tight pants tucked into boots. A long sword clung to her side.

"Welcome to the second competition," Ava spoke. King Silas remained seated behind her, while Nicolas leaned forward with elbows on his knees. Wind rustled his hair and he played with his lip between his teeth.

Irritatingly, I clearly wasn't the only girl noticing him. Celeste's eyes were purely fixated on Nicolas instead of Ava.

When the crowd had quieted enough, Ava went on. "Today's test will prove your strength. To be queen, you must be skilled with weapons. If the castle is under surprise attack, the queen is the closest person to the king, and you are his last line of defense. It will be your duty to protect your king. It is your job to fight for your country and protect your throne. Today we will see if you can do that."

She descended the stairs. We all looked at each other. Where were the instructions? Did we just begin fighting? Perhaps that was part of the test, to see who took the initiative first. Just as I'd set my hand on my sword, Ava reappeared at the edge of the arena where she walked in with us.

"Your test will be beating me in a sword fight."

My hand dropped from my sword. Nicolas stood, but the king pulled him back down. The girls were a mix between pleased and appalled. "She's twice our age," Bella snorted.

Ava's eye's narrowed till they were as sharp as daggers. "Just for that, I'll fight you first. The other girls can wait in the stands. This won't take long."

Bella's knees trembled and she fidgeted with her sword while shooting us a desperate look. As a guard motioned for the remaining girls to climb to the stands, Ava curled her hand over her hilt with a devilish smile. "I must warn you; I was trained by the late queen."

That didn't mean anything to me, but as soon as she began it was clear that she was something to be feared. Bella held a tight frame, but Ava thrusted her weight forward and coiled her blade around the other girl's, disarming her within mere moments. The crowd booed.

Bella hung her head in her walk to the stands as a more confident Tia stepped up.

Tia deflected two combats before lunging to strike with a motion that nearly knocked Ava from her feet. Cheers filled the air. My elbows dug into my knees as I leaned forward to study Ava's movements—how often she attacked, what stance she used to defend, which angle she swung at—it all helped me understand her better.

Ava made a daring downward slice that would have cut off Tia's neck had she not dropped to her knees. She wasted no time striking up, her blade finding Ava's side where metal connected with metal and a hallow bang sent Ava to her knee.

The air stilled. Ava dropped her sword. Tia had beaten her.

All the girls forgot they were in competition with each other as they rose to their feet to clap. Tia absorbed the praise, taking her time to bow to each side before making her way back to the stands with a smug grin.

Nadine went next. At this point Ava was at an unfair disadvantage as her chest heaved with breaths, but she straightened as Nadine approached and twirled her blade in her hand.

All signs of exhaustion left as soon as she began fighting. I richly desired to have met the late queen who could teach someone to fight like that.

Nadine lasted for several minutes until she began to crack under the weight of Ava's sword. But in a movement so fast it was hard to follow, Ava's blade relented just enough for Nadine to push back.

Ava withdrew and raised her hand. She was yielding.

As the girls roared with cheers, my eyes narrowed. Ava was stronger than Nadine and her moves were far more advanced. She had her beat—but she let Nadine win.

I found Nicolas through the dusty air. He was frowning. He bent to whisper to the king, who shook his head, but as he pulled away King Silas tipped in his seat to watch more closely.

Cathleen went next. She fumbled with her blade and stepped back each time Ava advanced. Still, with her first attack she was able to disarm Ava.

This time I was certain. Nicolas's eye found mine from across the arena and his lips drew in a tight line. Ava was letting her favorites best her, which wouldn't apply to me.

The next few girls were taken down, but they put up a good fight. Blaire still hadn't arrived, until it was only me and Celeste left to compete.

"Best of luck," Celeste muttered. She gave me a little smile that I couldn't read through.

"Thanks," I said flatly, standing to join Ava in the arena.

Ava wiped the edge of her sword as I approached and gave me a low grin. Sweat covered her face and her breathing came quick, but she still raised her sword in the air to liven up the audience, only lowering it when I was close enough to hear her speak.

"Are you ready for this?"

My sword rose, splitting her image in two. "Ready."

She stepped forward, using both arms to bring the weight of her sword down on me. Dirt flew as my foot dug back to stabilize my body to absorb the thrust and I twisted to get out from under the attack. She didn't spare a moment before she curled around to slice again.

My blade beat against hers. I spun to the side and dropped back, forcing her to twist and reposition before she could attack again. In that time, I tightened my fists around the hilt, the warm steel burning into my palms as I drove the sword at Ava's side.

She stumbled, and I advanced again, sinking my feet into the ground to drive her further back. My teeth clenched down on my tongue until the brutal taste of blood singed my lips.

My nostrils flared. I withdrew to avoid her next swing and drove my sword between us. She deflected with a plate on her arm, but it pushed her back until she was almost against the planked wall.

Her eyes narrowed and a growl escaped her lips. Victory coiled within.

She charged me, putting all her weight into each attack until I was left struggling to defend. These were not the moves she made on the other girls. While she had been calculated in those attacks, she was unrelenting in mine. The crowd roared but their chants sounded like a dull buzz to my ears.

With the next advance, the loud clash of swords bit overhead and my legs buckled. As I dropped to a knee, Ava brough her arm behind her back, driving the sword across my arm.

A bitter sting was left in its place, followed by a dull ache. A red so dark it could be black dripped down my arm.

The buzz stopped. Either my mind was going numb or the crowd silenced.

Ava gave only a moment to recover before driving again, and I rolled out of the way. When I came up I faced the west, where the sun roared down to blind me. My sword came up to block an attack, but it was impossible to see where it came from. Ava used this to her advantage, pushing me again and again until I was cowering beneath my blade, fighting to stay alive.

Those girls have a killer instinct. Don't be afraid to throw in your sword to save your life.

Dana's warning clawed at my mind. No one would blame me for surrendering. I was of no use to this kingdom if dead.

My knuckles hardened over the sword. I was of no use to this kingdom if I broke so easily, either.

I spun in a circle, bringing my sword in a large arch to attempt to push Ava to the side so I could twist from the blinding light. But as my blade turned, she met it with a stiff hook and ripped the blade from my grasp, sending it soaring into the wood planks. It landed in the dirt too far to reach, while my neck froze under the cruel tip of Ava's blade. Behind her was the aghast look of her son, too far away to save me from his mother's malice. Nicolas threw himself at the railing to jump, but the king grabbed him back.

Ava's eyes sparked with untamed wildness.

"Would you kill me?" The words clawed from my hoarse throat, and I spat blood from my cheeks.

Ava wiped sweat from her brow. "For my son? Anything. I can tell when a girl does not love him. You will bring him nothing but heartbreak and a wasted life."

"You think I don't love him?" I asked.

"I know it."

She turned her blade and struck my face with the blunt edge, sending me sprawling across the ground. I rolled and held up my arm to block a second attack, praying she used the blunt end again. It smashed against my skin, rattling the very bone.

With great difficulty, I rose to my feet just to have her knock me down again.

Her age was of little importance to me now. I swiped for her feet, but she stomped on my hand, and I let out a cry.

"I wouldn't fight this hard for anyone else," I said breathlessly.

"You fight for a crown," she said, raising her hilt.

But the final blow did not come. Instead, her blade dipped until the tip met the ground.

I took several breaths before standing, as the crowd cheered at the performance. The girls didn't clap this time but sat still with pained expressions. It wasn't pity for me that stilled their hands. It was a harsh realization that I fought harder than them, and how far Ava was willing to go to stop me.

Or perhaps it was gratefulness that it was my skin that tore under Ava's blade and not theirs. A drop of my blood spilled to the dirt where it smeared under my boot.

The only one not shaken was Celeste as she rose for her turn. She was emotionless as she brushed by me to face Ava.

Ava gave the last of her energy into fighting Celeste, but it was clear who would win. Even if Celeste didn't possess a natural skill with the blade, Ava pulled back all her strikes. I'd just been on the other end of that sword; I could tell she wasn't giving it her all.

Ava allowed Celeste to fight for as long as I had until Ava's grip on her hilt fumbled and the blade came clashing down.

She didn't pick it up. She drew an arm across her glistening forehead and stripped off her arm plates. Celeste stayed by her side.

Once more, the crowd roared. Their favorite had won.

"Should we stand there, too?" Bella asked.

To that, Cathleen snorted. "You shouldn't." Bella stuck out her lip.

"Well my lord," Ava called over the dying roar of the crowd. The air settled like a heavy cloak around us while the unpleasant sting of blood still marred my mouth, and shocks of deep throbbing pain traveled down my arms.

Nicolas dropped into his chair. Guilt built up in my chest, hurting deeper than the cut in my arm or my mouth. I'd let Nicolas down by not winning today, and now it'd be difficult to convince the kingdom that I deserved the crown or their loyalty.

Ava's grating voice spoke, "I think we have a clear winner." Her gaze swept to the king and her son.

Nicolas clenched the rails while shaking his head at his mother, with a fire in his eye that I adored him for. He was not weak and would not stand by as his mother dictated matters of which she had no right. I needed someone with his strength in my life.

King Silas stood just as Ava's mouth opened to announce the winner. Her hand was already reaching for Celeste's.

"I think we do," King Silas said. At the king's voice, the audience completely silenced. "This competition was to find a queen who would fight for her kingdom and protect her king. Today I witnessed a girl willing to do anything to fight, even as her blood fell to the earth. That is what a queen should be, and that is why I'm honored to announce Princess Rowan as the winner of this competition. Lady Celeste, you have placed second."

The crowd lit up again, this time for me. A few girls patted my back in good spirits, and even though their jostling brought fresh throbs to my arm, I didn't pull away. Ava's lips turned down in a harsh line and she stormed from the arena. In her dust, Celeste wore a smile and cheered with the crowd, even nodding her head in my direction with no sign of animosity over placing second.

Nicolas gave me a passing smile as he pushed from the platform and followed for his mother. King Silas remained to see the crowds out, and the girls filed in a line back into the castle. There were no complaints today, and no bitter looks at either me or Celeste. The slender girl came to my side and squeezed my shoulder.

"You did well today," Celeste whispered. "I was impressed."

"You have skill, too," I confessed. She'd earned a bit of respect after her performance, though as soon as I said that she peeked over her shoulder at the retreating Nicolas, and my tongue turned sour.

We followed the other girls into the castle in silence. Celeste's sudden presence raised questions of her intentions, and her quiet nature raised my brow. If she came to fight for Nicolas's heart, she did so with a deep steadiness instead of aggressive assertion, either indicating a confidence or disinterest.

I laced my hand around her arm as soon as we entered the building and pulled her to the side. She raised a brow but obediently followed.

Broken light from a sheer, golden curtain hovered in the side hall, casting a golden glow over the cream rug, copper vases, and polished wooden frames of paintings. Our feet left tiny tracks of dirt through the shiny pine floors, but maids stood ready at the side to wipe it up. They eyed me and Celeste as we paused while the others moved on. I took off my shoes and held them up, which seemed to appease them.

"Can I help you?" Celeste asked coolly.

Her casual demeanor unnerved me, and I crossed my arms. "What are you doing here?"

Her face pinched in thoughtful expression, and she took the time to run her hand through her hair before responding. "I'm here for Nicolas, and for the throne. Both sound good to me." She said it so unabashedly, no shame or guilt in admitting she was here for the throne.

I wanted to ask why she thought she'd made a good queen, but the matter with Nicolas pressed far heavier on my chest. "You left him. It's been years. Now suddenly you're back?" It was suspicious, and enough so to suspect ulterior motives.

She shrugged, running a hand through her hair again. "I love him. Frankly that's the only reason I need." She didn't flinch as she said those words, but I did. They hit me like a gust of icy wind so powerful that the breath from my lungs fled with it, and my grip on my boots was the only thing tethering me to the ground. My toes curled over the smooth floor. All the girls in this competition competed to be the future queen, but I'd been naïve enough to believe I was the only one harboring genuine feelings for Nicolas.

Celeste didn't note my unease. "When he asked me to marry him, I was young and unbridled. But I've matured now, and I'm back to fix my past mistake of letting him go. I love him, and I'm here to fight for him and for Thames."

Another wind struck me with her words, and this time there was nothing to anchor me.

"He wanted to marry you." I exhaled the sentence, forcing my ears to hear it a second time so my mind would understand.

He hadn't told me that part. From his story, they'd just been in love and she left, then he turned all his attention to finding me. But how much could he have focused on me when he'd been ready to marry her?

A more sickening thought came. If she'd said yes, there might have been no one to wake me.

Celeste nodded. "He asked twice."

Her lips twitched in pleasure, only faltering as echoed footsteps taken in urgency sent the maids rushing to the side wall just as King Silas swept into the room with a brow set so low that it hid his eyes. His frown reached his chin.

"Celeste, to your room. Hurry."

There was a pressing seriousness to his tone that sent her obeying without hesitation. From behind the king came three guards who followed Celeste. She peeked over her shoulder at the escorts and hurried faster.

"What is it?" I asked. Three guards remained behind with the king, their stone faces showing no emotion.

King Silas's skin bore wrinkles of a much older man.

"Blaire has been found," he said. His gaze drifted to the maids waiting to finish cleaning the room, and his tone dropped low. "She's dead."

Chapter Twenty-Four

THE DOOR TO THE office banged shut as the guards shuffled to their set places—some by the windows and others barring the door. A few council members sat by the desk with pinched expressions as Nicolas paced the floor.

It couldn't be helped; when he came to sight, so did the thought of him proposing to Celeste. Twice.

One of the advisors, a lanky man with straw-like hair and a golden lion broach ran his hands back and forth together while keeping his head low, even as he spoke. "An attempt aimed for the throne or a trick to eliminate competition?"

"Either is dangerous," another piped up. She pulled at the folded hemline of her amethyst blazer and leaned heavily on the Thames accent. "And rumors will spread which are just as dangerous. Perhaps we call the competition off, no?"

"Agreed. The eligible daughters of wealthy lords all dying will bring this kingdom far more turmoil than we've yet seen. Call it off," golden broach man replied.

"The competition was working," the third said, a white-haired gentleman relying generously on his crooked cane. "We made progress. Saw rest. Hate to lose that."

Two hard knocks rippled at the door. The guards peeked through, then separated to let Ava and Martin in.

"Finally." Nicolas jumped toward Ava. "I need a word with you."

"We have a predicament." She held up her hand as if she hadn't heard him. He growled at it.

King Silas snorted. "I'd say; you are clearly biased against Rowan." He crossed his arms from where he leaned against an armchair.

Ava's eyes caught fire. She refused to look at me. "I think the dead girl makes for a bigger problem."

"I'm king, I'll decide what's the bigger problem." King Silas said. "Ava, from henceforth, you are banned from all dealings related to the Queen's Competition. It is your close friendship with my late wife that keeps you in my good graces, and nothing more."

Nicolas plopped himself into a chair. "Just so we are clear, there is nothing keeping you in my good graces."

"I am your mother," she said with a condescending look. "Being in your good graces has never been my job."

"Now about the dead girl," King Silas cleared his throat, and I winced at the word 'dead.' "I'm not ready to call off the competition. All the nobles have agreed to accept the results, which will be void if we cancel the final event. I say we move it up to tomorrow so the next day we can announce Rowan the winner and send the girl's home. If any more of them die after that, it's not on our hands."

"But one of them has already died," the woman with the heavy accent said. "That must be addressed."

"It will be, when we have all the details. For now, we keep this quiet and the other girls safe. I suspect this was more an attempt to scare us into halting the competition than anything. Someone is relying on the unrest of the people to further their agenda, and if the competition is finalized and the nobles are bound by contract then they will have little turmoil to feed on."

He pushed from the chair and straightened his jacket, moving toward the door. When none of us followed, he raised a brow. "It means the competition is working. We continue on. Move the third competition to tomorrow and prepare Rowan to be the future queen of Thames."

He pushed through the door as guards hustled in pursuit.

The three advisors bent their heads together in low whispers that lasted only a few seconds before they followed for the king in a flurry of head shakes and frowns. Golden broach man paused to shake my hand.

"Good luck, my queen," he said. "I hope you are prepared for what your rule may bring."

Ava frowned as they left.

I shifted toward the door, but hesitated. With one of the girls dead and my sword left behind in the arena, that left me vulnerable and wildly uncomfortable. There were no guards waiting to escort me.

I cast a look to Nicolas, who already moved for my side.

"Nicolas," Ava caught his arm as he tried to pass. "You can't be mad at me for protecting you."

He tore his arm from her grasp. "You don't get to make that decision for me."

"Martin?" Ava turned to her husband in a humane gesture, but he only laughed.

"I've long since stopped getting involved in your schemes. I love you both." He planted a kiss on his son's forehead, then his wife's.

"Useless," Ava whispered. But she leaned into his kiss.

Nicolas and I left, and his fingers laced through mine. "How are you?"

I examined my arm. "The cut from your mother's sword isn't bleeding anymore. But poor Blaire." I hadn't fancied the girl, but no one can think ill of the dead so soon after their passing. Death had a way of bringing out the better memories of a person.

Again, Dana's warning came. Blaire might have been dead before she'd said that. While I agreed with the king that one of the other girls wasn't guilty, I didn't completely pardon the idea.

After my performance today, they might think twice about coming after me.

Nicolas's eyes danced from side to side as we walked, inspecting every shadow lingering behind wide columns and every sound bouncing from windowpanes. His words drifted from him, but his focus was only half with me. "Listen, my mother is not a great person. But we don't have to deal with her if you don't want to. I'll do whatever it takes to makes you happy."

The sentiment might have been sweet if he'd looked at me once while saying it.

"Nicolas," I paused, pulling him to stop beside me. Even now his eye didn't stay on mine but peeked around for anyone who might be coming. "Look at me. I know you don't feel safe but we are okay right now."

"You aren't safe until we get this sorted," he said.

"And you will never be safe as king," I reminded him. "I signed up for this. This will not scare me off, and neither will the next time there's an attack, nor the next. I am here." My words stumbled. "If you still want me to be."

Now he dropped his head and stared at me. "Of course I do."

I rocked back on my heels, trapped between trusting his words and needing clarity on his feelings for Celeste. It'd been his word that told me of their relationship, while leaving out a big part. That neglect might have been to spare me hurt, but it could have been to spare himself the pain that still etched in his heart.

If he cared for Celeste, I needed to know.

Just as my heart had opened up to him, I felt the cold claws of fear beginning to close over it, protecting it from breaking.

Ask him and put yourself out of this misery.

"Did you propose to Celeste?"

His shoulders jerked back, and his breath stopped. My heart sunk with the realization that no answer he could give would make me feel better. He couldn't lie and say he hadn't. Hearing that she meant everything to him would hurt, and hearing that she was only a fleeting pleasure would make him appear immature.

Nothing could take away from the fact that he'd once cared deeply for her and hadn't told me about it.

My hands slipped from his. "Why didn't you tell me?"

"I told you about her. She broke my heart. That relationship was over."

I didn't miss how he said 'was.'

"You didn't tell me that you proposed twice to her. I looked like an idiot when she told me." Hot tears formed in the corner of my eyes.

Nicolas no longer checked for danger and paid little regard to who might hear as he pushed back. "Did you want me to devote my life to waiting for you? I couldn't be sure you were real! But you knew you would one day fall asleep and that someone would come to wake you. Did you wait for me? Or did you allow yourself feelings for another?"

I stepped back. Cassian shouldn't have been brought into this. And I never knew I would fall asleep. I always hoped I'd break the curse.

But I'd been honest about my past relationship. Nicolas hadn't. "That's not why I'm mad."

Nicolas folded his arms over his chest and took a wide stance. His voice lowered, but his words hit me harder this time. "Fine. Are you upset because she loves me, or are you upset because you don't?"

Loves. Not *loved.* My eyes narrowed, and the question squirmed from my throat, drenched in terror. "How do you know she loves you?"

"So you admit that you still don't?"

My nails dug into my skin. "Nicolas. How do you know she currently loves you?"

He sighed, running weary hands over his head. "She came to my room to talk last night."

Her collected coolness could now be depicted as only one thing. Confidence. The image of Celeste with her silky hair and curvy hips going to his room late at night sent goosebumps to my arm and my teeth clenched together.

This was worse than I thought. Instead of accepting that he'd proposed and explaining why he'd hidden it from me, he danced around the topic and made my chest tighten with frustration. "And you didn't tell me."

Nicolas threw up his hands. "I tried to! You wouldn't speak with me."

I focused on each breath, hoping they'd soothe my rising anger, but each gasp of air brought in more images of Celeste with Nicolas, her nails curled through his hair, her smile upon his lips, until squeezing my eyes shut was all I could do to block out the images.

"Rowan, I am here for you." When I opened my eyes, Nicolas had dropped his hands to his side and relaxed his face, though he kept at a safe distance. I released my fist, though my breath released sharply.

"Do you still care for her?"

He inched forward. "I respect her. She's an incredible woman and would undoubtedly make a great queen. I wouldn't have loved her if she weren't wonderful." His chin dipped down until he was close enough to breath in, and I kept my body rigid while waiting for his words.

"But I am only interested in pursuing you, Rowan Sordwill, the girl from the ice."

His rough fingertips trickled up my arm, making the hairs stand on end. By the time his hands reached my shoulders, I'd released my burning anger, and by the time his grasp coiled mine, I'd almost forgotten what we'd argued about.

"I won't apologize for not being in love with you yet." My eyes met his squarely. "I fall in love on my own time. I won't be pressured into it."

"Of course not." His nose grazed mine, and his grip tightened. "You wouldn't be the woman I cherish if you made this easy."

That one sentence made the rest of my frustration simmer as if it were merely a passing wind. Nicolas Zapallis, heir of Thames, was mine. Even though my actions were cold sometimes, even though I wasn't delicate like a rose or as beautiful as this castle, he chose me, and as a feeling of peace settled over me, it was enough to convince myself that this feeling could last forever.

"Am I forgiven for proposing to another girl?" He smirked while brushing his lips close to mine.

"Just don't do it again." I closed the gap, securing the moment with a kiss firm enough to show him I cared and soft enough to remind us it could all be taken away in an instant. This love between us was fragile and new, still a young emotion that burned in slow sparks over flickering embers, likely to either catch fire and burn forever or char us to ashes.

By the Fates, I hoped it would burn forever. I had nothing else in life to burn for but him.

Chapter Twenty-Five

AS I HEADED BACK to my rooms, a stricken voice in my hallway stopped me. I peeked inside an open doorway to Cathleen's room where all eleven other girls sat on the large bed together in one huddled mass.

Many had tears in their eyes. Tissues were strewn about. Noses sniffled. Everything in me said to run.

But Celeste looked up at the wrong moment, spotted me, and held out her hand. "We are mourning Blaire together."

I hadn't known Blaire well, but every way I phrased that sounded heartless in my head during their moment of clear distress. Their arms opened and I crossed the room to crawl into their close knit.

"I'm so scared," Bella was saying. She sat with her back against a pillow, hugging her knees as she rocked back and forth. Tia stroked her arm but was in no better shape herself. Her nose was rubbed raw and her eyes bright red.

"I know. We all are."

"If someone killed her, then someone could kill us just as easily," Bella said.

The rest of us just looked at each other while her words hung in their air, waiting to be absorbed. No matter what we did to keep them out, they slowly carved their way to our hearts where they took a strong hold.

Someone had killed one of the contestants. No one was safe.

"We are going to be fine," Nadine said. She held Cathleen's hand while Cathleen took silent heaps of breath between cries. A single tear drifted down Nadine's cheek. "We are strong. We will survive."

It was the right thing to say in the moment, but even then, there was little that could comfort us in the face of another's death. While I wouldn't want to be caught in fear, I found it healthy to maintain a fair level of awareness that troubles could come at any moment.

We fought for a dangerous prize, and it wouldn't be won easily.

"I heard her body was broken when they found it," Bella continued to whimper. "Her beauty spilled onto the floor."

"Hush," Celeste said softly. "It'll do us no good to think on that."

But as the girls stared at our hands all tangled together, it was clear we thought of little else.

"They'll station more guards to keep watch over us," I tried to comfort them. "We will be safer than ever."

"Still," Bella sniffed. "I doubt I can ever go to a library again without thinking of her body laid on the floor."

My forehead wrinkled. I'd fetched some books to study Thame's history, and the library was in the western wing, a part of the castle not used often and not well guarded. She should have known better to wander there. "What was she doing in the library?"

Tia stroked Bella's arm while the girl gulped. Her eyes met each of ours before she sighed.

"You may as well know now. She'd fallen in love with a cleaning boy. They met there sometimes."

All our jaws dropped open, while Nadine cursed.

"She never should have done that," Nadine said. "Or she should have told someone. Perhaps then she'd still be alive."

Her words felt cruel now, offering that there was a hope Blaire could have lived if she'd done something differently.

"Poor Blaire," Celeste said. "She was a dear girl."

We didn't say more but remained on the bed huddled together with tears and embraces and kind smiles. I had no words of comfort to offer these girls but being around them felt unlike it had before. We weren't competing, weren't trying to best one another. We were just girls, feeling lost and afraid in something bigger than ourselves.

Then a maid came in with Cathleen's meal, and one by one we drifted from the room with a last comforting smile.

Tomorrow the games might begin again. Tomorrow we might remember that we were in competition with each other. But for tonight, we'd laid down our swords and embraced each other, and that felt more powerful than any crown.

The next morning, my peaceful slumber was once more rudely cut short by Lucille shaking me fervently, her muffled voice breaking through my muddied mind.

"Wake me one more time, and I swear I'm hiding all the wine."

But there was more than just her voice. Another, sharp sound pierced the air, followed by other noises coming one by one as I fully woke. A high-pitched ringing echoed off stone walls and through hallways, bursting out windows to crack against the dark, night sky. Hurried footsteps traveled down long corridors and banged against the walls. A scream.

"Get. Up." Lucille struggled to push me from the bed. I fell to my knees and sprang up.

"What is that?" The noise came from all directions at once, growing louder every moment. Thoughts of Blaire came to mind, and I looked around wildly.

"Intruders in the castle. We have to get to the lockroom now." Lucille's nightgown wrapped around her long legs as she bustled from side to side, prying me from my spot and shoving me at the door. Isabel and Rosalie spent the night in their own chambers with Mateo, while Dana was with her husband, so it was only Lucille and I to collect from the room.

The front door burst open and we both screamed. A guard lept into the room, swiveling his head in all directions. When he spotted us, he waved an arm.

"Hurry. There's no time to waste. There's at least ten already inside." Then he was gone as soon as he'd come, leaving us with a final warning as he ran on to the next room. "Don't trust anyone."

Only ten men, yet the castle was in uproar. By now word would have spread of Blaire's death, and all it would take was one intruder to send us all to frenzy.

Lucille and I exchanged glances before hiking up our skirts and bolting after him. Neither of us cared to be the next found dead.

The hallway was a mess of people running in both directions, including a few of the girls in the competition who didn't know where to go. Bella stood in the middle sobbing into her hands, while Cathleen tugged on her arm. A few guards or maids paused to help them, but most ran to their own places, either a lockroom or to fight.

Celeste was the image of grace as she held a trembling Tia's hand and ushered others to follow her. She used a stern voice that rang of confidence while the others could hardly do more than cry. At her instruction, the last of the girls headed south.

It seemed the lockroom was down the south hallway, while the guards with hands on their weapons ran down the north hall toward the east wing stairs.

That led to Nicolas's rooms. The fight was near him.

"Come on." Lucille's voice was hardly recognizable as fear prompted it, but my bare feet dug into the ground.

"Rowan?"

My chest beat with such force that it hardly contained my heart, and my head rang as loud as the alarm. If I went to the lockroom, I'd be safe, but I'd have no way to help be certain Nicolas was. Before I could think too hard about my decision, I flew back to the bedchamber where I fumbled along the wall to find my sword. As soon as Lucille saw me with it, she squeaked.

"No. Come with me now." This time her voice was less afraid and more demanding.

"I can't lose him," I said, tightening my hand over the smooth ridges of my steel hilt. "You go."

The air clouded with dull clashing, frenzied stomping, and wild shrills. Amidst it all, Lucille growled. "You don't even know where to go," she said. "I'll take you to him."

Lucille carried the courage of a warrior and she didn't know it.

She changed directions to lead me toward the east wing. We climbed stairs to guards' disapproval until we reached the landing.

"You can't go this way! You might be killed!" A guard shouted as he sprinted past us. He stuck out his arm to lead us back, but I pushed through with the blunt of my sword.

"I know," Lucille grunted, ducking under his grab. "You try arguing with her."

As soon as we turned the corner, we both skidded to a halt. The sharp scent of blood hit our noses as the scene unfolded. In the middle of the wide hallway lit by the pale moon was King Silas, sword above his head, bringing his weight down with a grunt over another guard. The man fought back, but he was no use against the burly king. Blood stained his beard but he didn't hold back from his swings.

Guards fought against guards, and I had no way to tell who was good and who was bad. I could only hope they could.

Ten men was wrong. It was more like fifty. A full battle played out in the corridor, and we stood at the cusp of it in our nightgowns with nothing more than a sword to protect us.

Nicolas shouted, shoving a man down in front of him. He stood in white pants already dirtied with blood, and his teal sleeves rolled up to his elbows as he wielded his blade. He paused to press a hand to his chest where his old wound would still be healing, but he was given little time to breathe before another man came at him.

I held up my sword, but no one paid us any mind, and I didn't know who the enemy was to strike down.

"You need to be in your room," King Silas shouted.

Just as I opened my mouth to reply, Nicolas yelled back, "I can fight!"

"I don't doubt it," King Silas grunted as he struck down another. "But one of us has to live. Go, and take her with you."

Nicolas's brow clenched together, until through the chaos he spotted me, looking like a fool behind my sword thinking I was coming to save him.

My fingers tightened. I'd failed to protect him once, then lost in a fight with his mother. I wouldn't run today.

A guard rushed at me, not to cover me from danger but to bring his sword down. Lucille yelped and pressed her back to the wall while I pressed my feet into the ground and braced against his strike. Our swords met in the air, and his eyes widened ever so slightly at my display of strength before I twisted the blade around his.

He sliced his sword outward and snarled while swinging sideways, putting more power behind his advance this time. I bent my knees to drive forward and knock his blade to the side, then slashed upward to bring his sword above his head.

I dropped to my knees as his next swing came around, crouching under the blade to drive my own upward into the tender part of his side.

Lucille snapped her eyes shut as the man fell to the floor.

"Take this," I said, grabbing his fallen sword and thrusting it into her white hands. The tip hit the stone floor as she was unprepared for its weight, but she didn't let go.

Nicolas pulled from the chaos to place a hand over mine. "You should be in the lockroom."

"A queen fights to protect her king," I told him. "I'm fighting for you."

The sentence was made more impactful as in that exact moment someone snuck behind Nicolas and I blocked his attack with my sword. Nicolas spun around and drove his blade into the man before he could shield himself.

Nicolas sighed and looked at me. He opened his mouth, but the fight spread to us, and we were quickly surrounded by the madness.

"Rowan, behind you!" Lucille shouted. She'd pressed herself further back until her feet tipped on the edge of the stairway. I turned to meet the one she warned me about, keeping my side near Nicolas.

"Go downstairs," I called to Lucille. "Your mother will kill me if you die."

Lucille fled as swift as the wind, and I breathed easier knowing she was escaping the fight.

Keeping Nicolas safe was now my only priority. We kept our backs together as we held our swords up to deflect incoming attacks. A short man with strong arms came at Nicolas, but he was quick to disarm him. His back pushed against my own as he delivered a fatal blow to the other man.

His chest heaved as he faced me. "Are you alright?" he asked in the quick moment before more enemies arose.

Only Nicolas would pause in the middle of a fight to check on my well-being.

"I'm good," I promised him. He grinned, but his expression was still tense.

In an odd way, I cherished this time with him. It was a testament to the trust between us that I could fight beside him and feel safe with him guarding my back. And circumstances like this could bond us.

But while Nicolas fought with unrelenting strength, his expression said he longed to be free of the battle.

It wouldn't last for much longer. There had undoubtedly been more than ten men, but the fighting began to quiet and many looked around to find the last of the attackers.

A new fleet of guards stormed up the stairs, and we froze. My blade hovered in the air before my face, preparing to fight if they attacked, but instead they surrounded us and finished taking down the last of the men.

"The threat is diminished, sire," one said to the king.

King Silas drew deep breaths and kept his sword raised. He pointed it at us.

"Be grateful neither of you died today," he said. "Or else I would have killed the other for not listening. Get inside your room while we make sure there are no further attacks."

I brought my sword down to my side and nodded. The fighting was over, but Nicolas still gripped the hilt of his blade in both hands and studied every guard with jittery eyes, almost expecting one of them to attack. I slid my fingers through his arm and tugged. We stepped over fallen bodies while the guards formed a path for us to Nicolas's chambers, where they stood at attention while we shut the door.

The sound of it locking was the only thing that relaxed Nicolas. "There." He bent to catch his breath. "We are safe." The darkness of the night still cloaked the room, but Nicolas inspected every corner until satisfied it was empty of attackers.

At last, he kicked his sword to the side where it clattered against the wall.

"You should have gone to a lockroom downstairs," he said in a weary voice. "You could have died." He slid to his knees.

I set down my blade and sat beside Nicolas. "I wanted to know you were okay." I stroked his shoulder where his muscles spasmed. Bit by bit they relaxed under my touch.

He rubbed his hand over his eyes. "At least you're alive. This all happened so fast." His gaze bore into the ground with the memory. "My father, Silas, and I were in the office having a late meeting when a thoughtful servant came in with a marzipan cake. Everything was normal at that point. Only two minutes later a guard came looking for us, saying there were intruders in the castle. We couldn't avoid them on our way back to our rooms."

He stared at the floor for a while.

"The odd thing was the intruders seemed surprised to see King Silas. But if he was their target, I can't figure out why they'd be surprised to see him outside his own room." His forehead crunched in the way that it did when he was trying to sort something out, and his fingers tapped together.

I leaned against him, letting him feel my warmth. "It's going to be fine."

The corridor was quiet behind us, save for a few footsteps and quiet talking. If they found more intruders, the fight wasn't near us.

"I never wanted this," Nicolas whispered. "I never wanted to fight for my life." He leaned his head against his arm to peek at me. The moon lit the gold in his eyes. "And I want so much more for you. You shouldn't have to sleep with a sword by your bed or worry about intruders. You should be given a safe home and a happy life without the load of ruling." He rolled his head back down again. "I never wanted to be king."

I *had* wanted this. All my life I wanted to be queen as my birthright owed me.

But this relationship brought unforeseen changes to my heart. Now Nicolas's desire reflected my own—despite what I used to want, I'd do anything to keep him safe. Even if that meant losing a crown.

"Do you think these men are related to the ones we overheard in the tent at the carnival?" Nicolas asked.

"I hope so," I said softly. "Or else you have more enemies than you know."

As the soft blue light outside morphed into calming hues of orange, the entire castle settled down.

"You shouldn't have to see so much death," Nicolas said.

"I've seen death before. I told you, I'm not going anywhere."

We sat against the wall until his breathing had slowed almost to a rhythmic sleep, and the fear of the night fled with the sun of the morning. As he rested, I sorted through the situation in my mind, trying to find a way to free Nicolas from this responsibility.

If only the heirs before him hadn't died. If only King Silas could somehow live forever. If only being a ruler wasn't so hard. I could take on as much of the burden as possible, but I could never free him completely.

Just when I thought he was in a deep sleep, Nicolas's head popped up. "We should check on Silas. I want to be certain everyone is okay."

I nodded and helped him to his feet. We braced ourselves to see the death once more, but the guards had cleaned already and the halls glistened with traces of soapy water.

A repulsive scent hung in the air. All the windows would need to be opened and the stone meticulously scrubbed to be rid of such an odor.

Nicolas covered his nose as he inspected both directions. "I doubt Silas is in his rooms right now."

At our voices, the king's door opened from across the corridor. They made no effort to disguise his door from the rest by painting it in brilliant gold and carving a lion's head into the wood, making it clear that greatness lived within. It was magnificent, but it made for an excellent director to his whereabouts.

Silas poked his head out. His thinning hair was pointed in every direction, but his beard had been cleaned of blood. "Nicolas?" He asked. "Is that you? You'd better come in."

Beside me, Nicolas let out a breath. "Thank goodness there were no more intruders."

"I wouldn't be thanking anything yet," King Silas said somberly.

The look on his face wasn't a good one. I slid my hand into Nicolas's as we came to the wide doorway. The king's large bed faced us from the back of the room where two tall and gangly figures bent over it, white caps on their heads and cream robes over their bodies. They fussed with a person who lay unmoving on the sheets.

Ava curled herself into a chair by the fire, her cheeks stained with tears.

"I'm so sorry," King Silas said. He chucked off his overcoat to fold it over a chair. "That marzipan cake was meant for me, but your father had a piece first. It was poisoned."

Nicolas became a statue beside me. "What?"

Ava spoke up from her place beside her husband. Her voice cracked. "He's not dead yet, but there's no sign of waking." Her body shook with a silent sob, and she folded her hands around Martin's.

Nicolas's voice was only an echo. "My father is dying?" He stumbled toward the bed, while I did all I could to keep him up. He glanced my way. "He can't die." He repeated the words a few times while I held fast to him.

The orange light from outside no longer appeared calming, but instead turned harsh like a warning of a coming fire. Nicolas stared as the doctors continued to pry with Martin while he remained too still, too lifeless. Ava refused to move from his side.

"This isn't right," Nicolas whispered. "His death would be for nothing. He'd die for nothing. The attack was meant for me and Silas. Not him." Through Nicolas's grip I could feel him crumbling beside me, and I knew the intruders succeeded in one thing: they'd wounded the crown today. If Nicolas could, he'd walk away right now.

I never wanted this, he'd told me. *I never wanted to be king.*

As tears rolled down his cheeks, I squeezed my eyes shut. *Let me be strong enough to support him through this, so he'll never feel alone. I never want him to feel as desperate as I did in the ice while my family died around me.*

His face crumpled with pain, and nothing I could do would stop the tear that rolled down his cheek.

Chapter Twenty-Six

NICOLAS STAYED BY HIS father's side and I remained by his all morning until my stomach rolled with hunger and my lids were like iron bars over my tired eyes.

"Get some sleep," Nicolas nudged me.

"I'm okay," I whispered back. We'd taken to whispering as if Martin were only sleeping and noise might bother him. Frankly, I thought we should attempt loud noises to see if we got a response from him, but the doctors were convinced he'd wake if he was meant to. None of their antidotes had brought him closer to life.

We now waited to see if he'd open his eyes or if his hands would grow cold.

"I appreciate you so much." Nicolas kissed my forehead. "But you need sleep. The final competition is still this evening."

That snapped me to attention. I'd forgotten. "Do they still expect us to compete today?"

Nicolas gave me an apologetic look. "I heard Silas talking about it. The faster we get this done, the better."

I moaned during the entire time I pulled myself to my feet. "Okay. I'll get ready."

Ava was asleep in the wide, burgundy chair, and the doctors were taking a break. King Silas had drifted off to somewhere hours ago. The room was utter silence as Nicolas leaned his head on his arm to watch his father breath while I slipped to the door.

To my surprise, Celeste stood outside when I opened it.

"Oh." She took a step back. "I heard what happened. Is he alright?"

My muscles argued as I took a deep breath before holding the door open further with a cordial smile on my face. "You can go in. I was just on my way out."

"Thank you." She brushed by me and hurried to Nicolas's side. My feet were heavy stones over the floor that begged me to stay by Nicolas's side as a reminder to Celeste, especially as she fanned out her skirts to collapse into my seat and coil her hands around his arm in delicate strokes, each movement stoking a fire within me.

Nicolas peeked at her long enough to grin before returning his entire attention to his ailing father.

His sweet sentiments from yesterday ran on repeat through my mind until they gave me the strength to pry myself from the room. Each step that led me away brought further confidence that I'd made the right choice by leaving when there was nothing more to be done to help, and my exhausted limbs needed rest before the final competition tonight.

After that, Celeste would no longer be around to worry over.

I rubbed my fingers over the bridge of my nose. Jealousy did not become me. At this rate, I'd go gray much sooner than my mother had.

But it felt nice to have something worth getting this jealous over. I had a treasure worth protecting, even at the sake of my sanity. And the Fates knew this month had put my sanity to the test.

The last of my energy went into falling against my door to open it and stumbling into the warm afternoon light from the open windows.

The scene before me was anything but warm, and the air quickly chilled.

Rosalie clawed at her mother's knees while Isabel hunched over my bed, her elbows deep in the plush comforter and her face buried into the unmoving shoulder of a man with hair dark as the night and a leg bandaged in cloth as bright as the day.

His fingers trickled through her hair, the tiniest of movement to show life, but other than that he lay still.

Dana set a washcloth over his forehead before whispering something to her daughter-in-law, who gave no reply. Lucille held the soberest look on her face as she poured dark stew into a bowl and brought it to the bedside. When she saw me, she placed a finger over her lips as if I might have yelled otherwise.

"It's my brother," she said, wiping her eyes with her sleeve. "Mateo was injured during the attack." Her hands shook before she squeezed them together, blowing a mouthful of worry into them with one long gust.

Rosalie gave up at her mother's heels, and instead crawled for Dana's.

"Will he live?" I asked.

"Yes," Dana replied, her sharp ears missing nothing. She bent to retrieve her granddaughter from the floor. "He will live." Her eyes clung to Mateo's leg for several moments before trailing over the rest of him with tight-pressed lips.

"But he may never walk again," Lucille whispered. "The cut is deep."

My heart broke for her and her family. Even though I'd never met Isabel's husband, his family had quickly carved out a special place in my life, and their pain was not easy to see.

I'd gone from one mourning room to another.

"Should he be in the hospital wing?"

As soon as I asked it, I wished for the words back. Dana placed one hand on her hip while bouncing Rosalie on the other. She came near us to let Isabel and her husband have quiet. "Are you questioning my skills? Do you forget that my talent with the needle saved your man?"

I blushed. "Of course not. You are truly a magician."

"Hospital was full anyway," Lucille whispered as she poured herself some stew. Her gaze flickered to her brother multiple times. "I hope they are taking good care of Karl."

Dana snorted. "That one may die."

I'd not heard of this particular gentleman, but the way Lucille gasped and clutched a hand to her chest made me guess at a new lover.

"Mama, how can you say such a horrid thing?"

Dana only shrugged. "He doesn't deserve you. I've never cared for that boy, and don't expect me to start now just because he suddenly fancies you. Perhaps Rowan can teach you a thing or two about taste in men." She waddled back to her son's side while Lucille blinked after her.

"Mothers are the worst." She turned to me. "Do you want stew?"

"Yes, but not as much as I want sleep. I'll be on the couch if you need me. I hope Mateo is okay."

I hated feeling helpless. Helpless to save Nicolas from the strain of ruling, helpless to heal his father, helpless to aid Isabel's husband. But if I didn't get sleep, I might be hopeless in the competition this evening.

I moved to the couch where the warm sofa greeted me and I wrapped the soft blanket like a cloud around my body, and the heaviness of the day pulled my lids shut until I was asleep in mere minutes despite the stress going on around me.

It was so comfortable that I might have stayed there all day, caught in the dream world where worries didn't exist, had Lucille not dropped the pan of ash at the hearth of the fire.

Her body froze as my eyes peeked open. The light clawed at my pupils, and I groaned. "Lucille, am I destined to be awoken by you every day for the rest of my life?"

"I am so sorry!" she whispered with a hand over her mouth. "I didn't mean to."

My reluctant feet hit the floor. "It's fine, I should get up anyway." The competition would begin soon, and it'd do me no good to sleep through it.

"Good, because I lied, it wasn't an accident." Lucille grinned, and I glared at her. Her hands flew up in a casual gesture and she giggled. No one could say Lucille wasn't bold. "You'd sleep all day if I let you, and you need to get ready. It's an important day for you."

I took my time to stand up. "Just once, I'd like an unimportant day. A day filled with nothing but sleep and laughter."

Lucille tucked the last of the ashes back in the pan. "Win this competition, and we'll have a day such as that."

Mateo still lay in the bed and Isabel stood at his side, but another man in a bloodied uniform had joined them. This one didn't look injured, and I wondered whose blood it was on his lapel. He nodded as he spoke with Mateo, who took a deep breath.

"Who is that?"

Lucille barely looked over there. "A man with information on the attack from today."

I perked up. "Do they know who tried to kill the king?" I asked the man. All three figured looked to me, and the guard frowned.

"I'm not to say more."

"As someone living in this home where the attack took place, and someone very close to Nicolas, I'd like to know where the threat came from so I may be on guard." I let no uncertainty linger in my tone and set my back straight. "Please."

The guard exchanged a look with Mateo, who gave a small nod. I liked him already.

"All I know is one of the captured men gave us some useful information. They are sending out an ambush now and should overtake the rebels by nightfall." The guard patted Mateo's hand. "The worst may be behind us now."

A thing such as that deserved to be celebrated, but merriment couldn't take place as Isabel stood beside her husband who may never walk again, and Nicolas knelt at his father's bedside waiting for a sign that he'd live.

And I knew better than to expect permanent peace. Such a thing wasn't obtainable.

This threat may be alleviated, but another would come. There would always be another to challenge the throne, to raise unrest, or to put pressure on the kingdom. We might be safe from these particular rebels, but more always came. Being a ruler meant being in constant danger.

And sometime, when an assassin aimed for the king's heart, they might hit mine.

"I should go see Nicolas," I said, grabbing a shawl to protect my arms from the evening draft.

"I believe another lady is with him currently," the guard said before I'd finished tying the shawl.

I froze. "Celeste?"

He coughed but nodded. I tried to read the expression on his face, his pinched eyebrows and puckered lips, and the way his fingers rolled over the bed's headboard, but he nodded once more to Mateo and strolled from the room.

I could only imagine what conversations had taken place between Nicolas and Celeste in my absence, or what memories had been brought up while I slept.

Lucille pushed a bowl of soup across the cart. "You ought to eat. The competition begins shortly."

"Fine." I pushed the door shut with my foot. "I'll check on Nicolas tonight. First I'll excel at this final test."

Chapter Twenty-Seven

The Final Test

THERE WERE TWO DISTINCT differences between the first two tests and the third.

First, the villagers were not in their usual place behind a gate, but the gates had been opened and they flooded the courtyard in swarms of color and smiles that made me fidget. They didn't hold signs but still cheered our names as we paraded from the castle and into the dying light of the evening.

For the first time, my name was among the top called.

I smiled, raising my hand and letting my long sleeve drape to my elbow as I waved to the audience. The click of our heels on stone was drowned by cheers floating on the wind. I was glad to have chosen a warmer gown for tonight, one of cherry colored cotton and lined with white fur that crept over my open neck. I'd done my own hair tonight due to the rest of the family being busy with caring for Mateo and had opted for a simple knot on the top of my head with a delicate crown pinned to the front.

The crown may have been bold, but I was a princess, so it was my right to wear such a thing.

Twelve guards led us in the front and twelve trailed behind, worming us through the crowd until we were a part of them. Many shouted Blaire's name. They must not have heard yet. Likely they were equally ignorant about the attack we were under today and how many of the girls had layered on rogue to hide the puffiness in their faces from crying.

I searched the front for Nicolas, but the king stood alone. His absence carved a sadness in me. During each of the previous tests, it'd been his presence that comforted me enough to keep going, knowing he was there to watch and was cheering me on above all others. But for this final test, I'd be facing it alone.

Somewhere along the way, he'd become a part of me that I felt incomplete without.

I don't want to live without him, I realized. *I want a life with Nicolas.*

At last, I'd found the certainty I searched for, and it wasn't when Nicolas was present. It was how I felt when he was gone. What had Isabel said? She knew she wanted to marry Mateo when she wanted to be with him all the time.

I was finally ready to make a life here. Now I needed to fight one last time to earn it.

As we took our place at the front, I realized Nicolas wasn't the only one absent. The delegates didn't sit in their usual looming stands near the king. Only King Silas stood on the dais, the crown wearing visibly heavier on his head today as he folded his hands over his lap to watch us enter the courtyard.

He'd been through much today, and yet he stood tall as he leaned on his hands over the railing and smiled at the crowds.

As the king spoke, he spoke to us all.

"Today has brought challenges unseen. These girls have already faced an unplanned test to see if they are brave enough to stay in the face of danger. Two have decided to leave. We do not question them but send them home with love in our hearts."

Two have left? I wasn't the only one with raised brows looking through the mass of people to see who was missing. Celeste stood by Nadine, both keeping their heads forward as if they'd known this already. Those were the two I hoped had gone, and yet the two least likely to do so.

Cathleen was not here, and neither was Bella. Two I wasn't worried about anyway. Now Blaire's absence would look like she'd left on her own, and none would question.

"The remaining ten will participate in the final test. After that, the advisors and I will come to a decision on who is most deserving of being the next queen of Thames. We welcome your opinions. Please leave your votes in the boxes to the side."

His arm swept across his body, bringing every eye with it to the shadowed wall of the castle where three long, wooden tables were laid with garland beside slips of paper and ten boxes each bearing a different name. A mass of guards flanked each side to oversee the voting, many of them Nadine's personal guards. If possible, the number of soldiers attending her had increased over the past few days. They stood at the side ready to help, but their livery stood them apart.

They glanced at the boxes as we all did, though I doubted those small crates sent a buzz of terror though their bones as it did ours.

Girls' arms brushed mine as each squirmed with nerves. The boxes stared at us, reminding us of how important this final competition was.

A queen would be named after today.

I ought to feel secure knowing I was the intended winner of the competition but sweat pricked my brow. Nothing about these competitions had gone according to plan, and I would be a fool to expect simplicity now.

King Silas waited with slow eyes scanning the crowd until we'd settled enough for him to move on.

"We do not wish to test your patience, my dear people. We will decide tonight and Nicolas himself will announce the future queen tomorrow to the court. We will make a public announcement tomorrow night."

The air hummed with the eager whispers of the townspeople. It lit up the air like a fire, making it difficult to concentrate.

This test held so much importance, and for the first time, I was going in completely blind. I had no clue what to expect from tonight.

"The test is simple," King Silas said.

That brought no consolation. The first test was meant to be simple, and I'd failed that one. The second test was more complex, and I excelled.

He continued, "A queen must know how to be among her people. Ladies, your job today is merely to interact with the townsfolk, converse among them, hear out their concerns, form friendships. If you can do that, you are on the way to becoming a great queen."

No delicate embroidery. No exhausting sword fights. Only talking with people.

And yet, this one terrified me more than the others. Forming friendships was not my strong suit.

Some of the girls had already lightened, smiles brightening their faces and bouncing on their heels eagerly. Undoubtedly every girl here felt better about this task than I did. Even had I been warned, there was little chance Dana or the girls could have prepared me for this. I was hopeless.

King Silas's hand raised over the crowd. "The test begins now and ends at sundown."

For Nicolas, I thought, and I turned to the people around me.

The woman nearest reached for my arm, her slender hand protruding from within an oversized, pearl-colored sweater draped loosely atop a stained, linen dress. Tight curls framed her round face, bouncing as she moved.

"You must be Rowan." She fawned over my name, then her eyes grew wide. "I'm so sorry, I mean lady Ro—no, Princess Rowan." Pink spread over her cheeks. "So sorry."

"That's alright," I said. Then added, "You may call me Rowan." I felt a tinge of victory that I'd thought to add that last bit. Surely a queen would let her people know her and call her by her informal name. I glanced to the king to see if he'd noticed, but even if he were looking in my direction, which he was not, he couldn't have heard that.

Her shoulders relaxed. "Very good. Ah, you're just as beautiful up close are you are from afar. It's no wonder Nicolas traveled so far to wake you. Tell me, how do you get your hair so shiny?"

My mouth opened but nothing came out. Dana used a cream on my hair, one that was not easy to come by. One that a villager likely couldn't afford. There was no better way to drive a divide between people than bringing up money.

"Um," I began a shaky sentence. Before I finished, another grabbed at my arm, sending relief coursing through me.

This was a plump woman with big teeth and a bigger smile. "It's so good to meet you. Would you come to my home for dinner sometime? It's right past the candle shop, you can't miss it."

Never before had relief turned to dread so quickly. Was I allowed to say yes to that? I wasn't even allowed to leave the castle right now but turning her down would appear beyond rude.

Another hand pulled at me, this time a tiny hand clutching my skirts. A girl with red hair like mine gazed up at me. "What was it like to sleep for a hundred years? They say you turned to pure ice."

"It that true?" The plump lady asked. "How did you survive a hundred years?"

From every direction, eyes swarmed me as people leaned close to hear my reply. The other girls must have been pulled away by their own crowds, for as far as I could see was only townspeople pushing to get close. From the group, a mother hushed her child saying, "This is the girl who was cursed. There's magic in her."

Of course. They were more curious in my past than what I'd offer them in my future.

"It was quiet in the palace where I slept," I started. "And alone. Until Nicolas came, I hadn't been around anyone for a hundred years. I don't remember much from that time."

At the sound of their prince, they sighed. "Are you in love?"

A new idea came to me. If I could sell my and Nicolas's love story, I could get votes from that.

"Yes," I replied. "Very much so. He's all I have in this lifetime."

A chorus of awes drifted around me, but a curly-haired gentleman with hard-set brows raised his hand. "Besides the kingdom of Thames, you mean? If you're queen, can you love our kingdom as if it were your own?"

That shattered fast.

"Of course I will," I said. "I'll do everything I can for this kingdom."

From the left, Celeste pushed through the thick crowd with little apology. As folks complained, she didn't glance at them for more than a moment. My brows knit together. She wouldn't win anyone's approval with that attitude, and it was so different from her usual charismatic personality.

She reached my side and wrapped a tight hand around my wrist.

"I need her," she said.

The few around me complained while others turned to seek out the next girl. I yanked my wrist from Celeste's tight grip.

"What are you doing?" I hissed.

"Saving you," she hissed back. "These aren't the people you need to talk to. The delegates are hidden in the crowd. Find them and speak with them. That's the only way you'll win. It's part of the test."

I stopped walking and peered through the crowds. All the faces appeared foreign to me. No one was even remotely recognizable from prior meetings. I definitely didn't see the solemn looks of the advisors who normally watched the tests with blank expressions.

"I don't see them."

Celeste sighed. "That's why it's a test. One last clever trick to see if you're fit to be queen. They want to test if we are smart enough to remember the delegates' faces and seek them out in the crowd, since they are the ones whose approval we need to win. The townsfolk's votes mean nothing. Nicolas told me about it this afternoon, did he not tell you?"

From my frown, she got her answer.

"He probably just learned of it this afternoon," she said, then pointed to a group of huddled people in brown garb watching the other's swarm. They didn't melt into the crowd, but kept at a distance, and while they'd done their best to dress down, the tips of their shoes from beneath long robes showed wealth.

Celeste was right, they were here.

"Go," Celeste ordered.

I planted my feet. "Why are you helping me?"

She sighed again. "Because I care for more than just Nicolas. I care for Thames. If I'm not queen, I believe you are the next best person to lead this country. I need to be certain one of us wins today."

I'd been lied to before, but Celeste's intense gaze held no games behind it. If this was manipulation, she was quite adept at it, but somehow, I believed her words.

This time when she nudged me, I headed straight for the delegates.

Chapter Twenty-Eight

FROM THE CORNER OF my eye, I watched who Celeste veered toward, so I'd know who the next delegates were. She'd seen them one less time than I, and yet she remembered them much better. Perhaps the way the curled mustache twitched on one of the delegate's face was familiar, or how another always kept her head at an angle, even to watch me approach. The sharp smile of the third paired with piercing gray eyes was not something I recalled.

The three delegates shifted amongst themselves as I approached.

"Good evening," I began politely. "How are you doing today?"

"Fine," Gray Eyes said. Then silence.

I looked at the other two. They said nothing.

"Is there anything you'd hope the next queen accomplishes for you?" I pressed.

Tilted Head leaned to Curly Mustache. "Straight to business," she whispered, with an expression as close to indifferent as it was to impressed.

"What would your rule look like?" Curly Mustache asked, avoiding my question.

I clasped my hands in front of me. "Well, Thames has great relationships with neighboring countries. I'd do everything I could to preserve those. Keep the country from bitter war. I'd continue the late queen's blanket charity program, as well as any other programs she partook in, and do everything I could to keep the people happy."

They glanced to each other. Those were all bland answers, nothing of substance to show specifically what I'd do as queen or what values I held dear that would benefit Thames. A child could have given the same reply.

Only a few minutes in and I was already failing this test. I needed something more.

"I'd set up People's Day," I said, remembering traditions from Elenvérs that I adored. The delegates raised a brow, and I rushed to continue. "It's a day where the king and queen dress down, open the castle doors to invite anyone in, and they sit with the people to get to know them and hear their complaints. Look at how excited everyone is about this one opportunity to speak with the potential future queen. They could have that every month. It builds unity for the kingdom and loyalty among the people."

There were other traditions from Elenvérs that stood out to me: the unique way we had of granting knighthood, the Full Moon Feasts, the dancing under the stars, but the delegates nodded with small smiles, and none of the other traditions were as beneficial.

"Unity among the people would be good," Tilted Head said. "Especially in a time such as this. Good answer."

Curly Mustache brought a hand to his chin. "How about a more personal question. You know Thames has an uncertain situation with the heirs, being as most of the rightful ones have died. To prevent this from happening again, Nicolas needs to have many children. Are you prepared to take on that task?"

They stared at me unabashedly while my stomach dropped.

They were right, the next queen should produce many heirs to keep the line secure and prevent future fighting over who ought to be king. And for any others, that job would be simple. It would be an honor to bear Nicolas's children, and they'd look so cute with his caramel eyes and curly hair. The image of them running through the halls with sticky fingers and wild giggles melted my heart.

But it also shattered it.

Because I'd forgotten something extremely important. Something that never bothered me before, and had gotten pushed to the back of my mind as I struggled to uncover if Nicolas was the one I wanted to spend my life with.

Now I knew that he was. But remembered a reason why he might want a different bride.

Once more, my past haunted me, and this time, it was a memory from my birth. From the day the fairies gathered around to bestow their gifts upon a crying infant and prepare her for her future.

The final gift had been forgotten.

Your daughter will never have children, so this curse cannot continue. She will never know your pain.

The fairy had spoken these words to my mother, and she'd thanked her in return. I'd been spared a great heartbreak by never knowing what it'd be like to lose my daughter to the same curse that separated me from my parents.

But I'd never know the joy of having a child, and neither would Nicolas. I couldn't give him a baby.

The advisors waited for the answer that should have come easily, while the words clawed like heavy stones through my throat. "It would be very wise of the future queen to have many children, I agree. Any woman would be lucky to give that to Nicolas. I'd love nothing more than to do that."

An answer honest enough but hid the grief that built into hot tears over my eyes. I ducked my head. "I should move on to others, thank you for your time."

They didn't ask further questions and I pushed myself back into the crowd, hoping no one stopped me until I'd recovered enough to open my mouth without sobbing.

A strong-jawed woman came in my path, one with eyes so piercing blue that they'd be impossible to forget, but I didn't abandon her to find more delegates. Her questions about sleeping for a hundred years were a welcome distraction to keep me from more questions about future children I'd never have.

The evening sky brought its stars out early, and the final test came to an end before I spoke to another delegate. I could only hope the three I'd spoken to were enough to solidify my place in their minds.

The townspeople scrambled to cast their final votes, and it was impossible not to watch my box as they swarmed around it. Their bodies created a wall too thick to see through, but as the crowd filtered out, I saw a few slip votes into mine.

Maybe tonight hadn't gone as terribly as I thought.

"Thank you all for attending," King Silas said. The circles under his eyes grew darker as the night settled around us. "You are invited back tomorrow night to hear the results. Guards?"

He motioned to the side, where twenty guards came to escort us back into the palace. The guards watched the crowds with jittery eyes, no doubt frazzled by the earlier attack. We'd never been so protected as they brought us inside the stone walls and locked the door behind them.

As the girls filtered to their rooms for the night, Celeste peeked over her shoulder to me. She gave a small thumbs-up with a question on her face, and I only nodded. She smiled, then trotted off. Maybe to bed, maybe to find Nicolas and report how well she'd done. I'd seen many put names in her box.

I dragged my tired body to my bedchamber to eat dinner before seeking out Nicolas. My stomach needed filling first and my thoughts needed to be sorted through before I saw him again.

An important decision would be made tomorrow, and he deserved to know that if he married me, he'd never have a child of his own.

Chapter Twenty-Nine

LUCILLE WAS THE ONLY one in the room. The bed was made and the windows were drawn shut while she knitted by the fire. She threw her needles aside as I slumped into the room.

"How did it go?" she asked.

I groaned, searching the cart for dinner. I ignored the steamed vegetables and stacked crispy potatoes and thick meat with a brown gravy atop my plate, then sat on the edge of the bed.

"Where's Mateo?" I asked, ignoring the pit in my stomach that only grew as food hit it.

Lucille squinted but replied, "He's better, so he's resting in his own room with Isabel while Mama takes care of Rosalie. Do you want to talk about it?"

The mention of Rosalie sent a fresh river of pain covering me.

How could I have been so foolish as to forget I couldn't have children?

I turned my face away. "No. I'll eat quickly then I need to find Nicolas." I filled my mouth with more food so she couldn't ask further questions.

Two bites in and there was a knock at the door.

"Don't answer it," I whispered. "I don't care to see anyone right now." Lucille froze with a hand stretched to the knob, which she slowly retracted.

"Rowan? Are you in there?" Nicolas called out. His voice sent shivers of anxiety spiraling through my veins and settling so deep into my skin that I feared I'd never shake it free.

This was worse than facing an army. This was worse than facing a curse. This was misery at its finest.

Just as I'd allowed myself to fall for a man, I had to give him a reason to walk away. If he did so, I'd be alone to nurse my broken heart and find a place in this world that never should have been mine.

Blast. A hundred years later and the curse was still taking something from me.

Lucille didn't move, but she arched a brow and gestured to the door.

Slowly, I nodded. "Let him in."

The door creaked open and Nicolas stepped into the room. His jacket was unbuttoned, his hair pressed to the side and creases marred his face as if he'd fallen asleep on wrinkled sheets. He scanned the room until he found me as a tired smile came to his face.

I set my plate aside.

Lucille didn't need prompting. "I'll be out if you need me." She hurried from the room and closed the door behind her.

Nicolas took a deep sigh and moved to my side where I leaned against the bed, bracing my hands behind me. He crossed his arms and settled close while the hairs on his forearm brushed mine.

His breathing was slow and he didn't say anything. For several moments he just, *was.* Still. Quiet. As if being by me was his comfort. Like I could relieve the stress of his day merely by standing near him. His shoulders sagged with obvious burden and his eyelids closed, but he didn't unload any of the stress on me.

It further cracked me. He was that person for me as well, my comfort after a long day. I'd do anything to take the pain away that I was about to give.

"How's your father?" I asked, contemplating if it was acceptable to give him further bad news if his father had just died. For a moment of horrid virtue, I wished his father had passed so I had an excuse to spare him from further pain.

Horrible, horrible person.

"He's the same. The doctors say that's a good sign that he hasn't passed yet. Gives them hope," Nicolas said. He ran his hands through his hair. When they settled back on the bed, one covered mine. "It's hard. I've never been close with my father. Clearly, I'm not close with my mother either. But he's a good man, and I love him. Family is important, and I'm scared of losing that."

I stared at my feet as he spoke.

"But we got news that the pursuit of the threat has gone well; the men just returned with the belief that the trouble will subside now. All there is to do is get the delegates to agree that you deserve to be future queen, and the unrest hanging over my rule will be over. We can have peace, finally."

"It sounds so simple," I said, knowing politics often turned out much more complicated. Some of the delegates wouldn't agree on the winner. Some people could still revolt. The promise of a peaceful rule was never one to be held by kings, only the promise of unseen tribulations.

"Are you okay?" Nicolas asked.

That question broke my resolve. The crack within me opened and a wave of sadness washed over me, spilling out through tears that pricked behind my eyes.

"We need to talk," I began. He shifted on the bed to hold both my hands, and I forced myself to look at his face.

I didn't want to lose this.

While my heart cried out for me to stop and preserve this relationship, my lips moved. "You need to know this isn't something that I meant to keep from you."

His eyes narrowed but hands kept hold of mine. I savored their touch.

The air burned my dry throat as I took a deep breath. "When I," my voice cracked, "was born, fairies gave me gifts like gracefulness and laughter."

His forehead crinkled further. "Alright."

Large tears rolled from my lashes. My mother had been so grateful for the final gift, thinking she was saving me from a pain. She might have been, but she'd never know the pain she replaced it with or the future the fairy stole from me. I'd gladly take eighteen years with a child than nothing at all.

I clutched one hand over my stomach, forever barren.

"The final fairy took away my ability to ever bear a child." He gasped, and his frame went still as stone. The sobs couldn't be contained now as I freely cried. "I'm sorry Nicolas, I can't give you an heir."

He took long breaths while stroking my hand while his mouth dipped open and his eyes darted through the space between us. For a while he said nothing, and the only sound was my soft cries and his calculated breath.

Then he looked up. "Why? Why would she do that to you?"

His image was faded through my glossy eyes. "To spare me the pain of losing my daughter. The same curse that took me would have passed to any daughters we had."

"But not our sons?"

I wiped my cheek on my shoulder. "There's no way to know if we would have a daughter or a son. My parents were assured I was going to be a boy, otherwise they never would have had me."

He let go of my hands to rub his together in the motion he did only when in deep thought. "But you are fine. You woke up. You get a full life. And they got to know you. I would have taken that over no child."

Fresh tears caressed my chin. "I woke up, but not before everyone from my time died. It's a pain I can understand wanting to spare me and my daughter from. But right now I agree that it hurts."

He stood up and crossed his arms. "We can never have a child."

My voice cracked. "I'm so sorry."

He blew the air from his cheeks. "Then we are a couple who never has children."

My heart warmed, but the tears didn't dry.

"If you weren't the future king," I said. "It would be easy. But you have duties to your kingdom, such as providing heirs.

As queen, I couldn't give the kingdom that stability. In twenty years, the unrest would return as once more the people looked to their own favorite sons and attempted to put them on the throne. Our reign would forever be shadowed by the lack of children."

His eyes widened with each word, until his head dropped into his hands. My fingers clutched the sides of my skirt to keep from fidgeting as fears ran wild within me.

His feet dragged against the floor as he stumbled about the room in thought. He paused. "Adoption?"

I sniffled. "Would fill a hole in our hearts, but the legitimacy of the child would always be in question. They would still have to fight for the throne. Nothing but a true heir could provide Thames the stability it desperately needs."

I'd secretly desired him to hold me close and tell me it was okay; that he'd risk the security of the throne for me. But he paced the floor with such intensity while rubbing his hands together, back and forth, back and forth, until he could have worn through the soles of his tan shoes. The silence killed me.

"Please say something," I begged.

He stopped walking long enough to give me a helpless look. "What am I to say? How can I guarantee the stability of the kingdom when it is already in shambles? How can I deny my heart something it yearns for? I want a child, Rowan. I long for a baby of my own."

I thought the weight of never having a child had crushed me, but I'd been wrong. Those words—they broke me. Fully and mercilessly shattered me until I was nothing but breath clinging to broken bones.

As soon as he said them, he crossed his arms. "But I also want you, dearly. I love you."

My head snapped up at those words. I'd never been told that before by a man. I'd never been truly loved.

Yet the sentiment wasn't spoken with tenderness but regret. It was his love for me that bridled him against making the easy choice to pick another girl, leaving him uncertain of what to do.

"I'm sorry I didn't tell you sooner," I whispered.

He shook his head. "You're telling me now, before it's too late."

Before he officially chose me before the court tomorrow, he meant. I closed my eyes.

"I'm sorry Rowan, I need a moment." Nicolas turned on his heel and headed for the door. He hesitated in the doorway, until his hand clutched the knob, swung the door open, and closed it tightly between us.

It felt as though he'd closed the door on us as well.

I tipped into the pillows and let the tears drown my face, hoping they'd drown the sorrows with it. But the misery only grew until it engulfed me, and sleep could be my only escape from the agony of the day.

It wasn't fair of me to ask Nicolas to stay knowing he wanted a child. And yet, I found myself dreaming that he'd stay anyway out of complete love for me.

Because I loved him desperately. As much as I wanted to fix this for him, I was helpless to do anything but wait for him to decide if a life with me was enough for him.

Chapter Thirty

NICOLAS DIDN'T RETURN THAT night, nor did he appear with the first sign of the morning. As I slid from bed to carry my uneaten dinner plate to the cart by the door, the handle clicked, and my eyes watched intently for who would come in.

Lucille peeked in, and my chest dropped.

"Still not in better spirits?" she asked, placing one hand on the cart and the other on her waist. "What happened at the competition last night?"

"I'd rather not speak of it," I told her. "It's quite personal."

I turned away from her hurt expression and waited for the quiet roll of the cart and lock of the door to turn back.

The silence of the room surrounded me. I could wait all day for that door to open again, and Nicolas may never be the one to walk through it no matter how hard I wished him to. One night wasn't enough to decide who to spend his life with— the girl from the ice who couldn't have kids or the girl that the kingdom loved, but today the kingdom would be expecting their answer.

He'd spent months telling me he cared for me. Today I'd find how deep that love ran.

The anticipation curled around my skin until I thought I might suffocate from it. I stripped from my old clothes to find new ones, a dress of rose with cream tones coming out in the sash and bodice, then pushed through the door.

I needed to know what he'd decided. I couldn't wait for this afternoon.

My shoes clicked in the empty hallway as I headed for his room. I paused as I always did at the corridor opening to stare through to his window. The yellow scarf billowed in the wind once more.

Giermo and his love had patched things up. Perhaps it was a sign that Nicolas and I could as well.

From around the corner, Nicolas strode into view, his feet moving fast over the stone and his head facing the floor. He looked up with I called his name.

His feet faltered. "I didn't think you'd be up yet."

My brow crinkled. Was he not coming to see me?

I took a timid step forward. "How are you doing?"

He sighed, taking a few steps of his own near me. He didn't come all the way though, pausing just out of reach. "It's been a long morning. I met with Silas and the delegates to discuss the results of the competition, and there are two girls they have agreed to support should they be chosen. They've left it up to me."

"Celeste," I figured. Even to me, she was a clear answer. She wasn't frail in the face of danger, she held her own against Ava's sword, and I'd never seen her as anything other than kind to the people around her.

Plus, she had a legitimate claim to the throne. I didn't.

Nicolas nodded. "She was their first choice."

That stung. I feared to ask if I was the other, but Nicolas went on. "They agreed to you as well."

Not wanted but agreed.

He moved closer, but he didn't come to me. Instead, he moved past. I angled back with a frown. "What do *you* want?" I asked. His eye didn't stay on me but shifted to his feet. I braced myself for the answer.

He took another step away.

"I'm sorry, Rowan. There's a lot to be figured out first. I can't give you answers when I don't have them myself." I planted a hand on the windowsill to still myself as he retreated.

"I have to go, but if everything gets sorted, I'll give you answers soon. I'm sorry," he repeated the apology a few times as he crossed the hallway and hurried down the other end.

I stood like an idiot watching him leave, unsure what to do now. I might've preferred no answer to that one. Clearly, he still wasn't certain about me.

Dana came from behind, whistling a tune that halted when she saw me. Her brow curled up. "Are you just standing here?" she asked, shifting a basket of laundry on her hip. Her gaze danced down the empty corridor.

"I'm—" I stared at the space where Nicolas had gone. "I don't know."

"Well come inside and let me fix up that hair of yours. If you're to be announced our future queen today, I want you looking your finest." She bustled past me, nudging the door open wide enough to fit the large basket through and gesturing for me to follow. With one last look over my shoulder, I followed her inside.

"Now." She set the basket down and stretched her back. "I've a special hairstyle planned for you today. Isabel was kind enough to let me practice on her last night."

I dipped into the cushioned seat before the vanity to allow her fingers to comb through my hair. She fluffed the curls a few times, taming some wild ones and twisting others so they'd match in spiral, before starting with a few sections near my ear.

"How is Mateo doing?" I asked to get my mind off Nicolas and how he'd rushed away from me.

A little smile came to her face. "His stubbornness has returned, so he's doing fine. He insisted upon returning to work, so they placed him on simple duty—guarding the dungeons, where he won't have to do much but sit at an old table all day."

"I'm glad he's better."

"Me too." She was silent as she braided a small section of hair and wrapped it as a band over the top of my head, tucking it behind my other ear and spreading out the sections to give it a full look. The rest of my curls she allowed to stay down.

When she'd finished, she stood back and sighed. "Masterpiece."

"Thank you," I spun to stand from the seat, and her gaze trailed me.

"Are you excited for today? The other girls will finally be going home."

I pressed my lips together. What would happen to me if I wasn't chosen? I had no home to retreat to. If Nicolas chose Celeste as his queen, would I remain here in her shadows or would I venture on to Elenvérs to find a quiet place to live out my days? The other girls had a place and people waiting for them elsewhere, while I had nothing but a kingdom full of strangers.

A tear rolled down my cheek. Today could cost me everything.

Dana folded her arms around me.

"Could I," I spoke through the tears, "stay with you if I don't get chosen today? Just for a little while until I find other lodging."

Her head pulled back and she stroked my cheek. "You can stay with me forever, if you desire." She tightened her grip again and didn't let go until my tears ran dry and my shaking chest remembered how to breathe normally.

"Thank you," I whispered.

She smiled. "Certainly. Though I don't think you have anything to fear. It's clear Nicolas loves you by the way he looks at you. He'd give up a kingdom for you."

Maybe. But could he give up a child?

I wiped my tears dry. "We will see."

I painted rouge upon my lips and took a sip of water. There was only enough time to eat a small lunch before the gathering with the council to announce the next queen, though my uneasy stomach might reject anything it was given right now.

"The leaves have started to change color," Dana said, gazing out the window. She fluffed a dress out before folding the sleeves in. "A new season is coming."

Today was the epitome of that sentence. A new season was coming, and I feared for what it would bring. A season of preparing to be queen, or a season of heartbreak. Either way, tomorrow would look very different than yesterday.

A tender knock came to the door, then the handle turned.

Ava glided in with high heels on her feet, a black dress with diamonds white as ice across the hem, and an apple the color of blood between her fingers. She stopped at the sight of me, and after a moment, she smiled.

"Beautiful. Fit to be queen."

I didn't say anything. My body didn't possess the energy to fight with her today. She came closer, drumming her fingers over the skin of the apple before stretching it out to me.

"This is for you."

I took it, still silent. The weight of it settled into my palm, and she smiled again.

"In our country, it's a sign of peace to offer an apple. I want this to be the start of a friendship between you and I," Ava said.

Of all the things today would bring, I didn't think this would be one of them.

"My son is important to me, and you are important to him. This apple is my promise that I will be on your side from now on."

She said it with certainty, unaware that things between Nicolas and I were anything but certain. It was he who I desired to reconnect with, not his mother. I wanted little to do with her. Without her previous antics to drive a wedge between Nicolas and I, we might have been strong enough to deal with my barrenness together.

Dana busied herself with the laundry, but she kept a close watch on Ava. My eyes narrowed at the fruit. "This is your apology for the past few weeks? This apple?"

She laughed. "I know it doesn't look like much, but it comes from a genuine place in my heart. In fact, the last queen once gave me an apple with similar meaning." She folded her hands and sighed. "Jezebel and I did not get along when we first met. But she knew the importance of friendships, so she brought an apple to me one day and offered a truce. With that truce, came a friendship neither of us were expecting."

Ava strolled to the couch and sat down, then patted the space beside her. I brought the apple with me to sit by her side. "You see, everything I've done since you arrived has been out of love for Jezebel. She had a masterful hand when it came to being queen and a specific way she wanted things to carry on after she died. One of those wishes, and one she held very dear to heart, was that Celeste take her place. She loved that girl and believed her to be the best possible queen for Thames. It boded well for us that Nicolas loved her too, until they split."

Her eyes rolled over me. "And then you showed up."

She paused and put a soft hand over mine. "But the late queen never met you. I've been fighting so hard for her wishes, when they might have been different had she the chance to know what a strong woman you are. So, with my son's interests at heart, I'm offering you a truce."

I studied the apple. It was hard to hold bitterness against her when she fought so hard to carry out the wishes of her dead friend, but the strain she'd put upon her own son while doing it wasn't easily forgivable.

The timing of it was peculiar. In a very short time we'd both be in the court hall with the rest of the castle to find who won the Queen's Competition, and if Celeste won then there would be no need for her and I to make amends. Her coming with a truce gave me hope that she knew her son's decision, and that it was me.

A smile crept to my face, and Ava mistook it for her.

"Thank you," I said. "I will think on this."

Her smile faltered, and she didn't move.

I raised a brow. "Is there more? If not, I believe we have an important meeting to attend."

She brushed her skirt as she stood. "Very well. I will see you there." She gave one last look to the apple before withdrawing from the room.

I stared at the apple. It was such a small thing that came with such a big apology. From the moment I got here, I'd struggled not only to find my place with Nicolas but also to keep sane from Ava's ploys. The strain she'd placed upon Nicolas's and my tender relationship wasn't easily forgiven, especially if the relationship crumbled today.

"It's a strange tradition, and not one I've heard of," Dana called from the closet where she put away clothes.

"I don't think I'll accept it," I said.

Dana poked her head out. When she saw my face, she chuckled. "You have as much fire as Lucille. Will you give it back?"

I tucked the apple between my two hands. "I think I will. She doesn't get to control our friendship." Once decided, the determination set in me like stone. Many factors of today were out of my hands, but I wouldn't be forced into a relationship with Ava that I didn't care for. With Nicolas or without, my life would be much easier if I didn't have to deal with her.

That much, I could control.

I stood and filled my chest with breath, hoping courage came with it. "I ought to go. The court is waiting."

Dana took a moment to stroke my cheek. "Be brave, dear one. Today might be the beginning of your happy ending, but either way, there is always tomorrow."

There is always tomorrow. I nodded and took the first steps to uncover my fate.

Queen of Thames, or unwanted girl from the ice.

Chapter Thirty-One

THE WINDOWS WERE OPEN to let in autumn air that curled around the pillars and draped us in the scent of crisp afternoon.

I hadn't the time to give the apple back to Ava before taking my place, so I hid the red fruit in my palm behind my plethora of skirts as I faced the daunting room and the moment before me.

The king's throne had been moved to the side of the dais until it was almost upon the edge, far enough that the king melted into the crowd pushing at his side. The entire castle showed up for this event, maids in their caps near the back, stable boys jumping to see over heads, and the eager court at the front with all eyes upon us. Even the cook was there with her bright, white hair knotted on her head.

We stood in a row on the dais off to the right. They'd placed Celeste and I at the head of the row, nearest the center, as if the coordinator knew one of us was the winner. Celeste was closest to the throne.

That throne, the queen's throne, sat alone in the middle as it waited for who would take its place. It was made of gold that shimmered in the sunlight, with pearly-white cushions and roses carved into the legs, wrapping around the arm rests and up the back. Very soon, one of us girls would sit upon its seat and the kingdom would acknowledge us as the future queen.

They would soon have their queen of roses.

I held my breath as Nicolas appeared from the crowd to climb next to the throne. He studied it for a long moment, running his hand over the engraved edges, before pivoting to address the crowd.

He hadn't looked to me.

"Kingdom of Thames. I'm humbled to stand before you today to announce the next queen."

They cheered for him, and he kept a hand on the throne as he raised a hand to acknowledge them.

Beside me, Celeste fidgeted. She wore a gown of deep red with a high neckline and necklace of pearls. Her hair was pinned up, so I could see as her jaw clenched. Her chest didn't rise with breath. She must be holding it just as I was.

Did she know it was between me and her? Did she know Nicolas got to choose the winner? Perhaps that's where he'd been off to in such a hurry this morning, to find her and tell her the good news.

I bit my lip. There was no need to torment myself with further questions when the answer was about to come. All I could do was stand strong and brace myself for what would happen.

When the crowd quieted, Nicolas went on.

"The queen we have chosen is one who will serve you well, and I think you'll all agree with me that she was born to rule. She is kind-hearted, intelligent, thoughtful, and brave. This woman will be a jewel for the kingdom."

My entire being froze as he stretched a hand toward us. The moment was here. From beside me, Celeste's hand found mine and she squeezed. I squeezed back.

"Kingdom of Thames, please welcome me in celebrating your new queen, Lady Celeste De'Amos."

The room exploded into celebration while my world went dark. Celeste's hand slid from mine as it covered her mouth and a sweet laugh escaped her lips. With a dagger in my heart, I watched as she picked up her skirts in a dainty hand and walked to Nicolas's side.

He smiled to her, and she nodded back. Something had passed between them.

Then she turned to the room, bowed her head, and lowered herself into the throne.

Behold, the future queen of Thames.

Each moment was torture for me, each cheer was grating to my ears. I didn't cry, didn't process the information correctly. All my mind seemed capable of doing was repeating that moment where Nicolas said her name instead of mine, then repeating it again until I understood what it meant.

In the end, he'd chosen her after all.

Perhaps there was something I could have done differently. I could have fallen for him faster. I could have given him my whole heart. I could have tried better to get along with his mother. I could have told him as soon as I knew I loved him.

But now he'd never know how much he meant to me, or how much my heart shattered at losing him.

I'd lost the one who braved the frozen mountains to wake me from my sleep. I'd lost the one who taught me to skin squirrels in the woods and make fire. I'd lost the one who'd made me feel like home, even when home was far away.

I'd lost the one who had kissed me as if nothing else mattered in the world, because I gave him a reason to walk away.

The floor couldn't be felt beneath my feet, but somehow, I moved with the other girls from the stage to allow Celeste her attention. We tunneled through the crowd—no one caring about us anymore—and to the side door. My steps were slower than the other girls', who'd already disappeared by the time I reached the slender door to take me out of the room.

My hand paused on the handle, and I risked one look back upon Celeste and Nicolas.

The dense crowds prohibited me from seeing him, but I saw her clearly. She sat on the throne in a comfortable position with her hands on each side and a wide smile on her face. Her gaze wafted over the court to soak up all the praise that would be hers for her lifetime.

I closed my eyes and pushed through the door.

It didn't shut immediately behind me, and a hand caught my elbow. When I turned, Nicolas slid through the doorway with me, closing it on the sound behind him and leaving us in the narrow corridor alone.

My breaths came quickly, and I shook my head. "Why?"

"I'm sorry Rowan," he said. "I'm so sorry."

Chapter Thirty-Two

NOTHING HE COULD SAY would heal the crack in my heart, but I didn't want to turn away. I'd give him every last moment I had just to be near him again.

"I understand that it's too much to ask you to choose me instead of the chance at having a child," I told him, forcing words through my tight throat.

The other girls must have fled to their rooms already to pack their things and retreat from the castle. I'd soon be joining them. For now I savored my final moment with Nicolas, wishing I'd given him my heart when he'd asked for it.

This was where he'd explain that he wanted to have kids someday, and the thought of losing that was too much for him to bear. He'd tell me how sorry he was, and how he wished me the best.

But instead, Nicolas closed the distance between us and gripped my hands in his. He frowned at the apple, still in my grasp, and moved both his hands to one of mine.

"No," he said. "It's not too much to ask."

I looked up in confusion, and he grinned.

"Rowan, I choose you. I'm giving up my right to rule and giving it to Celeste. You and I will have our own life, away from the pressure of ruling."

Once more the world dropped from beneath me and I struggled to make sense of his words. A moment ago I thought I was going away. Now I didn't understand what was happening. Was he allowed to give up his right like that? What would that mean for the kingdom?

Nicolas laughed at my confusion, tugging me closer.

"That's why I left so quickly this morning. I was sorting through the details. We are leaving the kingdom in good hands, and if you want, can retire to my childhood home on the seaside cliffs to live a peaceful life."

I tightened my grip on his hands to keep myself upright. "I didn't lose you?"

He smiled and brushed the rough edges of his fingertips in a line down my cheek, circling under my jaw where he caressed my chin. "You'll never lose me. I choose you."

My cheeks drowned once more in tears, but these ones were not induced from sorrow, but rather from joy. Everything I thought I'd lost a moment ago came back to me, and I promised to cling tight to it.

I started by throwing my hands around Nicolas's neck and kissing him fiercely. His lips melted beneath mine, and the sweet taste of him drifted over me. He was mine, forever.

"I can't believe you did that to me," I said, half laughing and half crying into him.

He pulled back. "Believe me, I wouldn't have done so if I had another choice. I had to be sure we could do this before announcing it, and by then there wasn't time to tell you."

"What did King Silas say when you told him?" I asked through a sniffle.

He ducked his head. "Actually, I didn't yet. He'll find out soon enough though. I only had time to read through boring rulebooks written in fancy cursive to verify that I could abdicate my right at any time. King Silas can't oppose. But the delegates are all very fond of Celeste, so transitioning the title of heir shouldn't cause problems. And I'm happy to stay here until it gets sorted, as long as you'll stay with me."

His words stirred unspeakable joy within me.

He'd never enjoyed the thought of ruling, and while I'd decided to take on as much of the responsibility as possible to make it easier for him, he'd found a way to save himself entirely.

We wouldn't be trapped here, worrying about plots against Nicolas's life or pressures of not being able to have a child. We could live a quiet life in the seaside manor away from the court and the king and his parents where the only thing that mattered was each other.

We were free, and we were together.

"What is this?" Nicolas asked, bringing my arm up to inspect the apple. I let it drop in his hands. "It's a gift from your mother. She called it a truce."

He snorted. "She's never given anyone a truce in her life."

"Apparently the late queen and her had one to settle their differences," I said.

His brow furrowed as he cleaned a side of the apple on his sleeve. "Not from what I saw." He held the apple before his lips. "Her and the queen were thick as thieves from day one."

I frowned at her strange lie, while the apple gleamed as Nicolas crunched his teeth into it.

Pieces started coming to me. The way Ava hesitated before leaving after she'd given me the apple. The way her eye stayed on me during the court gathering. The way she'd always hated me.

"Nicolas, give me that apple."

I was too late.

Nicolas staggered forward, dropping the fruit on the ground. It rolled to the side as he fell into me.

"Nicolas?" I cried out. The weight of him pulled me down, and I struggled to lay him on the floor. "Nicolas?"

His eyes rolled up, then they shut.

My heart stopped. Poison. She'd poisoned the apple.

"No," I yelled, grabbing his collar. "Please no." I ripped his shirt and pressed my hands to his chest. Breath still came, but no matter how hard I shook him, he didn't wake.

"Help me, someone help me!" I kicked at the door, pushing it open. "Someone help! The prince has been poisoned."

The crowd parted in confusion, many tipping their heads to get a look at me and Nicolas sprawled across the ground. It wasn't until guards came running that the people backed off.

"It was the apple," I said, pointing to the fruit as a few guards approached me. My throat tightened and I struggled to form words. "He took a bite. He fell. I don't know what kind of poison it is."

Ava pushed through the crowds to kneel at her son's side. "First my husband, now my son. Must everything be taken from me?" Tears already ran down her cheeks. "What happened to him?"

I tightened my grip on his hand. "The apple you meant for me was eaten by him."

Her eyes widened, and a hand flew to her chest. After a long pause she pushed out the words, "I have no idea what apple you speak of."

I growled. "The one you gave me this morning." The crowds pushed in toward us to get a better look, and from amidst them, King Silas and Celeste appeared. Celeste's face whitened when she saw Nicolas on the ground.

Ava placed a hand on a guard's arm. "I've never seen that apple in my life." Then her expression hardened. She folded an arm protectively over her son.

"It's clear that in Rowan's jealousy over not being chosen, she poisoned Nicolas so no one could have him."

"He did choose me," I told her. "He was leaving with me. He loves me."

A few snickered, and I shot them feral looks. "He told me just now. He was giving the throne to Celeste but he never intended to rule with her."

Celeste didn't move, but her lips drew in a thin line.

"Rowan," King Silas spoke. He came to Nicolas's side to touch his forehead while the guards kept others back. In a low voice he asked, "Did you poison the prince?"

The accusation hurt most coming from him. A tear rolled down my cheek as I shook my head. "No. I promise, he planned to abdicate and leave with me."

He sighed. "Did he tell anyone else of this plan?"

Below my hand, Nicolas continued to take deep breaths, but his body didn't stir. I closed my eyes. If only he'd told another about his plan. "I don't know," I confessed. "But I didn't poison him, Ava mistakenly did."

Her tears were borderline hysterics, and they only worsened as I blamed her again. "I would never hurt my child."

King Silas placed a hand on Ava's shoulder. He looked over Nicolas with a frown, then turned to Celeste. "You won the right to be queen. I'll leave this decision to you."

She didn't move for the longest time, then swallowed. Her mouth opened slowly. "I sentence Rowan to the dungeon where she is not to be given food or water until she tells us what poison she used on the prince."

"I agree," King Silas nodded. "Guards?"

Without hesitation they grabbed my arms, ripping me from Nicolas's side.

"No," I cried. "I didn't do it! I didn't hurt him. Please, you must believe me. I love him!"

But my cries fell on deaf ears as my feet were dragged beneath me toward the dungeons. I hardly got a last look at Nicolas, who could very well be dead the next time I saw him.

This morning, I thought nothing could be worse than Nicolas choosing another. But this was. This was much, much worse.

Chapter Thirty-Three

LIKE IRON BONDS AROUND my wrist, the guards yanked me toward the dungeon while ignoring my relentless pleas to let me go.

"Quiet," one guard snapped. "We're only doing our jobs."

"I didn't do anything wrong," I cried. "You're arresting the wrong person."

They had no reply to that as they tugged me harder. My wrists throbbed where their fingers pinched, and my toes scrapped against the floor. My shoes were long lost in the struggle, and my skirts were a tangle about my legs.

They brought me down a set of stairs where solid walls blocked all sunlight, and a sharp smell pillaged the air. I made one last desperate claw for freedom. Their hold tightened.

Another guard waited at the bottom of the stairs, and he leaned forward at the commotion. I recognized that face, and he recognized mine.

Mateo's eyes widened. "What is this?" He shifted backward on his chair to give us room and moved his cane to his lap.

"Mateo, you have to help me. They think I poisoned Nicolas." My head twisted in an awkward angle to see him as my feet tripped over stairs.

He looked up at the others for explanation, who dragged me past him and through a door. The smell grew worse. "The prince was poisoned," one explained. "Until we have answers, she stays in here." He grabbed a key from beside the cell door and unlocked the bars. Then he shoved me inside.

I planted my feet on the ground and hurled myself back toward the door, but it was shut too soon. My elbows met the wood with a crack, and my hands coiled around the bars to yank.

"I didn't do anything. I would never hurt him."

My throat turned hoarse from yelling, but they were trailing back up the stairs. One guard looked back, but he wasn't looking for me. He held up a finger at Mateo. "Don't let her out. You'll likely be killed if you do."

I'd felt trapped before, but for the first time a literal cage held me. My sword couldn't save me, my yelling was useless, and all I could do was growl at the bars in frustration while pleading through the door for Mateo to save me.

He looked at me with a pained expression, then back up the stairs. Finally, he let the wide, outer door to the dungeons close between us, so not even my cries could be heard.

My knees hit the cold floor as I hunched over and wept.

Nicolas would die. I would be killed as punishment. It was a very tragic ending that waited for us.

A strange feeling swirled within me. Unexpected happiness at the future Nicolas planned out for us tarnished by the uncertainty of his condition. A great deal of anger toward his mother mixed in there as well. Frustration that I hadn't seen it sooner. Bitterness toward Celeste for putting me here. A little hurt that Mateo hadn't come to free me already.

I'd let that man bleed in my bed.

Now he let me fret in a cell, and long after my tears had dried and my body welled with exhaustion, he still hadn't come, until the hour must have grown late and all hope of being freed soon was replaced by acceptance that I would be stuck here until either someone healed Nicolas, or he died.

Hours passed. I begged for freedom, for food, for a meager blanket to cover my shivering body, but no one came. After a long while of tossing and turning on the small cot and pacing by the tiny window to peer out of the cell, the outer door finally squeaked open. I fled to the door and gripped the bars over the window.

"Mateo? Have you come to your senses?" I asked.

But it wasn't Mateo who stepped through first. It was his wife. Isabel tiptoed into the darkness with a candle lit before her face, illuminating the deep frown.

"Isabel," I sighed. "Thank the Fates. The key is right by the door."

She didn't come closer.

"You're here to free me, right?"

Her head lowered, and my heart plummeted with it. I yanked at the bars. "I don't belong here. I belong with Nicolas."

"If you'll stop raging so much, she can give you news," Mateo said, peeking from around his wife. He tapped his cane on the floor. "She's not being killed for freeing you."

Isabel shifted.

"What news?" I asked, draping an arm through the bars. "Is Nicolas awake?"

The creases in her forehead deepened. "No. He's not. But his father is."

News of his father meant little to me now. "Tell me Nicolas will live."

She glanced back to Mateo. "The court apothecary inspected the apple and uncovered it was a sleeping curse that holds him. As long as his true love kisses him, he will wake."

I closed my eyes and let out a moan of relief. "Thank you. All I have to do is kiss him."

In the heartless dungeon, spark of bliss found me. Once, Nicolas woke me from my sleeping curse. Now, I'd wake him.

But Isabel wasn't smiling. "You don't have permission to go to him."

My brows bent over my eyes. "Then who do they think will wake him?"

My face paled just as she gulped. "An event is scheduled for the court to witness Celeste waking the prince with her kiss tomorrow morning. It's supposed to be the crowning moment that begins their monarchy."

It might sound romantic if it didn't send a pit to my stomach.

He once loved her. She loved him now. Her kiss may work.

I yanked at the bars again and roared. "You have to free me! He and I were going to leave together and live a simple life by the sea. I don't wat to lose that. She can't wake him."

"Rowan," Isabel said, taking a step near me. Her candle flickered in the dark, and a bit of wax dropped to her hand. "Even if she wakes him, she can't make him fall in love with her. If he loved you before, he would love you now."

That calmed my fast-beating heart. But then Isabel coughed. "Then again, if she can't wake him, they might not let you out to try. He'd spend forever sleeping, waiting for a kiss that never came."

Shadows covered half of her face, and she kept the other half tucked into her shoulder to keep the smell away. Though the prisons were empty besides me, they smelled like rotten death that made my stomach queasy. Even so, the thought of not being there to wake Nicolas from an eternal slumber brought knots to my belly tighter than any horrid smell could.

If I didn't get out of here to save Nicolas, then it would have been better if he'd never woken me. I'd rather me sleep forever than him. My knees crumpled and I sank behind the door. "Get. Me. Out. You know I deserve to be free."

"That's why I'm not letting you out." She came to the bars to peek through to my humble surroundings. Her lips pulled together, and she looked away. "If I free you, it makes you look guilty. You must believe in the power of the truth."

I believed in the power of a sword. In the power of true love's kiss. The truth was a tricky concept, often deceiving or misleading.

In this case, the truth that I loved Nicolas was not enough to help him.

She sighed. "I'm really sorry. I'll see what I can do. Don't lose hope."

Hope had mocked me recently. It'd held itself within my grasp just to slip through my fingers so many times. This time, false hope could cost me more than a broken heart.

Isabel's footsteps retreated and the door shut. Darkness surrounded me once more.

This time when I woke, alarms were going off. Mateo was hobbling on his chair, using his injured legs and cane to push the seat through the large doorway and push the heavy door shut. His body heaved with raspy breathing.

"What is happening?" I asked.

He looked over his shoulder. "An attack. Blast, I can't lock this door."

"Mateo, let me out," I pulled at the bars. "I can lock it for you."

He stared up at the set of keys just out of reach. He jabbed at them with his wooden cane but couldn't free the silver links. His black hair matted against his forehead with sweat and he cursed at his broken legs, which worked only enough for him to twitch, but not stand upon.

"Looks like you don't need to yell at me anymore," Mateo huffed. "I couldn't free you even if I wanted to. Nor can I protect you."

"I don't think intruders often come to the dungeons to wreak havoc," I said, though my fingers stiffened over the bars. Little could be said to ease my worries as the alarm repeatedly blared through the stone walls. It warned us of dangers we couldn't see, and dangers we could do nothing to stop.

I might be in a better position than Mateo at the moment. At least I could stand. If they came through those doors, there'd be nothing to keep him safe.

"Do you not even have a weapon?" I asked, eyeing his bare belt.

He massaged his legs while sending me a look of fury. "I was positioned to sit outside an empty cell. I hadn't the strength nor the need to arm myself." He waved his cane in the air. "But I will bash anyone who comes through the door with this."

I bit my tongue against mocking his meager cane, which a sword would laugh at.

The bars chilled my cheeks as I remained pressed against them in silence, doing all I could to not think of Nicolas as helpless as I was.

Suddenly Mateo's cane didn't seem as useless. At least he wasn't trapped in a sleep. Would Nicolas feel pain if someone pierced his heart, or would it be a passing as gentle as a midnight slumber?

Mateo took a sharp breath and his body went rigid. His fingers tightened around his cane and his jaw clenched together.

The sound of metal broke through the alarm. The fight drew closer.

"Get back from the door," Mateo whispered. "And pray you aren't seen."

I only had time to step back before the handle turned and the door opened.

I flung myself backward and out of sight just as Mateo yelled and raised his cane. There was a crack, then a willowy laugh.

The laugh was female, and eerily familiar.

"I see I've greatly overprepared," Nadine's cool voice slid though the dungeon. "I was ready to take down a group of men, and yet I find just one cripple between us."

Between us. Between her and me. What did she plan to do with me?

That wasn't the only question going through my mind, but I failed to think properly enough to put the rest in sentences.

Mateo growled at her. "There is nothing for you down here."

"I don't think that's true."

He roared with pain as if he'd been stabbed, and I clutched a hand to my heart. His roar turned to smaller grunts, and I guessed it more likely she delivered a sharp blow to his pained legs than a blade to his heart.

"Now." Her voice drifted closer. A moment later her face appeared outside my door where she smiled at my place in the corner.

I felt like a rabbit trapped while the hunter licked his hungry lips outside my cage. I pulled myself straighter.

"What do you gain by killing me?"

Her lips turned into a wry smile. "I thought a crown. But looks like you didn't earn that, did you?"

She meant those words to hurt, but the crown mattered little to me.

"As it is," she wiped a finger across the bars and inspected it. "I've come to see for myself the great Rowan brought so low. I thought I'd kill you, but this may be a more delicious ending than I could plan. You in this cell for the rest of your life, while Nicolas sleeps forever. Both of you so close and yet unable to help one another."

It was a wicked person who could smile at that, yet her teeth shone.

Then her mouth closed tight, and she took one last look at me. "Goodbye, Rowan. It's a pity you won't see me crowned."

She left Mateo cradling his legs as she went back up the stairs with a few soldiers behind her. I cursed at her back, but she didn't turn.

I'd underestimated what that lithe girl was capable of. No doubt remained in my mind that she'd been the one to kill Blaire after the first competition, and yet she'd held Cathleen's hand as she cried and wiped away tears of her own.

She outplayed us all. Perhaps well enough to get the throne.

I couldn't say I feared for Celeste's life, but I prayed King Silas was unharmed. He was the only one left to reason with to free me from my bonds.

After an hour, the alarms stopped and the castle fell still. We waited for someone to come and tell us what happened, but the door never opened again. I begged Mateo to crawl up the stairs and find out, but he remained in too much pain to trust his legs to bring him that far.

I cradled on my cot fighting sleep until it beat out my worries. My head rested on my knees and my tired eyes shut out the insanity of the day.

Chapter Thirty-Four

WHISPERS WOKE ME. I stumbled to the door to peer out where Isabel knelt at her husband's side. Their hands were clasped together and foreheads bent close.

"Isabel," I whispered. She turned to look at me. "Tell me what happened."

"Nicolas is safe," she told me. "As is my family. Many others cannot say the same. Lady Nadine's men attacked without warning and showed little mercy." She closed her eyes, and her husband stroked her hair. "But His Majesty and Lady Celeste still live."

My chest dropped a little at word of Celeste's survival.

"So Nadine accomplished nothing?" I asked.

Isabel's gaze hardened. "She killed many of my friends today. Celeste's rule will begin with heartbreak and bloodshed."

I quieted. My pain was not the only pain in the castle today. These walls were soaked with the heartbreak of many families.

"Please," I asked Isabel once more. My voice was soft. "Free me."

She just gave me a sad look. "I'm sorry, m'lady. I dare not."

Another day passed, and it was as long and painful as the last. But at least this time food was brought and a blanket for the bed. It comforted me to have the blanket but also scared me. This cell was one step closer to becoming livable, as if I might stay here forever.

Mateo kept to the other side of the door, perhaps to keep himself from my grumbling. The day was quiet and still until at last, the door opened.

"Let me out!" I didn't care who it was this time. I needed to save Nicolas. Every hour he spent trapped in that sleep world was a thousand times more difficult than my hour in this dreadful cell.

He deserved to be awoken before the next attack brought a sword to his neck.

From the darkness, Celeste stepped into the smelly dungeon with her dress balled up in her hands and her crown glittering on her head. My jaw fell open, then it clamped shut.

"What are you doing here?" I spoke through my teeth.

"I'm sorry," she said in a mocking tone. "I thought you wanted someone to free you."

I stepped back and crossed my arms, waiting for what she would do. She approached the door and reached for the keys. "There. You're out." The wood scratched across the ground as she held it open for me.

I brushed by her, but she grabbed my wrist. I tore it free. "I'm going to find Nicolas," I growled.

"No, you're not. I'm taking you somewhere else."

A new guard stood in the doorway while Mateo leaned against his side. Together they hobbled as Mateo's cane tapped against each stair, until at last they'd reached the top. Celeste walked after them, and I had no choice but to follow.

At the top I prepared to make a run for it, but the guards stood in my way. I was pretty certain I could barrel through Mateo, but the other was twice his size and could snap my neck without hesitation.

"Let me wake Nicolas." I turned to Celeste. "And he will explain everything."

Her lips folded into her mouth and her brow lowered. It was a look of anger mixed with confusion. I might have pitied her—a girl who for a moment thought she'd gotten the kingdom and the one she loved just to have the man poisoned and a girl claiming he'd sworn to run off with her—but she'd put me in the dungeon, and for that she got no pity.

"He will explain when I wake him tomorrow," she said. "Nadine's attack pushed the ceremony back a day."

"Why wait until then and put him through this torture?" I asked.

Her jaw clenched. "It's for the symbolism. If you wish to live, follow me."

I cared to live more than I cared about defying her, so I trotted behind her as she led me upward through the castle. We passed a few who stopped to whisper behind their hands, but I gripped my dirty skirts in my hand and continued putting one foot in front of the other, despite their stares.

Outside the sky had darkened and stars peeked over the kingdom. Two days had passed and Nicolas still slept.

Celeste led me to a small hall in the quiet western wing where she turned a golden key in a lock and pushed a door open. The edges of the lock were odd, as if someone had messed with them recently, but it wasn't until I stepped inside that I discovered what it was.

They'd been switched. Instead of locking people out, they locked someone in.

"One cage to another," I said.

"But this one is much prettier," Celeste said as if I had nothing to complain about. "And you're hidden now."

I didn't want to look, but an odd sight caught my attention.

It was one large room instead of a series of rooms like I had, and quite small in comparison. There was no fireplace, no closet, no sitting room, and no vanity. There was only a dress folded on the floor next to a bed, though it could hardly be called that.

It was one bed on top of another, on top of another, on top of another.

Numerous mattresses stacked over each other until they almost reached the ceiling. A thin ladder led up to the top where a lush pillow and heavy blanket sat.

I had no words.

"There's twenty of them," Celeste said. "If you're counting. Twenty mattresses. You wanted sleep? You'll get it tonight."

"Why?" The question spilled from my lips. "Why?" I didn't understand why someone would put so many beds together. If it was a joke, it wasn't one I understood. There appeared no meaning behind this.

"You'll sleep here tonight," Celeste said, looking over the bed. "And in the morning after I've awoken Nicolas, you will pay for what you have done to him. He will give us the answers we seek."

I pressed against the ladder and crossed my arms. "And if he doesn't wake?"

An emotion as cold as the floor beneath my feet stared back at me. "Then you'll die as an enemy of the kingdom for poisoning the man that I love."

Her heels clicked as she strode toward the door, echoing off the blank walls and almost empty room. I watched her go, torn between wishing she would wake Nicolas and hoping her kiss would be futile.

More than anything, I wished for him to wake.

"Rowan." Celeste paused at the door with a small hand on the frame. Her head turned over her shoulder to look at me. "Is it really torture for him to be asleep like he is?" She licked her lips. "He looks so peaceful."

It wasn't torture, necessarily. But if it was like my sleeping curse, he'd be somewhat aware of his surroundings and confused if he could ever wake up. I could picture him straining against the sleep to open his eyes, but no matter how hard he fought, he was trapped in a still body.

An unpleasant experience for anyone. I knew to sleep. Nicolas would know only to fight.

"Yes," I said. "He is as trapped as I am. Behind that peaceful body is a man screaming for someone to help him."

Her back went rigid, she nodded once, then pulled the door behind her.

It locked, and my second cage was built.

Chapter Thirty-Five

ESCAPE WAS MY FIRST plan. The peculiar number of mattresses would work splendidly.

The distance from the window to the ground was too high to jump from, and years of wind whipping at the wall had smoothed its edges so no grooves would be deep enough to support a climb down. But if I dropped the mattresses one by one out the window, they'd provide an ideal landing.

The ladder was intriguing, but there was no way to attach it to the window, nor would it be tall enough if I dropped it to the floor. I ran multiple scenarios through mind to put that ladder to use, but all came up folly.

"How bad could it hurt to land on so many mattresses? I'll be fine." I said, scoping out the size of the window. It'd take some squishing, but I had all night.

"Dump mattresses out window. Jump. Wake Nicolas," I plotted. They should have left me in the cell.

The ladder groaned under my weight as I climbed up where I balled my fists against the top mattress and shoved. It went nowhere.

My foot shifted from the ladder to dig between two mattresses, bracing myself as I pushed again with all my weight. The ladder wobbled, but the mattress did not.

"I don't understand," I grunted, grabbing the blanket and pillow and hurling them to the floor. "Why so many mattresses? I don't get the reasoning."

My teeth clenched together as I pushed again. No matter how much force I used, it held like stone.

I shoved. I pulled. I jumped on the top. Nothing moved it.

My hand slid between the top mattress and the one below it and was able to slide through effortlessly. "So they haven't fastened them together." But when I twisted my elbow upward in attempt to knock the mattress free, it clamped tight.

An odd tingling coiled about my fingertips, intertwining at my wrists, and enveloping my arms.

Magic was about.

My breathing quickened, and I eased down the ladder.

"I don't understand," I repeated in a whisper, staring at the large bed. "I don't understand what's happening."

If I couldn't mount my epic escape through the window, I'd have to break down the door.

I threw the force of my body into the door with little thought before backing up to do it again. It moaned but didn't break. As I prepared once more, a grumpy voice called out, "Knock it off. I'll only tackle you as soon as you leave, and I don't care to fix a door."

Even if I broke the door, I was unarmed and drained and hungry—no match for guards. Even Mateo stood a chance at this point.

Black from the night pooled into the room. I ought to sleep, but I couldn't do anything other than pace through the thick darkness and fret over Nicolas. He must be terrified right now. Was he alone, or did Celeste hold his hand? If his father went to him, would he hear his voice and know he was okay? Was he thinking of me, or had he succumbed to sleep?

I'd slept for a hundred years. I wouldn't make Nicolas wait that long.

I curled the heavy blanket over my shoulders and let it catch my slow tears. That was how the morning found me—awake, exhausted, and unable to think of anything other than Nicolas.

As the sky beckoned in the first colors of morning, soft lavenders and silky blues, the door unlatched and Celeste slid in.

"Is he awake?" I asked, dropping the blanket and pulling myself to my feet. Celeste looked me over.

"You didn't even change into the dress I left you," she said, pointing to the floor. In the deep darkness, I'd forgotten it was there.

"I would have preferred food. Is he awake?" I asked again.

"The ceremony isn't until this afternoon. Did you sleep at all?" She walked in a circle around me, inspecting the bed and kicking at the pillow on the floor. She wore a satin dress of pure white and her blonde hair braided over her shoulder, which she twirled between her thin fingers.

My nails dug into my palms. "Why haven't you woken him yet?"

She stopped, bent to the floor by the mattress, and sighed. Dark circles formed under her lids. Her arms trembled as if it required their entire strength to be wrapped around her body. From the ground she peeked to me.

"I can't. I tried."

Half of my heart celebrated that her kiss hadn't worked, while the other feared for what that'd mean for me. Would she give me a chance, or would she kill me? Her love for Nicolas might bind her to raging jealousy, and I'd be at her mercy.

"I didn't want anyone to know that I tried," she said, wiping a tear from her eye. "If it worked, I'd have made him pretend to sleep until I could officially wake him in front of the kingdom. It was going to be perfect. But I kissed him, then I kissed him again." I closed my eyes against the image of her lips against his.

"But it didn't work," she said with heaviness. "He still sleeps."

Another tear caressed her cheek, and I softened my tone. "Celeste, you must let me wake him. Please."

"I wasn't going to let you try," she said. Her hand dug under the bottom mattress until it came back with something small and green. "If you had slept. But you didn't."

Her palm opened, and a pea rested within.

I took a step back. "What sort of magic does it contain?"

She rolled it around her hand. "To the honest of heart, it does nothing. But this small item draws the cruel-hearted to a sleep that never would have ended until I'd removed the pea. No matter how worried you might have been for yourself or for Nicolas, if you weren't a kind person, you wouldn't have resisted it's lull."

She let it drop in her pocket. "You weren't asleep when I came in." Clear disappointment marred her face. She wanted me to be asleep, so her conscious held clear as she sentenced me to death. But I wasn't. I was awake all night. "Now I can't deny you Nicolas."

At last, my chest took a deep breath. Though the grime of the previous day clung to my dress, it melted from my mind and was replaced by a timid flicker of hope that the future Nicolas planned for us would come to pass.

"Where is he?"

She held out her arm. "Follow me."

I followed at a distance, wary of any last twists she might pull. But she led me directly to Nicolas's room where two guards stood outside. They straightened as we rounded the corner, and she halted.

I thought the guards frightened her, but she turned to me. "Before we go in there, I must know. Maybe my heart needs to hear it once more to believe it. Did he truly promise to leave with you?" she asked in a voice lower than a whisper. She braced for my reply.

"Yes." I answered as plainly as I could, not bragging about our relationship but not dismissing it either.

With rigid shoulders, she turned back to the guards in front of Nicolas's door. "Let us through."

They parted, and Celeste opened the door.

The windows were shut, drapes pulled closed against the coming morning, and room empty except for Nicolas.

"Where is his worried family?" I asked.

"The king is tending to his kingdom in the wake of Nadine's attack," Celeste said. "While Ava is with her husband as he heals."

I shook my head. "Probably too hard for her to look upon her son when she did this to him."

I crossed to Nicolas and held his hand in my own while Celeste stayed at a distance. Nicolas's chest rose and fell lightly, like the faintest of breath clinging to his body. His touch was warm and his face serene, but I could only imagine what was happening in his mind.

"I'm here," I said, placing a hand on his cheek. They'd left him in his clothes from days ago, the pressed suit and ribbons dangling near the sparrow-tailed collar.

I'd looked at him in this outfit then thinking of how handsome he was and how I'd lost that. Now it'd be what he wore as we started our lives together.

The bed sunk inward as I sat next to him, taking his arm and draping it over my lap where I intertwined our fingers.

"You woke me once," I said, leaning into him. We hadn't known each other then. I was no more than the girl he'd been searching for and he was nothing but a stranger to me. I hadn't even known his name. I hadn't known of his love for hunting or for his childhood home by the sea. I hadn't known about how hard he'd fight for me or how much I'd love him.

But I knew those things now.

I wondered if he'd hesitated before kissing me, taken in the details of my face and wondered if he was making a mistake.

I'd never been surer of anything as I brought my lips to his and kissed him.

He remained still for a moment, but as I kept my lips there, his began to move. A soft, slow press into each other. Then his eyes opened.

"You're awake," I said through a smile, keeping my face close enough that our noses touched. He grinned and settled his other hand firmly on the curve of my waist.

"Of course I am," he whispered back. "A fellow would be a fool to sleep through a kiss like that." He grunted as he sat up. "That's twice now that true love's kiss has saved us. Care to admit I'm your true love yet?"

I laughed as joy bubbled inside me. "I love you," I told him. His cheeks cracked with a wide smile and his eyes lit up until they shone brighter than the morning. "I love you," I said again. "I love you so much."

"One more time," he said, leaning closer. "I shall never tire of hearing you say that."

I brought my lips to his so he could feel them as I said, "I love you."

Celeste left behind us, but this time as she closed the door, she wasn't trapping me alone. She was leaving me with the love of my life and a bliss so deep it would last me a lifetime.

"I love you, Rowan," Nicolas said back. "Forever and ever."

Chapter Thirty-Six

TINY DAISIES ADORNED MY dress, falling as a train behind me. Nicolas's hand held mine, the soft fabric of his suit grazing my arm. He looked ahead with a blank expression as his mother knelt before the king.

The court gathered around in silence. All wanted to hear what her sentence would be.

Celeste sat in the queen's throne wearing a gown the color of blooming flowers and a frown. Her gaze occasionally drifted to us where her frown would deepen, but then she'd take a deep breath and look forward again.

Ava's forehead swept the floor as she knelt on her knees.

"I never intended to hurt my son," she said.

"But you intended to hurt someone," King Silas said.

Her eyes sliced to us, where she did not answer.

Martin sat in a chair at Nicolas's side with lowered brows and hard eyes. He'd never looked so upset in the short time I'd known him. From what Nicolas told me, he offered his wife no forgiveness for her sins.

His body remained weak, but it was healing from the poison. He'd leave and return to the seaside manor with us, where Ava was not welcome.

"I did what was best for my son," Ava said with a glance to Nicolas. Even on her knees with hands bound, she looked upon her son lovingly. "And I did what Jezebel wanted. She wanted Celeste on the throne. I guaranteed she got there."

Celeste shifted in her seat. No doubt it wouldn't bode well for her to be associated with Ava right now.

But King Silas saved her. "Lady Celeste won the position of heir all on her own. And I'm certain my dear wife never would have wanted this. Her heart was gold and her actions pure. You have acted out of malice, and there is no place for that in my kingdom."

The room held its breath for his sentence, while Ava bent her head once more.

"You are stripped from your title, but you are not banished. You are free to live in any of the towns in Thames doing whatever idle work pleases you for the rest of your life."

A gentle punishment that shouldn't burden her too hard. With Nicolas and Martin leaving, there was nothing left for her here. But she still threw back her head and wailed as if he'd ordered for it to be chopped off.

"Remove her," King Silas said with a dismissive wave. That sent her to further hysterics.

Celeste didn't flinch as she was dragged past her feet and out the side door. Nicolas did.

"That is all," King Silas said to the full room. "You can all leave now." He folded his hands and melted into his chair. He cast a look after Ava, then closed his eyes and shook his head.

"We can wait," Martin tugged on Nicolas's jacket, "until the room has cleared. I'm a slow man and don't want to be knocked over."

"Alright, Father," Nicolas said. "Do you suppose Mother will be alright?"

Martin laughed. "That woman is resourceful. She'll be just fine. As for us," he turned in his chair to give me a wink, "we will be living a good life by the sea. The air is clearer there, and it has a way of making everything else drift away."

He settled back with a grin and a faraway look in his eye. He hadn't hesitated when we asked him to accompany us and hadn't questioned Nicolas for giving up the throne. Instead he'd hobbled about the room to throw his things in bags and set them by the door. We'd leave in the morning.

Upon learning how Ava had been the one to poison Nicolas, Martin had exchanged a harsh word with her and demanded he get the last years of his life in peace. She would not be joining us.

"Are you certain?" The deep voice of King Silas came as he stepped from the dais to us. "I will miss your companionship, Martin."

He chuckled like the king had said a joke, but the king's expression was a sad one. "You'll be quite fine. I imagine this castle has some excitement left in it for you."

King Silas shook his hand before shifting to Nicolas. He clasped his palm over his shoulder where he stood for a moment, looking over the one who might have been king.

"You would have made a fine ruler, son."

"Perhaps," Nicolas said. "But I suspect Celeste will make a finer one."

Celeste remained on the throne with a tall back and raised chin as she watched us. She didn't smile, but didn't look away, and gave a slow nod as Nicolas glanced to her.

King Silas helped Martin stand. "Very well then. Go with my blessing. May life bring you nothing but bliss."

"And to you, Silas," Martin said. "And to you."

We took slow steps to leave the room, partly from Martin's weakness and partly from the nostalgia of the place. It wasn't the same as leaving Elenvérs, a feeling drenched in despair and unthinkable sorrow, but rather one laced with excitement for tomorrow.

We couldn't know what life by the sea would bring, but it would be a life with Nicolas, and that was what mattered most.

Sleep will be the start of a great adventure for you, Mother had said. She'd been right, and I suspected the adventure wasn't over.

Epilogue

A delightful year later

THE MIGHT OF AN entire army couldn't compare to the power of the waves as they crashed against the sharp cliffs, blanketing the escarpment in salty mist. My chair rocked back and forth on the white porch as summer's breeze curled around my bare neck. I'd taken to tying my hair up each day with a thin, black ribbon just to savor that feeling.

"The shipment reached Riju a few weeks ago," Martin said. He pushed open the back door with a pipe in his mouth and a yellowed letter in his hand. "Very good. The storm didn't get them after all."

"I knew it wouldn't; Rogers is a fine captain," Nicolas said from his seat beside me. The wind frolicked amidst his curls.

Martin grunted and slipped back inside. He no longer hobbled when he walked nor did he take so long to stand up. The distance from court had been like magic for his bones, each day healing his soul. After a year, he was a younger man.

Nicolas sighed, and not a worry in the world rested in his breath. The merchant business had been good, the silence of the house comforting, and the smile on his face ever-present. I joined my hand with his.

Little troubles found us here on the edge of the world where water danced in frothing waves and clouds hid the harsh light of the sun. The only struggles came from a storm a few months back that brought down many houses in the nearby village and took out some of our windows.

It'd claimed many lives as well. We'd gathered the bodies and gave them back to the sea.

But that storm carried blessings through its cruel destruction. A blessing Nicolas and I never thought we'd receive.

From above, a child cried out.

"I'll get her," I said. Old wooden boards creaked under my feet as I circled up the winding stairway to the upper room where a feathered rug and rosy colored chair sat beside a crib.

A girl with black hair and midnight blue eyes sat in the crib as tears flowed down her plump cheeks. She quieted when she saw me and held out her hands.

My arms wrapped around her tiny body and her little chin settled into my shoulder. Her hand went to the ribbon in my hair to pull on while I swayed. "Good morning, little one," I whispered. She gurgled back.

Even from up here we could hear the waves lapping at the rock face. The sound sang us to sleep each night and woke us each morning. It was the tune that I swayed to now as Everly held tight.

She'd lost her parents in the storm. She'd been given to us—the couple who thought they'd never have a child to love. While we mourned her parents who'd been dear friends of ours, we cherished what they'd left us.

She was as beautiful as the sea and as calm as the misty mornings when the water clung to the air, draping itself like a cloud on the surface of the cliffs.

Nicolas came from behind to brush his nose against Everly's. She'd never remember her real parents, but she already loved Nicolas fiercely. He could make her laugh like no one else could.

But when she cried, her hands always reached for me, and my shoulders dried her tears.

I'd happily wrapped my old sword away, trading it for the honor of motherhood. One day I'd get the sword out again to teach Everly everything I knew. For now, her hugs were all I desired.

"Something else came with this morning's delivery," Nicolas whispered. He held up a scarf made of vibrant yellow. "I asked Dana to send one for us to hang in our window and fly in the wind."

"It's perfect." I'd spoken many times how I loved the bright scarves from the Thames castle. Now we'd have a scarf of our own. Perhaps one day we'd fill the windows with scarves that each carried their own meaning, so as others looked to our home they'd see brightness over the sea.

But this yellow scarf held the meaning I loved most of all.

"The yellow scarf was back in your window before we left the castle," I remembered. "You never told me how Giermo and his love made up."

Nicolas's forehead crinkled momentarily. Then he grinned. "They hadn't."

I tilted my head to see him over the mass of Everly's hair.

He explained, "I'd hung that scarf for you."

I'd been so nervous during my last week at the castle that I'd lost Nicolas's love. But he'd hung a scarf in the window to tell all about how much he loved me, and I hadn't realized it until now.

This yellow scarf meant even more to me now.

Nicolas went to the window to tie the scarf. It caught the breeze and stretched out toward the sea, dancing up and down.

A symbol of our love to adorn our home. He grinned and turned back to me.

"Because our love is as eternal as the sun," he said.

He wrapped Everly and me in his embrace and my heart was complete.

"This," I said, looking up at him, his cheek resting against our daughter's head, "this was worth waiting a hundred years for."

He kissed my forehead as Everly clung to us and the scarf fluttered in the wind and the peaceful waves hugged the shore and I decided nothing would ever compare to this feeling right here.

I'd found my family, and I'd found my home. This was my happy ending.

A note to my readers

And a four-book series is done! I can't even begin to describe my emotions with that. Thanks for reading the final book in The Storyteller's Series! I've had so much fun working with fairytales and am now ready to move on to other stories.

Of course, that's what I say, then get an idea for a spin-off with Tarion and Elis, or a reverse little mermaid with Rowan's daughter. *sigh.* We'll see what happens.

The same as before, I'd love if you left a review for my book! Reviews are so incredibly helpful as they boost my position in the algorithm and let more readers find me. If you could take a moment to leave a review, it would help my career immensely. I'll read every review posted so I can hear your thoughts on my book! I love hearing from readers and am grateful for your time. You are also welcome to find me on social media to connect further! My inbox is always open to readers!

Thank you! Your support means the world to me.
-VM

Other books by Victoria McCombs

<u>The Storyteller's Series</u>
The Storyteller's Daughter
Woods of Silver and Light
The Winter Charlatan
(Heir of Roses)

<u>The Royal Rose Chronicles</u>
Oathbound
Silver Bounty
Savage Bred

<u>The Fae Realm Duology (Coming 2024)</u>
Mortal Queens
Shattered Kings

Acknowledgments

First, thank you to Jonathan for believing in me and supporting my dream of creating books. This is the first book that I've put together all on my own, yet you never made me feel like I couldn't do it. I love you.

Big thanks to my community of people on Instagram who listen to my story ideas and inspire me to keep creating. I've heard that it's best to follow artists over influencers, and you definitely make me believe in that. I'm encouraged by you all daily. Special thanks to Alexander who helped edit this, and to Ruth, Caitlyn, and Keira for being such steady friends.

Thank you to my family for being supportive, for listening to all my crazy ideas, and for reading through the story. You've believed in me for a long time, and I couldn't have done it without your encouragement. And of course, thank you to Jesus for being my savior.

About the Author

Some of the things I love most in this world are peppermint hot chocolate, peanut butter ice cream, golfing dates, Jesus, and game nights with family. And of course, books.

Fairytales were my first love. I became obsessed with the idea that if one was brave enough, they could defeat dragons, and that true love was real. I met my true love in college, and together we raise our boys. I have my dad to thank for my love of writing, and my mom to thank for allowing us to keep a wall of medieval weapons in the house, which cultivated my love for that time period. My dream is to write vivid worlds and charming characters that will leave an imprint on my readers hearts, the way that so many books have done for me.

Heir of Roses

"We will find a girl fit enough to rule. Pure, strong, and enchanting. A queen of roses."

Rowan's sleeping curse is broken by a stranger's kiss. Their happily ever after should begin, but they aren't in love. They struggle to develop feelings as plots of betrayal, mysterious deaths, and a sword-wielding mother-in-law challenge them.

When the king sets up a Queen's Competition as an attempt to settle unrest, Rowan's place is threatened. She must fight for the prince she ought to love to secure his position at court, while competing in challenges that seek to unravel her, bit by bit. For though they can force her to compete, she's the only competitor who knows she can never truly win.

Just as Rowan finds her place, a poison apple could destroy it all.

The conclusion to The Storyteller's Series is here.